DEATH TRANCE

DEATH TRANCE

A NOVEL OF HYPNOTIC DETECTION

R. D. Zimmerman

WILLIAM MORROW AND COMPANY, INC.
NEW YORK

Library of Congress Cataloging-in-Publication Data

Zimmerman, R. D. (Robert Dingwell)
    Death trance: a novel of hypnotic detection / by R. D. Zimmerman.
      p. cm.
    ISBN 0-688-11451-2
    I. Title.
    PS3576.I5118D43   1992
    813'.54—dc20   92-7963
                                               CIP

Printed in the United States of America

First Edition

1 2 3 4 5 6 7 8 9 10

BOOK DESIGN BY M. C. DE MAIO

DEATH TRANCE

Prologue

I stood on the edge of Lake Calhoun, hidden in the thick bushes, and my first thought was that I'd never seen anyone murdered before, least of all someone I knew, someone like Toni, whom I'd dated back in my college days. It was evening, most of Minneapolis was quietly at home, and she was out there, just past the beach and talking with that bastard, when the first shot was fired. And I thought, who'd have guessed this was how our tumultuous relationship would end after almost twenty years. Not in one final argument. Not in one last lustful encounter. But in sudden death.

It didn't end, though. Not just then. Not so quickly. Her mother may have once seen a demure little girl in her Antoinette, but the real Toni of medium height and long brown hair was nothing like that. No, not Toni the physician who loved photography and had run countless marathons. Beautiful, yes. Trim, yes. But also muscular and determined. A survivor now bending over, scrambling for shelter.

"Toni!" I screamed, my breath smoking in the cool April night. "Toni, look out!"

I was shouting because I saw someone charging them, rush-

7

ing through the night and along the edge of the lake, arm out, pistol in hand, racing in for the final kill. I dropped it all, her camera with the infrared film, the walkie-talkie, everything that was supposed to safeguard her, that was supposed to keep this from happening. Then I was running toward her, not knowing what I could do, how I could help. At the same time, that other guy, the one she'd arranged to meet, tore off toward the woods. How was this happening? We were sure we had this all figured out, so why did it look like he was racing for his life as well? Or had he tricked us, had he and his group connived to kill us both, Toni and me, right down here?

"Toni!"

I shouldn't have shouted. Not a second time, because she twisted around toward me, looked in my direction, and she didn't see that person—man or woman, I couldn't tell—running up behind her. Oh, my God, oh, no. If only she'd ducked behind the bench or taken shelter behind the tree because that's when a second shot was fired. I was tearing through the park as fast as I possibly could, feet over grass, over paved path, through sand, and then there was that horrible blast, a reddish one. I could tell she was hit, instantly so.

"No!" I cried.

I wanted her to shout back to me, say, Alex, I'm okay, don't worry. But she didn't. Instead she was stumbling, then falling. No, dropping, and I knew to expect the worst. She just fell so heavily, which only made me run faster across the beach, then across more ground, until I dropped to my knees, skidded across the grass, and to her side.

"Toni, where?" I begged, at first afraid to touch the body heaped in front of me. "Toni, can you hear me? Toni!"

There was nothing. No voice, no groan of any kind. No movement, either. I reached out, touched her, felt an electric shock of a realization zip through me. All that blood, so dark and sticky, was pouring out the side of her head, all over the ground, all over me.

I spun around, pleaded for help, looked toward the woods, saw the last of him, that son of a bitch, escaping in the dark, dashing to freedom and life. Turning the other way, I saw the flat black lake spread out in the night, then the other person, her killer, now zeroing in on me. The intention was clear. I saw that gun.

And as I knelt there clutching my ex-girlfriend's body, I thought, Toni, if I survive this, if I'm not killed now as well, I'll find out. I'll get that revenge. Once for your sister's death and once for yours.

Chapter 1

Her hands came up from the wheelchair and reached for my face, hovering at first, tentative, but then sure and probing, reading my skin, my eyelashes, my wrinkled brow. It amazed me how much she could read via touch, and I didn't try to hide anything. I'd never been able to, not from her, the great seer.

"Alex," said Madeline, my Audrey-Hepburn-look-alike sister, "you should have come sooner."

We stood on the long pier. Rather, I stood and my big sister—beautiful, wise, loving, funny—sat in her wheelchair, a light brown blanket over her lap, oversized sunglasses on her nose. She sat because she was paraplegic, and she touched me, ran her soft, long fingers over my face, through my hair, because she was blind.

"Give me your hand," she commanded.

Even though it was August, the air was chilly, and it blew off Lake Michigan, over us, around us. I lifted my arm, pushed back the sleeve of my mock turtleneck, the black one that looked hip back in Minneapolis and New York, of course, but very out of place on an island some ten miles southwest of Mackinac Bridge. Lush green trees, aqua-blue water, fine white sand filled every vista. It was all terribly Caribbean up here except there was no salt in the air, only lush pine scents, and, for sure, all of this lasted only a few months. Though it would crop up again next summer and the summer after that, etc., this wonder was temporary. A reward for the harsh winter.

Maddy took my hand, felt my wrist, caressed the thick hair on my forearm, touched me as if we were lovers. We hadn't seen each other since last spring.

"You've put on weight," she said.

"I haven't biked much this summer."

I hadn't done much of anything in the five months since Toni had died. Her death haunted me and was either a turning point or a black hole in my life, something that had tripped me and hadn't allowed me to get back up.

"Come on," said Maddy, letting go of me and placing her hands in her lap. "Let's go up to the house. This is going to work, you'll see. Trust me."

"Yes, Dr. No."

"Oh, stop," she laughed.

That's what I called her. Dr. No of James Bond fame. She lived that kind of unbelievable life here on her own private island. Only my Maddy wasn't evil at all. Just wonderful, so maybe she wasn't Dr. No and not even Dr. Madeline Phillips, a clinical psychologist-cum-stockbroker, but Dr. Yes. I smiled, my wide mouth exposing white teeth.

"Now just help me off the pier, will you? Give me a push. You can leave your things. Alfred will bring them up."

"What did I bring?" I asked, testing her.

"A large suitcase, a hard-sided one that made you groan as you lifted it from the boat and that made a hard noise when it hit the pier. Also a little carry-on that barely made any noise when you set it down. It's fragile because you put it down slowly, so I suspect that's your computer, your laptop." She paused. "And . . ."

"And?"

"Your black leather briefcase. It's still over your shoulder. That one I can smell."

"But how do you know it's black?" I asked.

"For the same reason I think that soft shirt of yours is black. You always want to prove yourself urbane."

"You're incorrigible," I said, taking hold of the back of the wheelchair.

"No more so than you, Little Brother."

I laughed as I pushed her plank by plank down the long pier. Water and fire, two potentially horrific dangers that she could neither see nor flee from, were really the only things Maddy was afraid of. I didn't doubt, however, that I'd be afraid of the same things if I'd gone blind in my late teens from congenital eye failure—retinitis pigmentosa, to be exact—then in my mid-thirties been struck by a huge, diesel-powered Chicago Transit Authority bus right in the Loop, right in broad daylight, right on a supposedly safe curb. So I eased her off the dock and to the asphalt path that led up to the house.

Her pier. Her path. Her house. And the boat, a huge fiberglass phallic thing driven by Alfred, her Jamaican manservant, that had whizzed me from the northern coast of Michigan over to Maddy's island. Her island. All of it, for Maddy had parlayed the $8.5 million CTA settlement into far, far more. She was that smart. Obtaining the best financial counsel, but mainly using her own wit, she'd plunged into the stock market before the Big Rise and ridden the crest of corporate takeovers and buyouts like a champion surfer. The blind paraplegic girl winning resolutely; she'd bought three million dollars' worth of *Time* at about $20 per share, sold it at over $140. Amgen had been another big winner for her, 150,000 shares rising from $15 per share to $125. The last I'd heard, Maddy had more than quintupled what she'd been awarded for having her spinal cord snapped by an inebriated bus driver who'd been thrice warned against drinking. A terrible tragedy that Maddy had, in capitalistic terms at least, championed over. How typical of her.

Behind us I heard Alfred charge the boat's engine and speed over the lightly capping waves. I glanced back, saw the long, cream-colored boat skim sleekly over the water, saw the coffee-black man at its helm as he circled through the sunshine and around to the boathouse.

I took a deep breath, sucked in the green-rich air. The cool wind off the lake faded as we reached shore and the protection of maples and oaks and strands of birches.

"God, it's wonderful here," I said.

"It is, isn't it? All the trees and all the water. It does wonders for the soul." From the side of her wheelchair she pulled down a wandlike thing, a probe like a blind person's cane. "I'll take it from here."

"No electric wheelchair for you, eh?"

"All this wheeling burns up lots of calories. If I had a motorized chair I'd just atrophy, and I won't let myself do that. I can't let myself go. And you shouldn't, either."

"Thanks for the reminder."

Maybe it was more like a fishing rod, that thing that was attached to one side of her chair and sticking way out. Whatever it was—Maddy had dreamed it up—she lowered it until it was just touching the path, so that it would lightly skim the paved surface ahead of her. That way she could wheel herself and didn't have to be pushed. That way she could go off on her own, zoom around the narrow blacktopped paths that she'd had laid like lace across the island, and pretend to be independent, not needy of Alfred or Solange, his wife, or all the protection her millions could buy.

Zoom. Her arms bulged and she was off. Christ, she could really tear along in that thing.

"Hey, wait up," I called, jogging after her. "I've only got feet."

"Come on, pudge, a brisk walk will do you good!"

"Hey, you crip, be nice."

"I just don't want to see a handsome guy like you lose it at forty."

"I'm not forty yet and, you know, you're almost as good as Mom at back-handed compliments."

"Gaaa-www-ddd!" she shrieked, disappearing over the top of a ridge.

Sister, schmister. I hurried along, just like the faithful brother I had always been and would always be. Long before her paralysis, even before her blindness, I'd been enchanted by Maddy. So much grace. And spunk, particularly as a child, charming all the kids, boys and girls alike. We were similar but different. I liked to think I was as smart as she, but I was never as outgoing, never as popular. Otherwise, while we both had the same chestnut brown hair, mine was long and curly, hers short and wavy. Whereas we were both tallish, I had a squarer body, my broader stature coming from Dad's side of the family. Maddy, too, had one of those long, movie star necks. Yes, I'd probably learned to like necks because of Maddy's. Toni's was almost as good, but not quite. Not so long, so elegant.

I dogged after her, through a grove of swaying trees. Always had been dogging after her. While she'd been the determined blind student and had gotten her Ph.D. in psychology and gone right into a very successful practice—she was on her way to the office the day she was struck by that stupid bus—I had dawdled in college. Studied languages, lots of them. French, Italian, Russian. I was good at all of them. And some German, too. I could get by in that one. I thought I wanted to be an interpreter for the United Nations, but while I got close, I fell short and somehow became a technical writer. That's why I left my hometown, Chicago. Moved to the high-tech mecca of the Midwest, Minneapolis, where I wrote installation manuals for some of the world's fastest computers. It paid well, but after my studies and travels abroad it was excruciatingly boring. Many of the people I worked with rarely traveled beyond Chicago, and the most interesting conversations we had were about who'd just bought the best garage door opener.

I came up and around a corner, saw Maddy atop a small dune, sitting there grinning, a huge beast on either side.

"Oh, for cute," I said in my best nasally Minnesota accent. I froze. "What are those?"

"Dogs, silly."

They were tan with black heads, and they stood so tall that their backs were at Maddy's eye level. A glistening glob of saliva hung from the larger one's mouth, and didn't I just hear a slight growl?

"Maddy, I don't think they like me."

"Nonsense, they're just very protective. Hold out your hand—palm down, of course—and let them smell you. And don't move."

"Have they had lunch?"

"This one's Fran," she said, patting the slightly smaller one, "and this one's—"

"Ollie. Clever. Very clever."

"They're mastiffs, Alex. I got them because we kept getting campers on the northern part of the island. A few prowlers, too."

"Not anymore, I bet. What do they weigh, two hundred?"

"A little bit more." To her creatures, she commanded, "This is my brother. Be nice. Nice, Ollie. Nice, Fran."

They came at me in a slow trot, noses high, ears perked. I was definitely the one with his tail between his legs, and I was quite still as they sniffed my hand, my arm, my butt.

"Maddy, I don't think I like this. Ollie's got her nose in my rear."

"Oops, sorry." Maddy clapped her hands twice, and shouted, "Scram!"

In an instant, they were off, bounding into the woods, and I could only imagine the havoc they'd wreaked on the deer population. A thirty-some-acre island was, after all, only so big, particularly for things like those two.

Maddy added, "It's only me and Alfred and Solange out here, you know. The dogs are really wonderful protection."

Maddy spun her chair, and we continued down the path to the old house that was perched on the southernmost tip of land. She rolled herself a bit slower, and I set my hand on her shoulder, squeezed. Maybe I'd stay a long time. Maybe quit my job. She'd always wanted me, in her own words, to mooch off her.

"I'm so glad you're here," Maddy said. Then, as if she were reading my mind, "Promise me you'll stay as long as you can and then some?"

"Promise," I said. "They still don't know what happened. The police—they've been pretty good, I guess. But they've lost steam, run out of ideas."

"I told you not to worry. Solange is fixing us some lunch, and then we can go right up if you like."

"Sure," I said, thinking it a rather ludicrous idea, but then what had we to lose?

Maddy had told me that the island paths—the ones she'd had blacktopped—had initially been laid out by Frederick Olmsted of Central Park fame, and we pushed along, in and out of groves, up and down ridges and silky, sandy dunes, with the majestic Lake Michigan bursting in and out of view. *Blam.*

Big sheet of blue blue water. *Whoosh.* A cool wall of greenery. Then, at last, of course, the biggest firework of all: the house, poised atop a hill to our right.

"God, it's beautiful. All the work shows."

"Really? Oh, good, but it still needs paint."

"Hell, yes, it's all peeling."

It was a big Victorian job with a hint of Colonial thrown in, and had been built as a summer house for a Chicago brewer in 1893. Soaring high up to a green roof, it was white clapboard and had a many-columned veranda on three sides. Perched overlooking this freshwater sea, the place had some twenty-five rooms, and when Maddy had bought it two years ago from the heirs, who'd only drunk from and never replenished the initial fortune, it was a candidate for demolition. Not anymore.

"The brush has been cut back and the windows fixed. You can't tell from here, I'm sure," Maddy rattled on proudly, "but it's all been replumbed and rewired. Structurally, the place is perfect. New boilers, too. Three of them. And all winterized. Can you believe it, only the servants' wing was fit for winter living. They used to have a caretaker that stayed all year long."

"You really going to stay here this winter?" I asked.

"Absolutely. I don't know if I'll ever leave again."

I stared at the magnificent house—famous for the Gatsby-esque parties once attended by the likes of the Wrigleys, Maytags, Sears, the Marshall Fields, and other Chicago name-brand families—and was struck by a rare gust of sadness for Maddy. Yes, this was perfection. Her perfection. Every piece of furniture, I was sure, in its exact place. The asphalt paths that she'd learned every turn and twist of. Everything studied and absorbed. This was her world, one she'd created so that it would never offer any surprises. No unknown sidewalks. Unseen curbs. And no buses ever again. This was what she'd bought with all that money. A world she could control; in that regard, her money had served her fabulously well. But so confining. Like a big prison.

"I'm happy here," she said, sucking in a double-bunch of air. "I really am."

Then again, I thought, what had I found out there beyond this drop of land and beyond those waters, what had I found besides speeding tickets, endless dribble about which was the best, the most perfect garage door opener, and, of course, murder? I turned and stared at my Maddy, that face sculpted from wide cheekbones to small chin, those lips so thin, nose so fine, and I realized something. In her world of darkness and frustrated movement, she'd been forced to look elsewhere, seek different meanings, and had, I suspected, found something I probably never could.

"Oh, and wait till you see the third floor," she gushed. "That's where we'll do it. We'll open the doors to the widow's walk and . . . and take off."

"I hope I still remember how."

"Nonsense, Alex. When I was still practicing, none of my clients were as good a subject as you. You can go under hypnosis like that," she said, snapping her fingers.

Which was why I'd come to Maddy's. A big, deep trance that Maddy would direct and I would fall into. A big, deep trance that would maybe, hopefully, turn up what no one else had yet been able to: who had murdered Toni, my estranged college sweetheart, and why.

Chapter 2

Under Maddy's direction, the inside of the house had grown even more incredible, from the open staircase that circled upward to a ten-foot-wide Tiffany glass dome, to the billiard room decorated with musty moose and deer heads, to the dining room with its table for sixteen, not to mention of course the broad living room, which opened onto an unparalleled vista of Lake Michigan. Much of the original furniture was still in place—the billiard table, the dinner table, several couches— because, I supposed, they were so damned large. You needed a place of such exaggerated grandeur to fit pieces like those.

"I could have had everything done at once," said Maddy, as we headed inside after our lunch of whitefish on the veranda. "But that would have spoiled the fun. All the mechanical things have been taken care of, and now I'm just doing it room by room. You know, most of the rooms haven't been wallpapered since before the Depression."

Not to mention the threadbare furniture or the torn curtains, the worn oriental carpets and more. Really, all of it.

I judiciously said, "Obviously."

"But I like that."

Maddy wheeled herself along, leading the way back through the living room, the entry hall, around the billiard table, and toward the back wing. I nearly forgot that she was blind, for she knew exactly where she was at every moment. One creaking board told her she was leaving the living room, a small carpet told her she was entering the billiard room, and so on. She had markers just like seeing people, only she sensed them in a way I couldn't.

"I like the smells," she continued. "The history of smells, you know? The layers of them."

Yes, I did. The house had a fragrance of age unlike anything I'd experienced before. Upon entering, you were first struck with the sweetness of the light woodwork that ran everywhere, then the mustiness of the wallpaper. Perfumy as much as mildewy. Dusty, too, like talcum powder. But washed—always washed—with the freshness of the lake breezes.

We headed through a rear door, into the back hall, and passed another staircase, one of two servants' staircases, Maddy said, laughing. Once there had been a staff of seven to maintain the house and an army of gardeners for the grounds. As she spoke, my eyes drank it all in. Old wardrobes, rich walnut ones, relegated back here years ago, and now filled with dozens upon dozens of paint cans. Wouldn't those be treasures in an antique store? Then two extra sinks—for cleaning fish? Two extra refrigerators, also, old ones with coils atop them. Water coolers, too. Boots. Mops, brooms.

"There's only one house rule," warned Maddy. "The back of the house belongs totally to Alfred and Solange. The kitchen, the sitting room, the servants' quarters—it's all off grounds to us. Please don't go farther than this hall. They're so good to me, I just want to make sure they have their privacy. I just want to keep them happy."

"Of course," I replied, realizing this meant none of the exploring I'd done last time I was here.

There was a clanging of pots from behind a cracked door.

"Solange," Maddy called into the kitchen, "we're going up. I don't know when we'll be down, but please don't disturb us. Perhaps a late dinner, all right?"

"Surely," replied a deep, sweet voice.

We came to a double set of doors, and Maddy groped for the doorknob.

"You're sure this thing is safe?" I asked.

"Don't worry, I had the ropes replaced with cables."

The elevator. Added in 1910 when the master of the house lost the use of his legs, it was a huge wooden room, easily six by six, that moved up and down. It necessitated a huge tower affixed to the rear side of the house, ran all the way to the third floor, and was originally rope-operated. The old man had required two servants not just to wheel him, but to hoist the ropes and pull him up and down.

"Remember when you first came out here last year?" Maddy asked as we boarded and she lowered the two wooden gates. "The elevator had been used as a broom closet for almost forty years. But it's all been redone and brought up to code— I had it electrified so I could operate it on my own."

With a jolt, we were off, moving past leaded glass windows, next past the back hall of the second floor. Lifting off on the first part of our voyage.

"We can just do a practice run today if you like," said Maddy.

"Let's just see."

Suddenly I was nervous. Was it hocus-pocus or would it work? Not to mention: Did I want to relive it all again?

When it seemed as if we might be hurled out the top of the house, the thing finally jerked to a stop. I lifted the slatted wooden gates—the one inside the elevator and the one on the third floor to prevent anyone from tumbling down the open shaft—and Maddy wheeled herself out. I glanced about as we went down a small hall. On the left were two servants' rooms stuffed with old racks of old ballroom dresses, dressers, stacks of mirrors.

"And look at this," said Maddy, stopping by a barrel and scooping her hand in. "Old soap flakes."

"What did the former owners do, abandon all this?"

"There's only so much shit you can lug through life."

"True."

Just as there was a servants' living room off the kitchen on the first floor, there was another one up here. This one, though, was filled with the jetsam of generations of a wealthy family that had, according to Maddy, more or less fizzled out.

"The family made their fortune in beer and lost it in alcoholism," mused Maddy.

I saw boxes packed with Venetian glass and crystal goblets. Chairs stacked three and four high. A wicker baby carriage, a brass child's bed, and piles of mouse-eaten mattresses. It was overwhelming, and depressing as much as it was amazing.

Maddy wheeled her way through it all, knowing the path perfectly. Pushed herself on and up to a door, opened it, and led me into a huge gymlike space, the main part of the attic.

"Oh, Maddy," I exclaimed.

Finally here was a place that was all hers. Maddy's. Here everything had been cleared out, the wooden floor painted white, the walls left bare wood. A huge, palatial space soaring some thirty feet to the peak, it occupied the entire front of this large house and was, oddly, the grandest space of all.

Maddy gave herself a double-handed push and roared into the middle of the room, braked one side and spun, screaming all the while.

"It's wonderful, isn't it?"

Just a big space. How freeing. I hurried after her, turned, saw the dome that capped the stairwell, above it the twenty-by-twenty skylight that allowed a core of light to strike the dome and flood into the center of the house.

"Come over here," said Maddy, not having lost a bit of orientation in her spin. "Look."

She led the way past the only furniture, two leather recliners—I glanced to the side, saw an enormous stereo against a wall—to two huge French doors, which she swung open. She rolled out onto the widow's walk, a small balcony cut into the sloping roof, and a blast of lake air washed over her. I followed, stood beside her, felt the exhilaration. The warmth, the cool wind.

"Oh, my God," I muttered.

Beneath us spread a sea of blue rolling and soft. To the very left I saw a trim of dark emerald green—the shore—and above . . . above a lighter blue. Sky blue. Fairy blue.

"This is why I bought the house," she said. "This perch."

"Yes." And for the first time I really understood.

"I come up here and feel the breeze and smell the air. I can sit here for hours. It's like flying."

"I feel like we're at the very top of the John Hancock Tower. Like we're standing outside on top of it."

She clutched my hand. "Absolutely, but away from everything at the same time." She laughed. "I have some friends out east who can't understand why I'd want to live up here—they think Lake Michigan's horribly polluted."

We were silent for a moment, then she asked me for a remote control, which I fetched from inside and brought to her. Seconds later there was this music that soared. Part rock, part New Age. Gregorian, too. I heard chanting voices. I closed my eyes. Yes, this was flying.

"Now for the fun stuff," she said.

"Fun? You think it's going to be fun?"

"Well, not going through it all. We don't have to do that today if you don't want. But going under. There's magic here, Alex. On this island and up here. Just wait." She turned. "Let's go back in. See the chairs? The one on the left is for you."

I knew she'd just bought it for me, suspected she'd had it special-delivered. A beautiful piece of furniture. Dark wood. Dark leather. It matched hers. I helped her out of the wheelchair and into her recliner, then went to mine.

"There's a lever on the left. Find it?" she asked. "Just pull."

I did, and my feet rose and my head fell back. The southerly sun poured inside and over us, warming, energizing, and the lake breeze came in whirls, washing and cleansing us. In the distance I heard the crashing of waves.

"Breathe in . . . out. In . . . out."

Hypnosis.

"I'm a little afraid," I said against the background of soothing music and rolling water.

"Has your big sister ever done you wrong?"

"No, but . . ."

"Shh. Let's just get into it and we'll take it from there."

Before the accident that had left her paralyzed from the waist down, Maddy had been a very good shrink. She'd always been very insightful. Intuitive, too. And compassionate, of course. All of which was heightened, I was sure, by her lack of sight. She'd always had a full load of clients, and her practice was with a successful group of psychologists who had a suite in a high rise in the Loop, just off Michigan Avenue.

"You're very good at this, Alex," said Big Sister, soothingly. "I think you should be writing novels, not technical manuals. You have a wonderful imagination. That's why hypnosis comes to you so easily. I'm a good practitioner of it, but you . . . you can really take off."

"Baloney."

"Don't baloney me. I'm serious."

Maddy had first learned hypnosis, I knew, from one of her associates, a woman some ten or fifteen years older by the name of Alecia. She was the doyenne of it all and was infamous for her work with hypnosis. I'd met her and found her uptight, was sure her patients did, too. Speaking of which, Maddy had later told me how Alecia had married one of her clients, something that occasionally happened back then, but for which today licenses were revoked. She'd married a guy whom I'd seen over and over and over again on television. Commercials, that's all he did. That's what he'd become famous for. Maddy had further leaked that Alecia had helped this guy, this Will, come to terms with his own mother's murder. I asked if that meant solve it, and Maddy had simply and only said yes. Hot gossip there, I was sure. Shrink marrying her patient. Murder in the family. Sounded interesting.

"In . . . out," chanted Maddy. "Lie back and relax. Clear your mind. Breathe in . . . out."

But while Maddy had told me of her own work with hypnosis, I really didn't get involved with it until that asshole of a bus driver had run her over. I learned it then to help Maddy with the pain. She taught me how to help her go under, slip into trance, then escort her far from the excruciating pain and to a place of calm. A pure place that didn't hurt. And that's what I did. Eventually we both became quite good at it. We traveled well together, and we'd slip under, brother and sister, and disappear into trance. To the Alps skiing, where Maddy would use her creative powers and imagine the exhilaration of rocketing down a slope. To the Mediterranean coast swimming, all that sun, all that beach. Snorkeling in Jamaica, her legs kicking and propelling her. They were guided fantasies of a sort, and we'd had a blast.

"I'm leading," she said. "This is your trance, but I'm leading."

"Just take it easy, okay?"

"Absolutely. I won't push and we'll come back just as soon as you want."

Now we'd both go under, of course. That was the way it worked in hypnotherapy. The therapist would go into trance as he or she hypnotized the subject. In our case, the leader was the one who put the other one under, made sure it was a deep trance, and watched out for the other person, bringing the subject back to consciousness if anything was too disturbing.

The music faded away. Yes, Maddy was directing, turning the volume down, preparing me for lift-off.

"Okay, Alex," she said. "I want you to keep your eyes open and at the same time roll your eyes up. Look up, look up as high as you can. That's: one."

I did as she commanded, and could feel the induction washing over me, beckoning to me. Stretching those brown eyes of mine up, I stared as high as I could. Up, up, up. To myself: one.

"Now, keep your eyes up and breathe in. Breathe in deeply and hold that breath. Good. Hold it. Hold it and while you're keeping your eyes up, I want you to lower your eyelids. Go ahead, close them. Two," she said with great emphasis.

I felt it now. The beginning of the trance. It came that quickly, always starting at the base of my neck and creeping up the back of my head. A numbing sensation. Oh, all right, I thought. I've already made the decision to do this. I give. Chanted to myself: two.

"Relax, Alex. Relax your eyes and let yourself fall . . . fall." Then the pronouncement: "Now breathe and: three."

The first time I'd tried hypnosis I hadn't been able to do it. Nor the second or the third. I'd caught bits and pieces of a trance, had tastes of it, as if I were learning to ride a unicycle and was able to go only a foot or two at a shot, but it wasn't until the fourth attempt that I fell all the way. Tumbled into it. Completely. Wonderfully.

"I'm not there yet," I said. "I'm a little out of practice, you know."

"Just let yourself fall, collapse into darkness."

Trance. It was coming. Crawling through my skull, into my mind. And my feet and hands, too. I could feel it there, eating from the outside, nibbling in. Now that I sensed it, I knew it was going to be great. Inner harmony. Hypnosis. I could be addicted to this, I remembered.

"You're falling," chanted Sister, riding my thoughts and brain waves. "And then all of a sudden . . . whoosh, a great net appears and catches you. Next you realize you're rising. Being lifted up."

I felt a great swirl of air blow through the open doors and wrap around and lift me. Yes. Up. I was rising into the air. In blackness. In darkness. Lifting right off that leather recliner that dear Sister had imported from the Big City. I'm rising, I thought. I'm going up. Higher. Lighter. Lighter into light. Yes, here it was: three.

An enormous rush of tingles surged through me. Oh. This was good. No, great. I saw myself floating into the air, magically and wonderfully. There I was now in sunshine. Secure but gone. Very gone.

From outside, from somewhere close but at the same time far away, a voice called, "*Alex, you're there now, aren't you?*"

Chapter 3

"**N**o shit," I called out of my trance.

"*I thought so.*"

"And how."

I sensed I was on some sort of magic carpet, flying out the French doors of this third floor, out over the house, out over the lake. Blue lake. Blue cloud. Oh, this felt good. I hadn't felt so relaxed in months. Ripples of air. Swirls that held me. Massaged me. Comforted me.

"*Let loose of everything, Alex. Let yourself go,*" called Maddy from back there, back on the other side.

"Trust me, I'm gone."

"*Don't worry. I'll make sure everything's all right.*"

"Who's worried?"

I felt as if I were in a dream that I could control. A dream, that's what hypnosis was like. A dream that I could direct, and that I could talk from. I was in trance, as fully under as if I were in the deepest depths of sleep, yet I was also completely awake and aware. I could be under and communicate with the outside—sister Maddy, for one—at the same time. It was an extremely odd sensation, as if I'd opened some magical door in my mind and disappeared into a secret part of my being.

27

In my trance, I felt myself sitting up and turning around. In my mind's eye, I saw myself way up there, in the sky. I looked back. There was the house with all its columns. So big and white. And there at the top, standing in the widow's walk, was my sister. Maddy. She was standing and waving. Looking at me. No wheelchair. No sunglasses. That's why she liked hypnosis, used it every day, for she could travel everywhere and see everything, both in my trances and hers.

"*Run with it,*" she called, waving to me from the widow's walk.

A swell of emotion erupted. Hypnosis did that to me. Made me free with my words and thoughts.

"Maddy, I'm glad I'm here. I miss you. I don't like living in different places. We had a lot of fun growing up in Chicago, didn't we?"

"*Oh, yes. The best.*"

"I worry about you, you know," I said, the truth serum of hypnosis pushing my concerns to the surface. "Do I need to worry about you? I do. A lot." Especially since our father died and we'd had to put Mother in a home. "I feel guilty, too."

"*Please don't, Alex.*"

"Why? I wonder why it wasn't me whose eyes went or who was hit by a bus. I mean, why didn't just one of those happen to me?"

"*God, then we'd have had a blind brother and a crippled sister, or vice versa. That would have been truly pathetic,*" she said with a slight laugh. "*No, Alex. You were meant for other things. Please don't worry. I'm not angry about any of it anymore and I've found an odd kind of happiness. I'm filthy rich, too, and I'm going to do some great things with that money. That's what I'm meant to do, that's my purpose. I might have a job for you, actually, if you're interested. Oh, and there's another matter I really do need your help on, but first things first. This is your trance.*"

"Oh, yeah."

My trance. That was why I'd come to Madeline's island. Touch base here, fly away. I was a flier, not a digger. Diggers went deeper and deeper into trance. Burrowed themselves in darkness, dug all the way to China. Not me. I started in darkness, for sure, but then I launched myself, flew higher and higher. I loved that part. Going up and up. Now I was up in the clouds. Cool, white, fluffy clouds. I'd come to Maddy's so she could launch me, so I could . . .

"Oh, I know why I wanted to be hypnotized," I said, my voice suddenly flat with sadness. "Toni. Do you remember her? She was from Chicago and she came up to Minneapolis and she was murdered."

"I know. She was a very dear friend of yours."

"It was awful." The words bunched up in my throat. "The . . . the police still can't figure it out, and I keep thinking there's something I know. Some clue. I was there, you know. The night she was murdered. I tried to help, to save her, but . . ."

"So what do you think; is there something you know that would help solve her murder? Is there something buried in your subconscious?"

It was clear to me, perfectly, brilliantly so. "Yes."

"What is it, then, that you know?"

"I'm not sure. But it's there, and it's the key, that's what I keep tripping on. This key. It's like it's right down at my feet, right in the grass, and if I can find it, then I'll be able to unlock the mystery of Toni's death."

"Of course. So are you ready to recapture time? Would you like to do an age regression?"

"Yes. Absolutely." I paused, momentarily lost myself in remorse. "I had to let go of Toni years ago. She didn't want to go out with me anymore. I did my best, but I don't think I ever really got over her, and now I can't get over her death. Not until I understand it."

"Not until you make sense of it."

"Right."

We'd talked about this on the phone. I'd called and told Maddy how I was all screwed up over Toni, kicking myself for what I hadn't done the night she was killed, beating myself for what I could have done. And knowing after the fact that I knew there was something I'd seen along the way. That key.

So Maddy had suggested an age regression. Not a big one, not a leap of years back to my youth or to a previous life or anything like that. But just back a few months to late April. Back to that week when Toni had come up from Chicago looking for her sister. My doorbell had rung, and there she was. Toni, whom I hadn't seen for almost ten years.

"In an age regression," prompted Maddy, *"you'll be able to go*

back and look at what happened. It's like a film that you can play again and again. At points you'll be able to speed it up. At other times, you'll be able to slow it down and look more carefully for what you might have missed the first time."

That was what I had to do, of course. Replay the film of that week, scour my memory for what I knew but didn't know about Toni's death.

"So I need to go back. But where do I start?"

"Just let the story come."

"Well, it started when Toni just showed up on my doorstep."

"Good." Big Sister breathed in, out. In, out. *"It all happened not very long ago. Just a few months. And it's all in your memory still. So just let yourself go back. Imagine yourself at the top of an escalator."*

I was up there in the clouds, and all of a sudden I heard a big *whoosh* and then right before me a door opened and there was an escalator. Weird. An escalator in the heavens. Leading down. But there it was, all shiny. I peered down it.

"Do you see the escalator, Alex?"

"Yes. It's right in front of me."

"Good. Now step on it. I'm going to count from one down to ten. When I reach ten, you'll be back there, back then."

Oh, I get it, I thought. It wasn't an escalator leading down somewhere. But an escalator leading back in time.

"One. You're stepping onto the escalator."

And I was. Yes, one. Yes, back. There I was yesterday washing my clothes, packing. Wondering about Maddy. Worrying about her. Would she ever marry now? Find someone? Probably not. There probably wouldn't be any grandkids to please our mother—I wasn't making great progress toward reproduction! Then again, grandkids . . . Mother barely remembered that she had her own children, so grandchildren might be too difficult a concept for her.

"Two. Let time go backward, carrying you back with it."

I mumbled, "Like I said, it started when Toni came to Minneapolis."

"Just let that scene play. Three. You have that power, Alex."

Smoothly, Maddy did the count, going back through the numbers, carrying me deeper into my trance, transporting me back into time. It all started back then, not long after Liz died.

That's what brought Toni to Minneapolis from Chicago. Her little sister, found drowned in the Mississippi.

And by the time Maddy had counted down to seven, then eight, there was a faint ring.

"There. Do you hear it, Maddy, the doorbell?" I asked.

"Tell me about it. Just drift back into time. You're getting closer to the bottom of that escalator. Nine. And . . ."

"It was Saturday afternoon, and I was getting ready to go out for a bike ride and . . . and . . ."

"Go on, Alex. Let yourself re-create that scene. You can do that. You can do that so you can better understand what happened to Toni." Deep breath. Pinch of lips. Exhale. *"You were getting ready to go out and then your doorbell rang . . . and then: ten."*

Chapter 4

The thing went: *wheeeeeee*! And again, but more deranged and lots longer: *wheeeeeeeeeee*!

God, I hated my doorbell, the intercom one that rang from the lobby downstairs. It was so damned shrill, and when I heard it I was tempted not to answer. Probably some kid selling candy; I mean, I wasn't against camp or anything, just . . . Or someone collecting signatures, trying to shut down the garbage burner. I was in my Lycra bike shorts, the skin-tight ones, and a blue T-shirt, and I was all set to go out. Bike ride. Around the lakes, three of them. Ten point four miles. That was the Sunday afternoon I wanted to set in motion. It was really the first warm Sunday of the year; the snow had been gone just a few weeks, the paths had dried, the leaves were ready to burst. So what kind of gearhead—which I was, to be sure, for I'd turned my second bedroom into a garage/repair shop for my three bikes—wouldn't want to be out?

The stuck-piglike intercom squealed again. Shrieked: *wheeeeeeeeee*! And I stood in the hall of my apartment, thought about sneaking down the back stairs and out the back door. Escape. For some reason that's all I could think. It flashed through my head: Don't answer the stupid door.

"But you did, Alex, didn't you?"

Yes, I thought better of it, realized I couldn't sneak away. It might be a friend. It probably was. Perhaps it was one of the Larses—only in Minnesota could you have not one but two friends with such a Scando name—who'd stopped by on his bike, curious whether I wanted to go for a ride. That's why I went to the intercom, pressed the button, felt as if I was throwing the switch of an electric chair.

"Hi, who's there?" I called into the box on the wall.

Pause from below. Then: "Toni."

My eyes opened wide. I took a step back. Toni? Of course, it was *that* Toni. I didn't know any others. And of course she was just walking back into my life. Hadn't I known she would? Hadn't I been waiting all these ten or twelve years or whatever for this?

Still I couldn't speak, didn't even know what to do. An old scene popped through my head. I was with a friend in New York, we went to lunch, and who do we sit next to in the restaurant but her favorite rock star, her idol of idols, Sting. My friend, Patti, who had searched the streets of NYC for years for him, who had rehearsed her speech ("Congratulations on your baby, Sting"), and who was never without a word, was suddenly speechless, mouth paralyzed, couldn't eat or say a thing, so I sat there for twenty minutes talking about garage door openers until Sting got up and left, after which Patti snatched the uneaten muffin from his plate and crammed it forcefully into her mouth, gummy wrapper and all, and then, with the mouth working again—horribly full of gooey bran and raisins and paper—Patti confessed: "I didn't know what to say, his baby's not a baby anymore!"

It was the same with me. While Patti had correctly sensed her future and that one day she would encounter Sting, so had I seen in my heart of hearts that Toni would drop again into my life. And like Patti, my opening line, recited backwards and forwards for years, was now outdated: "How's the residency going?" I had originally planned to ask her about that because that's why she broke off with me. Her medical career. Consuming. Or so she claimed and I had never believed. That was an excuse. There was something more, I was quite sure. An affair with another med student?

But asking about her residency was vapid and stupid because Toni, after all, had to have been a full-fledged practicing physician, an internist in Chicago, for at least eight years now. My premonition of seeing her once again had been correct, only off by about a decade. So there was no way I was going to press the SPEAK button and ask through the little intercom box, "Hiya, Toni, how's the residency going?"

My mind was as empty as if I'd had electric shock therapy; the only thing I could do was press the other button on the box, the one marked DOOR, which I did, thereby buzzing Antoinette Domingo back into my life.

Even then I knew it was a mistake.

My shrink—the one I'd seen some six years back when I was trying to come to terms with Dad's death in a plane wreck—had said forget about Toni, move on. But of course I'd always been eager to move backward, for her, for Toni. And as I pressed the button, allowed Dr. Antoinette Domingo reentry, I had this dark sense. This future sense. This notion that I was doing something that would render harm upon us both.

So I just stood there in the long, narrow hall of my condo. I opened the door just a crack, leaned against the dark oak woodwork that ran everywhere and for which I'd been willing to pay a premium. What a mistake—not the woodwork, but answering the door and letting her in. My heart swelled and shrank, swelled and shrank. Toni. Oh, shit. I should lock the door, run and charge out the back, hop on my bike, and pedal away as fast as I could. Right, I thought, I must do that, I should do that, because I knew—I knew, I knew, I knew—that one of us wouldn't survive this. Such was our relationship.

"*We can stop this anytime you like, Alex. Just let me know,*" called a protective voice.

Of course I couldn't stop myself. I had to see Toni. Just one more glimpse. One more encounter. Something I had to seize because if I didn't I'd never see her again. Of that I was certain.

As I feebly reached for the door, I heard her quiet steps padding up the stairs. The stairs were wood all the way up to the third floor. No elevator. A three-story walk-up, and Toni was winding her way up, a few floorboards moaning beneath her lithe step. Before I even saw her, I was hooked by the

sound of her. I stood there and stood there, leaning against the woodwork, hearing over the thump of my heart the sound grow more and more real. I bowed my head. Looked at my hardwood floor for some meaning in all of this. Oh, shit, what was I doing? Why was I making this stupid mistake? That chapter was done, over. Or was it?

I sensed a sudden presence, a lack of noise. Raised my head, tried to speak.

I whispered, "Toni."

There was just a long slice of her there in the crack of the doorway, but I could tell. She hadn't really changed since the last time I'd seen her, when she and her friend, Laura, a nurse, had swept through our apartment and moved her things out in only an hour. The same narrow shoulders, narrow waist, wide, flat hips. She wasn't particularly tall, though her legs seemed generous in length. I took it all in, all those markers. Yes. Dark hair that was thick and long and cut with haphazard bangs; it was the same except for a tinge of a henna. Dark skin that tanned on a cloudy day. Thick eyebrows, nice and brown, as were the eyes themselves, and a beautiful, slender mouth and narrow chin. She wore a white underthing, over that a loose tan shirt tied above those wonderful hips, faded jeans, and sawed-off cowboy boots, the kind missing the top part. White purse, too.

But the eyes . . . So very red. Red? Wet?

"Toni?"

She stormed the door open like a strong gust, blew into my arms, and I folded myself around her like a tree embracing the wind. Just as naturally. Just as quickly. We fit perfectly, me not too much taller, her head fitting into the crook of my neck. All this as if she'd not been nearly five hundred miles down Highway 94 for ten years, but only down the street for a few minutes. She was shaking, and I pulled her close to me, pulled her as tightly as I could, felt my fingers in her ribs, my hands in that hair that I'd loved to have trail over my stomach. Toni . . . Toni . . . Toni . . . why had we ever stopped? Or had we? Clutching each other in vertical embrace, I wasn't sure we had ever quit. Time seemed arbitrary. This was the way we'd been, the way we'd always be.

Then I heard a slurp, a good gooey one, and then I felt

the wetness, on my neck. God, those were tears. She was crying. For me? No, I wasn't so vain or that stupid. Tears of joy didn't come this fast, this thick. I planted my lips on her forehead, kissed her through her bangs. She raised her head, squeezed me, clutched me. And I kissed one wet cheek, then the other. Our lips met, brushed, but she turned, buried her face back in my neck before more was consummated.

She said, "Don't let go, Alex."

What an opening line to a heartsick old boyfriend, so I clutched back. It was great, this swell of emotion sweeping me back to some wonderful times. I would have stayed there, too, for a long, long time had she not started shaking, then sobbing so. Toni? I rubbed her back, breathed in the sweet, soft smell of her skin and hair. Toni?

"What is it, what's the matter, what happened?" I asked.

She sniffled, then choked on a word. She tried again but it came out garbled. My God, what was it?

Finally, Toni managed: "My sister . . . my sister Liz. She's . . . she's dead."

Liz? The last I'd heard, Toni's kid sister was a high school senior bent on going to school in the Northwest. So now she was dead? How terrible. A cute kid, that's what I remembered. Confused but cute and likable. What, however, did any of this have to do with Minneapolis, why the hell had that sent Toni into my arms, and why the hell was she blurting all this out to me, the chump she'd said she never wanted to see again?

Pulling back slightly, trying to see Toni's tear-streaked face, I asked, "Dead? What do you mean?"

"The Mississippi . . . she drowned."

I vaguely remembered seeing something in the paper a week or two ago about a young woman's body found in the river. I'd stopped reading, however, when I got to the part about the corpse having been mangled. I'd been eating breakfast and so hadn't gotten to the name, which I wouldn't have missed. Anything even faintly resembling Toni's last name— Domino, D'Amico—had always jumped out at me. I guessed I'd always been looking for another Domingo in my life.

"Oh, my God," I said, shutting the door behind her and ushering her in. "Come on in . . . let's sit down."

My apartment was a Pullman kind of place, long and occupying the length of one side of the building. Sunporch up front, living room, two bedrooms with connecting bath, then the dining room and kitchen in the rear. I ushered Toni down the hall, past the bedroom I'd converted from a guest room to bike central, into the living room, and to the couch. I didn't want to push things, so I sat in a chair next to her. When she reached out, I didn't hesitate to hold her hand on my knee. Same hands, just as soft, though slightly wrinkled. As were the eyes, with lines streaking from the corners like sunbursts. Yes, the same Toni, and yes, she had aged. We both had, only I hoped, but wasn't so sure, I'd deteriorated as well as she had.

She sucked in a lungful of air, let it out, said, "Oh, God, Alex, I'm sorry."

"Don't be silly," I said, though I was a bit surprised because I'd never seen her cry before.

"It's just that . . ." She withdrew her hand from beneath mine and sat back on the couch, threw back her head, stared up at the ceiling. "Liz drowned about two weeks ago, Alex."

That much I knew already.

"She'd been living up here for almost five years."

Now that was news, and from the way Toni said it, from the way she spoke the words without looking at me, I knew that Toni had been up here during that time. Perhaps lots of times. I was silent, caught in a flurry of rejection. And anger. Couldn't she at least have called?

"The funeral was last week. My parents can't handle anything more—they're getting a little old—so I drove up yesterday to close up her apartment. I'm staying at a hotel over by the U."

The U meant the university, so I was sure of it now. "You've been up here before?"

She nodded, and I left it at that. Why, however, had she contacted me now? Why not earlier or later? What had Liz's death set in motion, made it necessary for her to see me?

"I just went over to Liz's apartment, Alex," she continued. Then she stopped, caught her breath. "I didn't know it was going to be so hard—going in there, seeing all her stuff. It freaked me out, you know? It looked like she'd be back in just a moment—there was a cup of coffee and a half-eaten sandwich in her kitchen! I mean, a goddamned peanut butter sandwich just sitting there with bites taken out of it!"

As I sat there in silence, more of the newspaper story was rolling out of my memory. I remembered the headline. Well, not exactly. Not all of it, just the one scarlet word: Suicide. Which started me thinking back. Liz. There'd been problems in high school. Hadn't she dropped out or . . . No, she'd attempted suicide back then, hadn't been successful because she'd been found and her stomach pumped. She'd taken a whole bottle of sleeping pills. Sure, that was it.

Liz. I remembered her as some five years younger than Toni, and while she had the same thick, dark hair, she wasn't quite as pretty, face a little rounder, body a little shorter. She was wilder, too, than Toni. Much more so. More verbal as well. Right. She'd been kind of a mouthy kid, said whatever came to her head. Not rude, though. I thought back. Hadn't the family always seen Liz as the little girl who wouldn't grow up? Yes, but that really hadn't been it, had it? Liz and Toni's mother was an alcoholic, a wine queen, one of those who never got truly blitzed but always had that glow, wore a tiara of inebriation. And while Toni had been more the caretaker sort—which, I was sure, was why she'd gone into medicine—Liz had been the angry one, the one who saw the truth and wanted to battle it. So had she finally lost? Was that why she had killed herself?

"I went over to her place, Alex, but I couldn't stay. It was too much. I told my parents I'd go through everything, but I don't know. I don't know if I can. I walked in there, and when I saw that sandwich sitting there, I flipped out. I had to see someone. Someone who knew me and her. I'm sorry. I hope you don't mind. I got your address out of the phone book and just came straight over. I . . . I needed to see someone out of the past."

"I'm sorry about Liz, but I'm glad you're here," I said, and for whatever reason I truly was. "I remember reading about someone drowning in the river—it was downtown, right?"

She nodded.

"But I didn't know it was Liz. I would have called you or come down for the funeral or . . ."

Toni was bending her head forward, shaking it furiously. "It wasn't how they said it was," she said, having not heard my condolences. "Alex, everyone thinks it was a suicide—the police, her friends, even her shrink. But it wasn't, Alex. I know Liz. I know she was screwed up, but I also know she didn't jump off any bridge."

What was I supposed to say? What could I?

I muttered a cool, "Oh?"

Dr. Toni Domingo started wiping her wet eyes with the back of her hands, then went on to her nose. Most unhygienic, most unsuccessful.

"Let me get you some Kleenex," I offered.

I jumped up and hurried down the hall, through the extra bedroom and into the bathroom, where I pulled a long, flowing loop of toilet paper. Toni, here at last in my apartment. Unbelievable. And why, I wondered as I rushed back, had I offered Kleenex when all I ever used was good ol' tp?

Toni seemed not to notice my manners. I handed her the ribbon of toilet tissue. She mopped her face. Blew her nose. She seemed not to notice because she was holding something that was infinitely more important than my etiquette.

"I know Liz didn't kill herself because of this," said Toni, shaking the envelope at me.

It was a small envelope, note-card size, torn across the top, now dirtied and bent. A letter. How many times had it been read and reread?

"Is that from Liz?" I asked.

Toni nodded, drew in a trancelike breath. "I got it the day after—*after*—she supposedly killed herself."

"My God."

"We didn't even know she was dead yet—her body wasn't found until the next day. So . . . so here I get this great letter about her wanting me to come up and do some photos and—"

"Still doing that?" I asked, remembering Toni with either a stethoscope or camera always hanging from her neck.

"Whenever I can. It's my escape from medicine. Anyway . . . anyway, she wanted me to come up. Liz was always writing poetry, but she decided to try and break into free-lance journalism. She said she had this great story she wanted to write, and she wanted me to come up and take some pictures for her. This was going to be her big break, she said, and . . . and . . ."

I turned away, felt myself not wanting to know any of this.

"Stay with it, Alex. Let yourself stay with that experience, let yourself hear that conversation with Toni. What did you learn that's relevant to now?"

I asked, "Is there a date on the letter?"

Nod. Sigh. "The day before. It sounds," said Toni, pulling the letter itself from the envelope and studying several lines, "like she wrote it that night. I don't know." Then again, "I don't know."

Neither did I. We sat there in mournful silence. Toni blew her nose, gave it a good tweak. Then I knew what was coming. Sensed it quite clearly. This was why Toni had come. I understood now. But it was a mistake. The whole goddamned thing was a mistake. That didn't change anything, though. It didn't keep her from asking and it didn't keep me from doing what I wanted to do.

"Alex, I have a favor to ask."

I sat there in stony silence.

"Would you come with me to Liz's? I'm . . . I'm kind of creeped out about going over there alone. I'm sorry, you know, to show up after all this time and impose like this."

"Nonsense."

I could cancel my dinner plans. The woman I was supposed to have Thai food with at Sawatdee Restaurant wouldn't forgive me. But that didn't matter. I'd cancel, absolutely.

"Let me make a quick phone call," I said, rising.

I at least owed my would-be date that; it would have been our first date, so this was really nipping it in the bud. What was I going to say? My old girlfriend just buzzed her way back into my life and she was still the one to whom I compared all? Could I be that honest?

I stopped, one hand on the back of the couch, and asked the obvious. "There's only one thing, if Liz didn't kill herself, then what happened? Was it an accident?"

Toni shook her thick dark hair. "No. Nobody else seems to think so, but I think she was murdered. In fact, Alex, I'm sure of it."

My eyes scanned the floor. Over the winter, when chilly Minneapolis's crime rate was usually at its lowest, four or five young women had been hideously murdered, their butchered bodies found in snowy woods and fields. Everyone was reading about it, talking about it. Could Toni's sister have been the next victim?

"So will you go with me? I mean, to Liz's?"

My heart skidded to a halt. All my internal warning bells went off, screamed like my intercom-doorbell thing. It was like I knew what was going to happen, like I knew going over there—particularly right then—was not only stupid but dangerous, that it was another step along a path that led only to death. But hadn't I been waiting all these years for this, the opportunity to prove both my devotion and love for her, for Toni?

So I eagerly said, "Sure, just let me put on some pants."

And I was so excited that I rushed to change and forgot all about Thai food and making that one quick phone call.

Chapter 5

After that, it hit me, the realization that I was reliving it all hit me, and I started twisting and groaning. Toni in my arms? Toni to be killed? How was any of this possible? How could I stop it? I had to warn her, had to help her!

"Alex, let's take a break. I'm going to count from—"

No! I couldn't leave Toni. If I left her now, I'd lose her forever. I knew that much. I had to stay with her, protect her.

"Just a short break, Alex. A pause. Then you'll come back and Toni will still be there."

But . . .

"Ten . . . nine . . ." she cooed. *"When I reach one, you'll be back in the present and you'll remember everything, Alex. Everything will be fine. Eight . . ."*

I tried to battle that godlike voice calling me, tried not to hear her. But I couldn't block her out—she kept chanting, kept pulling me back, going on and on, reaching into the mesmerizing black hole I was hiding in, counting abracadabralike, grabbing and pulling me out of the darkness. I felt as if I were being sucked down a whirling drain from which I couldn't escape, from which—

"And one." Maddy paused a moment. "You're awake and you're in the present."

"Oh, shit."

Where was I? I opened my eyes, just as quickly shut them because I saw that I was back in Madeline's attic on Madeline's island. I groped for the recliner's lever and pushed it, which in turn catapulted me forward, head into hands.

"Are you all right?" asked Maddy.

"No, I don't think so. Am I really back here?" I said, glancing over.

"Yep." She lay motionless on her extended chair. "Well, I don't think you've forgotten a thing about hypnosis—I think you're just as good as ever."

"No shit." I shook my head. "That was a hell of a practice run, if you want to call it that."

A hell of a trance through time, through memory, whatever, to that night when Toni had shown up at my place back in Minneapolis. How was it possible? Yet even more so, how was it possible that I was back here?

I opened my eyes a bit, squinted at the bright light streaming in through the French doors. Heard the waves of Lake Michigan out there, bashing and rolling. Turned, and saw around me the huge empty attic, rising like a Viennese ballroom totally stripped of ornamentation. And my sister was right next to me, sunglasses over her failed eyes, her frozen legs completely still, of course. She looked every bit the elegant movie star resting on the deck of a luxury liner. So innocent, so lovely, yet what a sorceress.

"It was all so real. I mean, I was back there in my apartment, back then, in April. But it's August now, and I'm here, with you."

I stood, went to the screen door, looked out at the vast blue sea of Lake Michigan. It was like magic, all of this. Black magic. Witchcraft. What I'd just experienced, witnessed, seen—it hadn't just happened. No, it had happened long ago, months ago.

"She's dead," I said.

"Yes, I know. And I'm sorry."

"Do you remember her?"

"Of course I do."

"She's dead . . . and yet I just had her in my arms. I was just holding her, touching and smelling her. It was all so real."

"Isn't the mind amazing?" said Maddy. "I bet you thought you were beginning to forget her."

"Yeah, I did."

"But there she was in your imagination, just waiting for you to reach out to her. I hate our Western way of thinking—that life is linear and once you experience events and people, you leave them behind."

"Maddy . . . please."

"No, I mean it. Toni's out there somewhere, in a dimension just out of our sight, beyond our grasp."

A heavy depression was hitting me, washing through me. I couldn't bear Maddy's philosophy, not now. I didn't want anything to do with the methods Maddy had adopted to cope with the tragedies of her life. Toni was my tragedy, and she was dead, murdered, and nothing else really mattered.

I distanced myself from my sister, stepping out onto the balcony, where I was embraced by the strong afternoon sun, the powerful breeze. In the distance I saw a huge ship, probably coming up from Chicago, heading for the top of Lake Michigan, where it would pass into the other lakes, out the St. Lawrence Seaway, and to the ocean. To a world beyond. God, I felt numb with despair, as if I'd just held Toni—which I had—and as if I'd just lost her again—which was also true.

From inside, Maddy called, "Alex, do you want anything to drink?"

"Sure."

"Iced tea?"

"Sure."

I glanced inside, saw Maddy stretching to her wheelchair, reaching for a phone in a holster. She needed assistance, and I began to turn.

"No," firmly said my sister, hearing my steps and stopping me. "If I need help I'll ask for it."

Same old Maddy, I thought, turning back to the blue, watery vista. Hadn't changed since she was five. And sure enough, behind me I could tell she had the phone in hand, could hear her bleeping a couple of buttons on the phone and calling downstairs.

"Hi, Solange," said my sister. "Could you bring us a couple of iced teas? Wait, make that a pitcher, and bring extra lemons, if you would. Yes, we're still upstairs. Thanks."

I watched the whitecaps on the lake appear and disappear, little blips of white, and then I noticed something moving down below on the lawn, right in front of the house. Two big, long, gray things. Oh, yes. Fran and Ollie, the dogs. Was I going to be able to take a walk here, or was I trapped inside, Maddy's prisoner now?

From behind the screen door, Maddy said, "You loved her a lot, didn't you?"

"Yeah," I said over my shoulder. "But it was very complicated. Kind of weird, I guess. There's a whole bunch of stuff I never told you. Maybe it was a sick relationship, I don't know."

"Trust me, Alex, all relationships are weird."

I turned around, stared at her inside, and wanted to say—and was just about to—oh, yeah, how do you know? Maddy had dated some, might even have had a few flings, but as far as I knew she'd had no Mr. Wonderful.

Before I could blather my insolent superiority, however, she surprised me, confessing, "I had someone like Toni in my life. A man I cared for as much as you cared for her, I mean."

"What?"

"I fell very much in love with a man, and it was wonderful . . . and agonizing."

"You're kidding."

I stayed outside, on the other side of the screen door, as if I were in one side of a confessional booth and she were in the other. I hadn't thought it possible, or rather, if Maddy had been in love I assumed she would have told me, which she definitely hadn't. I'd kept secrets from her, to be sure, but she never had from me. Or so I thought. Then again, why should I have been surprised? She'd been a shrink, and shrinks were obsessive, even fascistic, about guarding secrets. They carried all their clients' deepest and darkest, a veritable fortune of dirty admissions, so why shouldn't she keep something about herself from me?

"It was before the accident." Which meant before the CTA bus. "About six months before, I guess."

Suddenly I heard a gentle knock. Iced tea. Maddy called out, and Solange stepped in. Through the screen door, from my vantage in the sun, I could see her dark shape. An attractive woman, skin a deep black. A gentle soul who moved with competence and attentiveness. She and her husband, Alfred, were in good employ here, and my sister was in their good care.

"Hello, Alex," she called to me.

"Nice to see you, Solange."

She set the tray down on the floor between the two leather recliners, poured one glass, lifted it carefully into Maddy's hands, poured the other, then left.

"Thank you," called Maddy.

We were alone again, and I stepped inside, sat on the edge of my chair, picked up my glass, sipped at it. And cut to the quick.

"But he was married?"

"He was married to his work—a very ambitious guy—but otherwise not really."

"What do you mean, not really? You either are or you aren't."

"The extra lemons are for you. Did you get any?"

I reached down, took another, said, "Well, was he married or wasn't he?"

"No, he was just divorced, but he was still sort of married in his head, if you know what I mean."

"Oh."

Maddy smiled, drank some tea, settled back into lounge position, a giddy expression on her face. "We've never talked like this, have we?"

"No."

"Well, I had a few boyfriends, you know. I went out on dates. Not a lot, mostly with blind men, though there were a few seeing ones, too."

"And him?"

"Seeing. Definitely. He had a Jeep or a Dodge-something, and he used to drive me out to the Indiana Dunes and then right down on the beach. He had a place where he could sneak down, you see, and it was all very exciting, racing along the edge of the lake and everything, all that splashing water." She sighed. "There was a moody side of him that I never really got to know, but he was special, really he was. Or rather we were special together. What's the saying? One soul in two bodies, that was us. Soul mates."

"Why didn't you ever tell me?"

"He worked in my office, you see, so at first we were very hush-hush about it. He was like that, too. Very secretive, you know. I got used to that, I guess. In fact it was kind of fun— we had a special secret. Eventually we told a few people, but then . . ."

Maddy's face fell. I watched her, my blind sister with the long neck and the Beverly Hills sunglasses, and I knew I'd seen her in pain before, but never in hurt. Her mouth grew tiny, her body still.

"But then?" I prompted.

"I was hit by that bus, you see, and I was in the hospital, and it really was very difficult for me to get around, and—"

"He never came to the hospital, did he?"

She shook her head.

No, he didn't. Otherwise I would have met him because I'd been there almost every day. All of Maddy's vast number of friends were there, and I knew them all now. But not him, this guy I now hated because Maddy had been deeply depressed in the hospital—I remembered that all too well—not simply because she'd been crippled, but also because there was no Mr. Wonderful in her life. Only Mr. Shmuck.

"Anyway, he could be like that, terribly abrupt, so I'm not that surprised he shut me out," continued Maddy with a helpless shrug. "He had this wonderful job opportunity out in the Bay Area. A private clinic was falling apart, and he went in, bought it, and turned it into a huge success."

"And you never heard from him again?"

She shook her head. "He must be happy because he must be rich now, which is what he wanted."

"What an asshole," I said.

Maddy mustered a smile. I set my iced tea on the floor, reached out, and touched her on the knee. She gave no reaction, and I realized, of course, that she couldn't feel my hand there, couldn't see it either, so I touched her on the arm, which brought more of a smile and most of the warmth back to her face.

"Thank you." She took a long, deep breath, tried to huff all that hurt out of her body, and said, "Now what'll it be? More trance or are we done for the day?"

"More trance."

I couldn't leave Toni. In hypnosis I'd found her, couldn't just drop her. I had to return.

But I couldn't stop thinking of my sister, either, and how hurt she felt and how little I could do for her and how little she really needed me—not to get the phone, not to pay for anything because she had all those tens of millions of dollars.

"Maddy, you mentioned earlier you needed my help on something. What is it?"

"Later, Alex."

"No, tell me. I'll do anything for you. You know that."

She put down her iced tea, took my hand in her glass-chilled grasp, said, "I do know that, Alex. Absolutely. And I do want your help. There is something you can do for me, but I don't want to get into that now. Let's finish this."

"But—"

"Alex, really, we'll get into it later. You can help me after we're through. First things first. I don't want to distract you. I don't want to detract from what you're trying to accomplish. What you're trying to do is both very difficult and very, well, exhausting."

Yes, there was the matter of Toni and who killed her. That was why I was here. To use forensic hypnosis in an attempt to identify her killer. All right, I thought, turning, settling back into the recliner, so Maddy was right. Again.

"Okay," I said, pulling the lever so the bottom part came up, caught my feet, lifted them up. "But you promise you'll let me help you?"

"Promise." She took one of those cueing deep breaths. "In . . . out. Are you comfortable?"

I squirmed a bit, wormed my way into the leathery folds of the recliner. "Yes."

"Then just relax. Take a deep breath. Hold it. Let it go. Now another . . ."

I did as she commanded, my sister the sorceress, following

her instructions, her induction into that other world, the hypnotic one that I lusted for. I took those breaths. Felt my body grow lighter. I rolled my eyes up, closed my eyelids, breathed again. It worked. Quite well, actually. Within moments I was on the fringe of another trance of another world. Several minutes later I was quite deep. I let her lead me, did as she commanded, and then I was gone. Very much so. Back into that black vortex.

And she called to me, *"Now, where were we?"*

Where were we? I knew, quite literally. Back in Minneapolis.

Chapter 6

Liz's apartment was close, but her neighborhood, across Hennepin and Lyndale and up a couple of streets, quickly changed from pseudo-yuppie to quasi-punk, which made it less boring but perhaps a bit more dangerous. After Chicago, however, nothing up here in Minneapolis really seemed all that threatening. Just last month a friend had confronted a burglar in her house. He'd broken in during the middle of the night, had been on the way up the stairs, and my friend was standing there in her nightgown, and when the burglar saw her, he said, "Excuse me," turned and calmly walked out of the house. Only in Minnesota.

So the neighborhood couldn't have been the reason I was afraid. But I was. I pulled over, parked behind a dark brown van, and Toni and I sat inside my Honda as the early spring light faded away. I looked up at the small red brick apartment building and felt a tremor of fear ripple through me. We shouldn't go up there, up those concrete steps, through that door.

"We can skip this part if you want, Alex. If this is too hard, we can pass over it and move on."

No, I had to push into this because I was certain there was

50

something to be learned up there in that apartment. Liz had left something behind that would tell us about her fate, so we had to go. I was sure of this, but why?

"Because you've returned to the past with knowledge of the future." The voice much wiser than I added, *"Don't worry, you'll survive what's about to happen. And so will Toni. Her time has not yet been called."*

Right. I knew that. But what was all this? Was I some sort of spy or hidden observer watching this or was I really back there, really doing my life all over again?

"Alex, just be assured that it's not the middle of the night and you're not down by the lake. There will be no man with a gun, not yet."

I felt a hand on my arm, which pulled me back into whatever reality this was. I looked down, saw Toni's long, thin fingers touching me.

"You look a little spacey," said Toni. "Are you all right?"

"What?" I asked, shaking my head, taking a deep breath, returning to that moment. "Oh, sure. Yeah, I'm fine." I reached for the car door handle. "Let's go. You have the key, don't you?"

She nodded, Toni who was supposed to have been gone forever, and climbed out of the car. I stared after her, couldn't quite believe it still, had to pinch myself. I didn't think I'd just lost Toni, I thought she had gone forever, disappeared over the horizon, never to return. I circled the car and was now just two steps behind her, having changed into jeans and a faded denim shirt. Toni was still in her tan shirt, jeans, and those too-weird hacked-off cowboy boots. And we were about to go into Liz's apartment, which I knew was stupid even though I did nothing to the contrary.

"Which is Liz's place?" I asked.

"That one."

Toni raised her finger without really looking, and I saw her point to a ground-floor corner window covered with a water-stained white curtain that hung limply from a rod. My pulse dialed itself up to high as if I knew there was someone inside there, lurking in a corner or hiding in some closet of the apartment. Come on, I told myself. Get a grip.

We entered a beat-up lobby, the tiled floor all chewed up, and I checked the row of brass mailboxes. L. Domingo's box was packed, letters and junk mail bulging out.

"Remind me to look for the mailbox key," I suggested.

"What? Oh, yeah. Look at that," said Toni, glancing at the box as she lifted a key to the front door. "Classy building, huh? You'd think John, the caretaker, would help out. He just lives upstairs. Then again Liz always said he was kind of dense. Oh, and a word from the wise. If we run into him, don't let him know you're from Chicago. He grew up across the street from Wrigley Field, and he'll corner you and talk for hours about the Cubs and the Bears."

The hallway was dark. Old green paint everywhere. Some old fixtures above. And a carpet that had had the life trampled out of it years ago. We turned left, and Toni lifted the key to the first door, put a hand to her mouth, closed her eyes. So she was just as unsure as I was.

"May I?" I asked.

She nodded, and I slipped the brass key into the lock, twisted, and pushed the door into our dubious fate. It was a dingy place—wallpaper old and faded, all the curtains and shades drawn. There was an old brown couch propped up on two dictionaries, a stereo, a haphazard stack of CDs, a big, fat upholstered chair. And not too much else at first glance. So what had I been afraid of? There wasn't anything in here except possibly, and probably, cockroaches.

"Come on," I said, reaching out and taking Toni's hand in mine. "It's all right."

Soft skin, doctor's skin, well scrubbed, smooth. That was what her hands were like. I'd forgotten that, but was reminded again of all our funny and wonderful times, as if her skin supplied a direct link to the past. I offered a small, reassuring smile, she looked at me and blinked her thanks, and so we went in, crossed the threshold, and entered the apartment a dead person had left behind. I didn't envy Toni this. I'd had to sort through my dad's things after his death, and it was awful, particularly since I'd had to do it mostly on my own. All the sorting and lifting of boxes.

"Sorry."

No, no, it was okay because Maddy had done other things. Some of the financial and legal matters. It was just hard. Mother couldn't face up to it. So I'd done it, which was why I knew how hard this was for Toni. Particularly if she believed her sister's death was not one Liz had bought of her own volition.

"Oh, God," muttered Toni.

It was depressing. Dark and dingy. Stale and stuffy. My eyes looked around, searched for the old peanut butter and jelly sandwich. It was around here somewhere, I thought, my hand falling from Toni's. The kitchen? I left Toni stranded in the middle of the living room and moved toward the rear of the place, with the oak flooring—which was in nearly every apartment and home within the city limits of Minneapolis— creaking under my weight like fresh ice. I entered a narrow hallway that led from the living room, passed down this gray corridor, and stopped at the entry to the little kitchen. And there it was. The sandwich. The coffee. Sitting right there on the edge of the chipped porcelain sink.

I should have stopped right there. I shouldn't have gone on. But I did. I couldn't help myself; it was as if some other sense had picked up an alien presence. So I went on down the narrow, windowless hallway and back toward a blackened doorway, which had to be to the bedroom. Behind me I heard something dragging across wood. I glanced back, saw Toni hauling a chair over, then heard her plunk herself down. She could do only so much, go only so fast.

Something else struck my ears, pricked at me. A soft scraping noise. Oh, shit, I thought. Was someone else in here? Had that been a heavy boot moving across the floor? I froze, heard something again. A gentle movement, a Hitchcockian one, as if a person were lurking, hoping not to be discovered. I stiffened, thought about backing down the hallway, retreating to the living room. I nearly called back to Toni, but why should I add to her trauma? Why should I spook her unnecessarily? It was probably a mouse or a rat or some really big bug. Something beating against the tattered shades, a Hannibal-the-Cannibal kind of moth.

Get a grip. There couldn't be anyone in here, could there? No, the front door had been locked. Still, I was in no hurry. There was no sense in announcing myself any more than I already had. I put one foot down ever so gingerly. There was a back door on my right, then another. I stopped. The door was thickly painted with the years of many tenants. Layers of them. I reached for the glass knob, twisted it. A black hole of a closet emerged. Coats, boots. Things stuffed in there, packed from floor to top shelf. No one could be in here, but—

But then suddenly something came crashing out. I yelled. This hard thing came ripping down, plunging toward my head, smacking me. I jumped back.

"Alex?" called Toni. "What—"

I yelled again, nearly jumped out of my clothes as a boxed Monopoly game tumbled down, burst open, showered me with the American-as-apple-pie cards and a whole suburb's worth of little green plastic houses.

"Oh, crap," I muttered. To Toni, I called, "It's nothing. Something just fell out of the closet."

Cursing, I stepped in and around the game paraphernalia scattered across the floor. Moved on. I needed to despook this place. Open all the shades, turn on the lights, open the windows, get rid of the chokingly stale air. That's right, I thought. This place needed to be reclaimed by the living. So I continued, glancing to the left and into the bathroom with its little hexagon-tile floor, tub with window above it, peeling white paint.

I heard it again. That slight noise. I froze. It was coming from the bedroom. My aroused heart took note and swelled with long, deep beats. But this was silly. Very silly. I took a step, another. No one could be in there. If no one was in there, though, then why was the bedroom door only partially open? What about the police—I'd forgotten to ask Toni if they'd already been here. Perhaps they'd come to ascertain . . . ascertain what? Next of kin? That it had indeed been a suicide?

Swish. That was what I was hearing. Nice and soft and slow. As if someone were hiding in the bedroom and moving very, very slowly. I didn't like this. I eased open the bedroom door, pushed it just a bit. There were jeans on the floor. A bra, dropped right on a small rug. I saw a mattress on the floor, too, and cream-colored sheets heaved aside. So what was unusual about this, how different was this than my own bedroom? Not very.

That's when I heard it again, that noise. My hand flattened on the door, slowly coaxed it wider, heard it perfectly now. I saw the source. A partially open window—pulled up some six or so inches—the wind billowing against the closed shade, the closed shade brushing against the windowsill. I shook my head. Had I seen too many movies or what?

I strode into the bedroom, made directly for the window, which I intended to throw open as wide and fully as possible. I was maybe halfway across the room, however, when I sensed something else. Something extremely odd. This time it was the bedroom door, and it was closing behind me. I froze, turned around. There was a figure there. A man taller than me, with a woman's stocking pulled crudely over his head. He'd been hiding behind the door, and now that I was in the bedroom, he was closing the door, then twisting the little lock beneath the glass knob.

Oh, shit. Here I was, trapped with some hood of a burglar, and Toni, my only chance at outnumbering this thug, was locked out of the bedroom. My mind bolted ahead, raced for a way to thwart all this, and—

"Alex, replay this scene slowly as if it were a film or a video. You've come back looking for something, a clue of some sort. You saw it all before, now you have time to study it."

Time banged to a halt. Freeze frame. I glanced to the left, saw a dresser. A cheap dresser made from pressboard. One of the drawers was yanked open. Several pairs of hose were dangling from it. So this guy, whoever he was, hadn't been expecting anyone. He'd searched Liz's drawers, found a pair of nylons, pulled one leg over his face. I looked back at him. Face grotesquely mushed beneath the nylon. Lips flattened, nose pugged out. No moustache.

"What's he wearing?"

He had on a T-shirt, black, with some sort of eagle on it. Beneath one of the sleeves . . . beneath the right sleeve, there was a tattoo. I caught only a hint of it, couldn't tell what it was, but it looked like a dragon. Yes, there was some sort of curling, serpentine tail—that's what was poking down. And jeans, of course. He wore ratty old black jeans and . . . and black high-top gym shoes. Canvas ones.

Shit, he dropped some papers or something from a folder, and from atop a dresser he snatched a shadeless lamp, a big, heavy wooden one.

I couldn't hold the scene still any longer.

In a flash of a second, in a lightning rush of adrenaline,

everything dialed back up to full speed. The guy came at me, lamp held back, ready to swing. Great. I'd come in here thinking I might find a mouse and instead discovered some thug who was apparently intent on batting me out of existence.

My eyes groped for something, anything, a tool, a device, protection, a weapon. A shoe. In the corner of my eye I spotted a shoe on the floor, and I scooped down and hurled it at him. The attacker laughed, knocked it away as if it were cotton candy. I eyed a pillow on the bed. Against a lamp of that size and weight a pillow would be silly armor. An alarm clock. I dove down, grabbed it, heaved, watched him swing the lamp Mickey Mantle-like, and a split second later I was showered with pieces of digital plastic.

There was pounding at the door, and a voice screaming, "Alex! Alex, what's going on? Alex?"

At the top of my lungs, I shouted, "Call the police! There's a goddamned burglar in here!"

I heard her kicking at the door, then nothing. Gone to the phone. Gone for a neighbor. Hurry, I thought, hurry!

In the faint light of the room, I danced a backward quick-step as the guy came at me. It was hopeless, I knew, but he kept coming and left me no choice. I had to fight just to defend myself. So when he jabbed the lamp at me, I dodged it, tried to grab his arm. He pulled back, coiled himself, swung the lamp, and I hopped backward and onto the mattress as the thing went wind-screaming past.

The tangled sheets were like a mass of angry snakes coiling around my feet and ensnaring me. I kicked, sensed my balance leaving me. That's when he came at me again. Even with my arms flailing, paddling, to keep me upright, there wasn't much I could do. He knew he had me, and he pulled the lamp back, swung it sideways, then hurled it right at my side. I raised my left arm, which broke the thrust of the blow. But it still bit hard, cracking against my forearm, then coming to a dead stop against my ribs. My vision exploded black, and I screamed but nothing came out because the wind had been batted clear from my lungs. I lost my balance altogether and felt myself in freefall, dropping across the mattress, hitting the wall hard with my head, which sent a thump that echoed through my body. There was another burst of darkness, then some light and I looked up, saw this L'eggs-masked vision towering over me, ready to pounce. He froze when he heard the pounding of fists against the door. I couldn't rise. Couldn't defend myself anymore. And there were voices. More than Toni's. Two or three people. I wanted to shut my eyes, shut everything out, but I knew I couldn't because I had to stay awake, clutch onto consciousness and try to protect myself.

Suddenly there was a thunk of something falling, and my eyes popped open. The lamp was on the floor, the burglar halfway out the window. I saw him, just the last of his black jeans and high-tops, yet I didn't move because I hurt like hell, and what did it matter if dead Liz's apartment had been robbed? Not much, really, so I simply lay there until Toni and the care-taker named John kicked down the door.

Chapter 7

We called 911, and as we waited for the police, Toni and I turned on a couple of lights, opened the shades, and sat in the living room. John, pale and tall and with a generous gut on him, stood in the open doorway. I stared at him, a big guy with a big face and balding, reddish hair, and I was glad he'd been around. Wearing a blue plaid shirt, jeans, and some old brown shoes that were all cracked and split, he looked as if he'd come from the north woods or perhaps the Iron Range.

"I wonder if I should call the owner," he said, touching his bottom lip. "I wonder what I should do."

"If you don't call her," said Toni, "the police probably will."

"Think so?"

"Absolutely."

"Yeah, I guess." He paused, then said, "I was sorry to hear about your sister."

Toni looked at the floor, nodded.

"She was real pretty. She played her stereo real loud, but that was okay because I—" John heard the first scream of a siren, leaned his big, puffy body toward the window, and announced, "Here come the cops. You don't need to tell them I was here, do you?"

Turning to him, Toni asked, "What were you going to say about Liz?"

"Nothing. Listen, I'm late for work, and the phone company don't like it when their repairmen are tardy, you know?"

"But—"

"I really gotta go. There's some phone lines down in north Minneapolis. A real mess, I guess. See ya," mumbled John, tugging on his lower lip and backing out.

I looked again at this guy with the disheveled reddish hair, and wondered when he'd last seen Liz and if the cops had bothered to talk to him about her death. Could that be why he was eager to avoid the police now? Had they given him a hard time? Before I could ask, though, John had slipped away.

Within the minute the cops dashed up the walk, started banging on the outer door. Toni let them in, escorted them into the apartment. Two of them, a Scando-looking blond guy, tall and wispy, and a woman cop, black, round face with large, smart-looking eyes. I pointed toward the bedroom, told them how the intruder had fled out the back window.

"Kind of tall," I described the guy.

"Race?" asked the Scando cop.

"White."

"Clothing?" asked the black woman.

"Um . . . black T-shirt. Black jeans, too."

"Hair?"

I drew a complete blank. "I don't know."

The white cop asked, "Bald?"

"Yeah, maybe."

They moved quickly, the woman cop hurrying out the back door of the apartment and into the alley. The other cop dashed to the front to his throbbing auto, where he barked the problem and the description of the suspect into the radio. Moving just as rapidly, Toni went to her white leather purse, took out a small calendar, cracked it open, picked up the phone, and dialed a number.

"Detective Tom Jenkins," she said into the receiver.

A voice blathered something that Toni didn't care for.

"No, you have to interrupt him," she insisted. "Tell him Toni Domingo's on the line. Tell him someone just broke into my sister's apartment and we were assaulted."

That did the trick, she got this Jenkins on the line, explained what had happened, and then she hung up.

Turning to me, Toni said, "He was the detective assigned to my sister's death. He said he'd be right here."

As we sat there, my shock began to cool and suddenly I began to ache with pain. I hadn't been in a fight since grade school—I'd duked it out with some tubby bully whose name I'd long ago forgotten—and I didn't really much care for it. I was appreciating the American penchant for violence less and less the older I got.

"I think the arm's okay," said Toni, probing my body with doctorly fingers that I found erotic even in my pain.

"What about the head?" I asked.

She ran her hand through my thick, curly hair, hit upon a hell of a sizzling egg, and said, "No, you're just as thick-skulled as ever."

She hugged me once, apologized, kissed me, so it was almost worth the pain. I could tell, though, that her thoughts were elsewhere, specifically on Liz and this break-in and if there was some sort of connection.

Even though the police soon had assistance, it was hopeless. The intruder had escaped. He was quick and scared of course, and so, some fifteen minutes later, suspectless, the two cops returned. Toni told them that she'd called one of their cohorts, a detective, and he was on the way because this was potentially related to her sister's murder—Toni definitely said murder, which definitely raised their brows—and then they asked questions. Not too many, just enough for their own reports, knowing this was a matter that the detective would assume.

Which he did. Detective Tom Jenkins arrived about twenty-five minutes after Toni had called, a confident guy, white, midforties, with receding dark, grayish hair. He looked like a former jock who probably once had broad shoulders and a trim waist, though things were now a bit the opposite, the waist looking a little bigger than the shoulders. He reminded me of one of my high school teachers whose name also was Tom. Jenkins had the same thick eyebrows, brown eyes, and easy smile, and he even looked as if he could solve our problems as simply as my teacher had once solved those math problems.

He introduced himself to Toni, and said, "It's finally nice to meet you in person."

She shrugged, shook her head. "Yeah, well . . ." she said, insinuating this wasn't the meeting she'd had in mind.

I gathered from their initial words that they'd only talked over the phone, that they had an appointment for tomorrow, and that, of course, he'd investigated Liz's death. It was also evident that Toni wasn't entirely satisfied or that she was frustrated or angry at him. Something like that. Something like he subscribed to the theory that Liz's death was nothing more than suicide.

Detective Jenkins spent a few minutes with the other two police officers, who told Jenkins what they'd found—essentially nothing—and then offered a couple of extra opinions. I heard the word "murder" muttered, saw the black woman eye Toni as the source of this information, and then I saw Jenkins give a slight but obvious shrug, making it clear that this was a matter of opinion and not fact. I glanced at Toni, who was following every syllable and body movement with angry interest.

Jenkins came over, sat down on a chair across from the ratty couch we were perched on.

"This might be connected to your sister, Toni," he began, "but it might very well not be. It could have been your average burglar. Just remember, this has been an unoccupied apartment for several weeks. Someone could have been watching it."

"Yeah, but . . ." replied Toni.

"Pulled shades and closed curtains are a dead giveaway," he was quick to interject.

Not to mention, I thought, packed mailboxes. That, however, I didn't mention, for I was determined to be one hundred percent on Toni's side.

Jenkins took out a yellow pad. "So tell me what happened."

Rubbing my head, I said, "I surprised some moron in the bedroom. Or rather, he surprised me and did some damage my way before escaping out the back."

"Go back earlier. Start from the moment you came in."

Toni took over, said how she'd been here a few hours earlier but had stayed only briefly. She described me as an old friend, nothing more, and explained how she'd come over to my place and asked me to accompany her. Which, of course, I did. So we'd come back, and . . .

"What about the door?" he asked. "Any sign of forced entry?"

"No." I shook my head. "I was the one who unlocked it. It seemed fine."

"Are you sure?"

"Close your eyes and picture it again."

I took a deep breath, and as if it were nothing more than a slide, I flashed the image of that door before my mind's eye. I saw everything. Brass knob. Keyhole. Even the wooden trim alongside the door.

"I'm positive. The door was pulled shut and locked." I motioned toward the door. "There weren't any signs that it was pried open, either. The paint and wood weren't dinged up at all—go ahead and check if you want."

The detective declined for now, and we continued with our story, Toni saying how she'd pretty much stopped in the living room and I had continued into the back. I thought I'd heard a noise, I explained, so I'd kept going, continuing all the way to the bedroom, where I saw an open window.

"How far open was it?" asked Jenkins.

"Ah, I don't know."

"Slow things down, look at the shade blowing, see the window handle, be there completely."

I thought back, remembered seeing the bottom of the window outlined against the shade as it blew back and forth, said, "About six, eight inches. No more."

"If that's how he came in," speculated Jenkins, "maybe he lowered the window behind him so as not to attract attention. Did you notice if the screen was on?"

I shook my head. That I hadn't seen, I was sure, because the shade had been pulled down over the window.

Then I recounted how the bedroom door had been closed and locked behind me, I had turned, seen this thug. I described him. Shut my eyes, breathed deeply, ran the scene in slo-mo so that I could reveal every little detail. Jenkins wrote it all down, clothing, height, that the burglar might have been bald, everything. I talked on, right up to the flight of the intruder out the window.

"Well," said Jenkins, "I don't know. I'll dust for finger-prints, perhaps we'll get a match. Can you tell if anything's missing?"

We all glanced around, saw the TV still sitting there, the CD player, the CDs. Even a camera. A small black camera sitting on a bricks-and-board bookshelf.

"Nothing's gone," said Toni, clearly not buying Jenkins's angle. "So it might not have been a burglar. Maybe he wasn't looking for anything to steal."

Jenkins suggested, "Or perhaps he just hadn't made his way to the living room yet."

"But the burglar did have something. What was it, Alex?"

It popped into my head. Papers or whatever. Right. The intruder had been holding something.

"Wait," I said, "he had something in his hands. Some papers." I could picture it now. "It was a folder or . . . or a notebook." I closed my eyes. Concentrate. Think. Remember. Go back, I told myself, to that moment and freeze the scene so you can study it. "That's what it was," I said, seeing it now in my memory and for the first time clearly. "A white notebook—maybe a spiral one—with some papers tumbling out. That's what it was."

I looked up to see both Toni and Jenkins staring at me. All of us disappeared into silent thought. A notebook? Why in hell would some guy break into an apartment to steal a notebook?

"Are you sure about that?" asked Jenkins.

I nodded. "Positive."

Toni said, "God, you don't think it could've been one of Liz's poetry manuscripts, do you? She was always carrying around a spiral notebook to write in."

"I've heard of weirder things." A moment later Jenkins put his pen away and rose. "I'm going to check out the bedroom, dust the window for fingerprints, and look for this notebook. Don't worry, I'll do what I can to get this figured out."

Toni reached for her purse, saying, "When you're finished, I want to show you the letter Liz wrote me. The one I told you about."

Jenkins sighed, said, "Okay, but then tomorrow I want you to go see her shrink."

"I still think she was murdered," said Liz, firmly.

"Believe me, I'm aware of that. As I told you over the phone, however, all the evidence we've gathered supports suicide."

There was one thing I didn't understand, and I asked, "What about the coroner's report? I mean, there was an autopsy, wasn't there?"

"Yeah, but . . ." muttered Jenkins.

Toni bowed her head, ran a hand through her thick hair, said, "Go ahead, tell him."

Jenkins eyed Toni, then reported, "The body got caught in one of the locks on the Mississippi. It was down there, hung up on a hinge, for almost four days until the gates finally jammed up. By the time the corpse was found it was severely mangled. The autopsy results were inconclusive."

"Oh."

Toni stared blankly ahead. "We knew she was missing, so I came up here. After they pulled out the body, I did the initial identification from a scrap of clothing. It was a blouse I'd given her—one of mine that didn't fit. A blue thing with stripes. The only way they got a positive ID was from her dental records."

I sat there, silent, wishing I hadn't asked, and now unable to stop myself from picturing a body crushed in the jaws of those enormous gates. Huge, meat-grinding gates powerful enough to block the flow of the mighty Mississippi.

"Well . . ." Jenkins moved on, motioning toward the bedroom. "We get a lot of break-ins around here, so be warned it could've been just a neighborhood punk who crawled through an unlocked window."

I cleared my throat, looked at Toni, and suggested, "Or it could have been someone Liz knew who came here looking for something specific." Then I turned to Jenkins. "Someone who knew Liz well enough that he wouldn't have had to break in through a window."

Toni eyed me, "What do you mean?"

"Well, we're assuming he broke in, but couldn't the jerk have had a key and just let himself in?"

And by the way Jenkins was staring at me, face long and flat, eyes glaring, I knew that was exactly the kind of grist he didn't want to mill.

Chapter 8

After the cops had left, after Jenkins had dusted for prints and was on his way, after we had locked up Liz's apartment, I suggested we go for coffee or wine or something, anything, where the two of us could just sit and perhaps catch up. Maybe even linger over memories.

"I haven't seen you in so long," I began as we both climbed into my Honda. "We need to catch up."

As soon as we were in the car, I could tell that it wasn't going to happen. Not yet, anyway. Toni was leaning away from me, pressing herself up against the door, and she had one hand to her forehead and was looking out, away. Okay, I got the picture.

Toni said, "Alex, I know we have a lot of ground to go over, but I can't. Not tonight." She turned and reached over and touched my arm. "I'm sorry, I just can't tonight. You understand, don't you?"

"Sure."

"Besides, you should get some rest. How do you feel?"

The aches mostly annoying, and I said, "Not bad."

"Good."

She offered a small smile, her thin lips parting, exposing

her front teeth, one of which was chipped at the corner. I'd never seen anyone else with a tooth just like that, a little angle of it missing, and the very sight of it took me back even more than the touch of her hand. Way back. She was a good kisser. I was a good kisser. Together we'd done very well and very much of that kind of stuff.

"Sorry you got beat up," she went on. "You were wonderful to drop everything and come over here tonight."

Tonight. Sunday night. Wasn't I supposed to be doing something other than this? I looked at my watch.

"Oh, shit," I said, realizing it was already ten.

"What?"

I shook my head. "Nothing,"

Karen, who I was supposed to have taken out for Thai food, probably wouldn't speak to me again, not after I'd stood her up on our first date. On the other hand, with Toni back, that might, perhaps be a moot point. I was determined to find out if it was.

"Listen," I began, "I've been working a lot recently and I've got some comp time. I'd like to take tomorrow off and spend it with you."

"Alex, that's really sweet of you, but I've got so much to do. I'm going to have to try and see Liz's therapist sometime, hopefully in the morning. And at some point I'll have to come back over here and make a start at going through Liz's things."

"Great. Let me just drive you around. I won't be in the way—I can wait for you if need be and I can help you here at the apartment, too."

"I don't know . . ."

"Toni, it's been a long time. Much too long." I wanted to reach out and touch her leg or arm, but I sensed I should hold back, not cross the boundary between the present and the past. "Besides, I know it's awful, having to deal with all this," I said, trying hard not to sound too much like a used-car salesman making his last-ditch effort. "So wouldn't you like some old, friendly company? Besides, I think I'm going to be hurting too much tomorrow to go to work."

She dove into her thoughts, bowing her head forward so that her long, thick hair tumbled over her face. She was gone, underwater, lost, and I could not guess her response. But when

she came up for breath, pulling and pinning her hair behind her head with one hand, I saw her smile and that chipped tooth.

She said, "Yeah, that'd be nice."

So we drove back to my place in silence, where she reclaimed her rental car and then headed off to her hotel, a Holiday Inn, of course, at Seven Corners. As she drove away in the small, spotless white car, as the red taillights faded down my tree-lined street, I wished I'd had the guts to offer her a room in my place. Her own room, of course. But I don't think I could have handled that, probably would have tossed and turned all night, thinking of her so close yet so far away and how it had taken me years to get over her rejection of me. Or had I gotten over it? Hadn't time just dulled it? On the other hand, had I asked she would have refused my housing invitation. Of that I was sure. In a certain way Toni had always been stronger than I.

As it was, I languished in the memories and tossed and turned all night as if I had in fact spent the evening with a ghost.

The next morning the only thing that really ached were my ribs. My head was fine, my arm just bruised and a little sensitive, but the ribs, they hurt, particularly when I first tried to get out of bed. I took my first cup of coffee into the shower and just stood there, sipping the steaming beverage while the hot water beat on my side.

First on the agenda was calling into work—I told them I'd had a bike accident and wouldn't be in today, perhaps not for a couple of days. I hit a patch of wet leaves, I lied, and took a good spill, so I wouldn't be up for any technical writing. That, of course, cheered me a great deal, which was why I was pretty smiley when I picked Toni up at eight. She, the doctor, inquired about my injuries, but I assured her that I was more than fine, delighted to be off from work.

We ate at Al's Breakfast, a tiny bowling alley of a diner with one narrow row of counter stools, a famous joint in Dinkytown, the university village. I wanted to charm Toni and I did. The Wallys—walnut waffles—were great.

Toni had been on the phone first thing that morning, and so a little before eleven we were downtown, parking in a garage, walking down Nicollet Mall, soaking up the first of what promised to be a brilliant spring day. We didn't linger, though, as we headed for an appointment with Liz's therapist. Dr. Edward Dawson had an office in the Medical Arts Building—the same building as my wonderful dentist with the tiny hands that didn't rip wide my mouth—and I wondered if he was a psychiatrist and not a psychologist, and if he'd had Liz on any kind of medication.

"How much do you know about this guy?" I ventured as we rode up to the sixth floor in an incredibly slow elevator.

Toni shrugged, brushed back her long hair, exposing a silver loop earring, and said, "He's got an incredible reputation, plus he's on the executive council of the American Psychiatrists Organization, so he's well known nationally. Liz started seeing him a couple of years ago, and I know she was crazy about him. She talked about him a lot—Dr. Dawson said this or Dr. Dawson did that—and she really seemed to get better. You know, more even, not so up and down. That's why I don't get this suicide stuff. She seemed so good the last six months, like she was out of the woods."

It turned out Dawson's practice was quite small—he had no partner and there was no receptionist. But he was obviously successful—the furniture in the waiting room was quite plush, a black leather couch and side chair, and a walnut coffee table that was littered with copies of *Architectural Digest, Harper's, Atlantic Monthly*, and the like. Nice soft light, too, from an expensive-looking lamp that stood in one corner. And it wasn't a handwritten note taped to the wall but a printed sign that told us to please take a seat, the doctor would be right with us, he was in session. We sat down in the small room, and I studied a couple of the framed nature prints—no, they were signed lithographs—on the yellow walls. Not my taste but good taste. Expensive, too. Squinting, I saw a framed book jacket on the wall, an anthology of essays edited by Dawson. A busy guy.

He was prompt. A little before eleven we heard a door open, some low voices—one of which muttered, "Thank you, Doctor"—and then another door opened and glided shut. So, I thought, the good doctor has another means of escape, a back way for his patients to sneak out of. An exit where the perhaps tearful, perhaps joyful client could leave in utter privacy. How tasteful.

As he came out, Dawson cleared his throat. I did a quick judgmental scan and in an instant I could understand why Toni's sister had felt comfortable here. He wasn't very tall. Maybe five eight. Mid- or perhaps late forties. He had a narrow face, a narrow head, and he was bald, a rim of graying brown hair circling the back of his head. It was the face, though, that seemed particularly soft. Easy. Rich blue eyes that were deeply set, and a mouth that looked as if it could as easily spout wisdom as humor. He wore baggy, soft-looking khakis and a white broadcloth shirt with a blue tie that went with the eyes, and he carried a manila folder that went with the profession.

"You must be Toni Domingo," he said, entering the serene waiting room that seemed a reflection of all that he wanted. "Hi, I'm Ed Dawson. I'm so glad to meet you. Fortunately I had a client who canceled this morning."

Toni held out her hand, started to rise.

"No, no, please sit down," said Dawson.

He took Toni's hand in his, shaking it gently, then sat in the armchair at a right angle to the leather sofa. My eyes followed the folder that remained guarded in his lap. A patient's chart. A big thick one. Was it Liz's or did it belong to the unseen client who'd just parted?

Dawson started, stopped, then said, "I don't know quite where to begin. Liz was a wonderful person, and . . . and . . ."

This time it was my turn to clear my throat. Me, the third wheel. I'd thought Toni and Dawson would disappear into his office, that I would be left here with the strewn magazines. But obviously not. This wasn't a session but a conversation, so it was taking place out here in the waiting room instead of in Dawson's office.

I said, "Toni, do you want me to wait outside?"

As if she'd forgotten my presence, she turned to me with a small start. "Oh, Alex, I . . . I . . . ." Then she looked back at Dawson. "This is Alex Phillips, an old friend of mine. He lives up here and—"

Cut her off, I thought. She doesn't know how to introduce me, so save her the awkward words. I rose slightly, pushing

myself up, but not sure if I should stand—an old formality?—
then reached out and shook the doctor's hand.

"Nice to meet you," I said. Then to Toni again, "There's a
coffee shop downstairs. Why don't I wait down there?"

"No, it's all right."

"You and I," Dawson suggested to Toni, "could step into
my office. Would you prefer that?"

"No, really, it's all right."

Toni was pressing down on my arm, lightly pushing it
against the leather sofa. I saw the tinge of anxiety in her eyes.
She wanted me to stay. Needed me to. This was going to be
heavy duty, of course, and the therapist's words intense. Dawson
certainly held some keen insights into Liz, perhaps some big
truths, and this was clearly of some concern to Toni. Obviously
she didn't want to hear them on her own. It was going to be
like looking into a casket, seeing the body of a loved one. And
Toni wanted someone's, anyone's, hand to hold as Dawson
opened the lid of Liz's mental coffin.

Dawson looked down, clasped his hands, looked up. "First
of all, I have to say that Liz's death shocked me terribly. I
thought she was doing just fine, that she was right on schedule.
Things were coming along so well and she seemed to be making
so much progress. She'd had some bad days lately, but I really
didn't sense any suicidal inclinations."

Toni tensed. I felt her tighten up, then squirm slightly.

"As you might have known," he continued, "I'd been seeing
Liz twice a week for the last two years. When she came she'd
been having trouble with depression and anxiety, so I started
her on medication."

"Really? I didn't know that—that she was taking any."

"Yes, and she responded very favorably. With her moods
in control, her therapy was intense and, I have every reason to
believe, rewarding. We concentrated on a number of family-of-
origin issues, her self-esteem, and her relationship with her
boyfriend."

"You mean Rob Tyler?"

"Right, the fellow from the College of Art and Design."

"But I thought they'd broken up?"

"Well, they had, but relationships are often hard to end.
You can't just flick a switch."

Amen, I thought.

"She wasn't seeing him anymore," Dawson went on. "At least not as far as I knew. He was calling her, though, maybe once a week. Liz didn't know how to handle it, she was a little afraid of him, which was the subject of one of our last sessions."

Toni lowered her head, shook it. "That guy's such a jerk. I met him once. Liz took me to some bar, and I couldn't believe it. He's just a skinhead. What in the hell did she see in him?"

"Honesty, at least that's how she put it."

"What? I mean, when I saw him his head was all shaved and he was wearing all this black leather and everything. He sure as hell didn't look like any Boy Scout to me."

"Well, that may be, but Liz felt he was being honest about how he saw the world. To him it was a dark, ugly place with many problems, and he was reflecting that. She liked that he didn't pretend the world was great and wonderful."

I glanced over. Toni was shaking her head. Unfortunately, it all fit, it all made sense, even to me. I'd never known Liz very well and hadn't seen her for years, but hadn't she been trapped, angrily so, between the perceived and real truths of the world? Absolutely. That was what her first suicide attempt was all about, an act of frustration, of rebellion, against an alcohol-ridden family that had pretended to be the Cleavers.

"I might also add," continued Dawson, "that that same thirst for honesty was why she broke up with Rob."

"What do you mean?"

"He became involved with some sort of gang. She tried to keep Rob out of it, but when she couldn't she finally broke things between them."

Toni shook her head. "Poor Liz."

Firmly, fatherly, Dawson strode into his role, clearly relishing it, and said, "Liz loved you a great deal. Rather, I should say she adored you. You must know that. In everything that she told me, it was always clear that Liz felt extremely close to you—she always, always spoke highly of you."

Her voice faint, weak, even shattered, Toni zeroed in on her main point of interest, "So you think it was suicide, too?"

"I'm afraid so."

He drew a deep breath, opened the file that sat on his lap. So all that, I thought, looking at the sheaf of papers, was info

on Liz. What she'd said. What she'd feared. Insurance papers,
too, and all those data of the official world. And from the stack,
Dawson pulled something I recognized. Stationery, small and
squarish, a tasteful off-white. Sure. Liz had written her letter to
Toni on the same stuff.

"I received this the day after Liz took her life," began Dawson. "This arrived, and I tried contacting her immediately.
She'd threatened suicide before, but always in person, never in
a letter. So when I read this, I was quite concerned. In fact, I
was the one who first contacted the police. Of course, they didn't
find her body for another four days."

Fingers trembling, Toni took the letter, held it, read it, in
disbelief. I read it, too. Peered over Toni's shoulder. Saw three
handwritten lines, short ones. Brief and to the point.

Dear Dr. Dawson,
    It's just too much, all of it. I can't go on, can't
continue like this. So this is good-bye. You see, in the
end I am master of my own destiny.
                                            Love,
                                              Liz

Quickly, I read it, reread it, even as Toni fell apart. Even
as Toni bent forward, hands to her eyes. I slipped the letter
from Toni's fingers, read Liz's letter once again, because there
was something about it that bothered me.

"What is it? What are you noticing?"

I raised my head, looked at Dawson with the question wrinkling my face. "There's no date on this."

"What?" said Toni faintly, looking up with red eyes.

"This letter's not dated."

Dawson took the note, scanned it, and his face flushed.
"No, it's not, is it? Funny, I'd never noticed that before. I have
the envelope it was mailed in—it's somewhere in here."

His fingers like ten worms in a stack of papers, he carefully
and thoroughly went through the folder on his lap. Obviously
this was a guy who was used to order; that he couldn't find the
envelope straight off was clearly disturbing to him.

"The coroner," he said as he searched, "figured that she'd

died on the Tuesday of that week, and I received this on Wednesday. I'm positive of that."

Toni was in her purse, rummaging around. Then she found what she was after. Her Liz letter. Same stationery. Same handwriting.

"I got this from Liz on that Wednesday, too," said Toni, holding out what she hoped would prove her sister's redemption.

All our eyes went right to the top of Liz's letter to Toni, and there, boldly scrawled, was "Monday." That made sense. Written and mailed on Monday, in Toni's Chicago mailbox on Wednesday. That would be mail service from the Twin Cities to Illinois in great but not impossible time. Mind whirling, I leaped to Dawson's letter. Written and mailed on Tuesday, delivered to Dawson the next day, Wednesday. Sure. Next-day delivery in the same city. That was typical.

"So what happened?" I asked. "She was fine, even great, on Monday when she wrote this letter to Toni. But then she took a nosedive, wrote to you, and then committed suicide. Is that possible?"

"Damn," said Dawson, almost a little panicky, as he searched the file, "the envelope must be in my office." He scratched the tip of his nose. "Possible? Yes, I'm afraid so. What exactly happened? I don't think we'll ever know. Perhaps she stopped taking her medication. Or perhaps it was something else altogether—an argument with a friend, a fight with her ex-boyfriend."

Toni said, "I'll be frank, I'm not a fan of psychotropic drugs. Liz knew that, which I suppose is why she never mentioned she was taking anything. You're a psychiatrist, right? What did you have her on?"

Unable to hide his distress, he closed the file, said, "I beg your pardon?"

"What did you prescribe for my sister?"

"Cazorp." Dawson glanced at me, then back at Toni, and said rather defensively, "It's a fine drug. I have a number of patients taking it."

"Believe me—I'm a physician—I know there are a lot of people out there on Cazorp. But I don't think it's the wonder drug some say it is. I see a lot of patients for side effects from it—diarrhea, jitters, dry mouth. I'm sure you saw the recent report claiming that prolonged use of Cazorp might cause sudden and severe depression."

"The test results on that were totally inconclusive."

Letting the issue slide, Toni moved on, saying, "My sister was never good about following directions. Do you know if she was taking the medication regularly?"

"She said she was and I have every reason to believe so. Unless a patient's in a hospital, however, you can't be absolutely positive. I can get you the dates of the prescriptions and the dosages if you want, but I think you'll see that everything was in order. I always monitor prescriptions—I don't just write them out left and right."

"No, of course not," replied Toni. "I didn't mean to imply that."

I didn't like it, either, this drug stuff. Liz could have overdosed, underdosed, or the prescription could have been wrong in some other way. On the other hand, maybe Liz needed to be straightened out with a drug like Cazorp before she could deal with certain things. Maybe she would have been dead years ago if she hadn't been on meds. However, Toni and her family were going to have to ponder the possibility of something chemical pushing Liz over the edge. And if it was something of that sort, then there'd be some vindication, some relief, that no, the family hadn't caused Liz death, but some concoction of the drug industry had.

Dawson pushed past the issue of medication, and spoke of Liz, praising her desire to get healthy, her sense of humor, her writing, which she'd been working at so hard. She'd told him about some big article she wanted to write. Something that would be startling. An exposé of sorts. She was doing the research and she was sure she was going to be able to sell it to *The Reader*, an alternative weekly.

At this, Toni nodded, said, "Right, that must have been the article she wanted me to do the photos for."

There was more, but not much. Dawson recounted several anecdotes that were purely for Toni's pleasure, but even after death, it was clear he wasn't going to breach Liz's confidence and get into the nitty-gritty of her life. The ugly stuff. There really was no need for that, either. No need to get into the crud that would hurt those Liz had already wounded by her quick departure.

We were there for almost an hour until it was clear that Toni was overwhelmed, and Dawson low on what more to say. So we left. Toni thanked him, he reiterated his admiration of Liz and what a tragedy this was, and I played the good friend, there at Toni's side for her support.

"Call if you have any other questions," said Dr. Dawson as we all stood, the audience over.

I eyed Toni, still thinking about the history of Liz's medication. That was what I wanted to know. Aside from what and how much she was taking, could Liz have been abusing drugs? After all, she was the daughter of an alcoholic; chemical abuse could have run in the family.

Toni, however, seemed eager to move on, and she said, "Thank you, Doctor. You've been very helpful."

"I'm glad, then." He looked away, shook his head. "She really was a delightful young woman. Such a tragedy."

"Yeah, she was a good kid." Toni took a deep breath, let it out. "You know, I was thinking about looking up Rob Tyler. Maybe I will."

"That might not be a bad idea." Dawson smoothed his blue tie. "I know they spoke, but maybe they even saw each other before she died."

"Maybe," muttered Toni.

A rush of fear zipped through my veins. Rob Tyler. Why did I sense as if we'd already met? What was it that I knew about him? We shook Dawson's hand, made for the elevator, but suddenly all I could see in front of me was the vision of a tall, lanky guy, shaved head, small eyes. Yes, a clear image, one that I didn't care for at all.

I turned to Toni, caught her eyes, and in that instant our minds broadcast the identical message: Yes, the sooner the better.

Chapter 9

He wasn't that hard to find, this Rob Tyler. Of course we didn't go to his place first off. No, we left Dr. Dawson's, rode silently down in the elevator, strode silently across the granite pavement of Nicollet Mall. Toni put on sunglasses even before we were outside and looped her hand in my arm and cried slowly and very silently. Then we headed for one of the few true remaining landmarks in downtown Minneapolis, Peter's Grill, where the turkey in the club sandwiches was real, not rolled and pressed, steamed or dry-cleaned, and the apple pie fresh and tart and made just back there in the kitchen. Real, original comfort food, not conceptualized fluff. Toni let me cruise-direct—choose the booth, order the food, ask for more coffee (which I really didn't have to do at all since the professional waitresses, aka grandmothers, kept the cups almost always topped off)—and she sat there, I would say, having trouble digesting it all. If she'd been a smoker, I know she would have been sucking long, deep drags. If she'd been an easy crier, I know she would have fallen apart in long, wet sobs. As it was, her few tears quickly ebbed.

"God, Alex, it was awful. I came up here a few days after she was reported missing. The police told me about those other women who'd been murdered, you know, all hacked up or something. That's all I thought about the first night I was up here, that she was the next one, the next victim. My biggest fear was that they wouldn't find her body for months. But they did— they found her that next morning." As we waited for our toasted sandwiches to be rushed to us, Toni said, "So maybe I'm wrong. Maybe she really did it . . . jumped off that bridge, I mean."

Frankly, it seemed that way; I thought it quite possible that the drugs had backfired or she'd overdosed or simply hadn't been taking them. The murder angle had seemed an odd one, a long stretch. Liz's letter to Toni now seemed the product of someone who was at the top of a tall high, while Liz's letter to Dawson seemed to have been written by someone at the other end of that spectrum, the low end. Unfortunately, the latter was apparently the more recent of the two and therefore the more accurate reflection of Liz's mental state toward the end of her life. And the guy we'd discovered in Liz's apartment? Sure, an ordinary dink of a burglar, just as Jenkins had suggested. All of that made sense, fit neatly into place. I could see why Liz's death had been so quickly judged one of personal choice.

"Yeah," I said, stirring my coffee, thinking that it was probably, obviously, suicide. "There doesn't seem to be a question in Dawson's mind, either."

But even if it was suicide, there were still a myriad questions, mainly, of course, why? And second, surely, what had precipitated it? Had Liz's whole life been leading up to that moment, just waiting for it? Or had it merely been a biochemical reaction, one leading to a black hole of depression? I was curious, of course, but I could have lived without knowing. Toni, however, probably couldn't, and my latest thing being resolution, I knew she'd be far more content for the rest of her life if she could piece together her sister's life and understand why it had fallen apart.

So I asked, "You want to look up this Rob Tyler?"

She smiled. Looked at me and smiled again, because our thoughts had always traveled in sync, and apparently they still did.

"Let's," she replied, and took a long, slow sip of coffee.

I then had the good sense to shut up and just let Toni slip into sisterly memories, to tumble into them, which made for a quiet meal in a restaurant full of din. Lots of lawyers and stockbrokers, men and women in their conformist suits, pumping up on caffeine.

After the pie, I told Toni I'd try calling this guy, and went to the phone by the johns, called the Minneapolis College of Art and Design, and asked for Rob Tyler's phone number. Which I was promptly given and which I promptly called. The phone was picked up on the third ring.

"Is Rob Tyler there?" I asked.

"Yeah, you got him," replied a deep, scratchy voice that sounded like it had been up too late boozing. "Who wants to know?"

"Alex Phillips, a friend of Toni Domingo's, Liz's sister. Toni's up here from Chicago, and she'd like to talk to you."

A stretched pause. "What about?"

Was this a moron or what? "About Liz." Apparently I had to spell it out, so I added, "Toni's just trying to find out a few things—what Liz was like the week before it happened, if she was up or down. You know, a few things like that. Not much. Toni's just trying to figure out why it happened, why Liz killed herself, and she was wondering if you might have talked to her."

"Nope." He grunted and groaned, then blurted, "Listen, Liz and I broke up a month or so before she jumped. She creeped me out. Got it? I didn't like her anymore, and I don't know anything." Then for a kicker, he said, "Gotta go."

And he hung up.

I stood there, stared at the phone, said, "Hello? Hello?" and when there was definitely nothing, muttered, "Asshole," and slammed the receiver back in place.

As I approached our booth, Toni looked up, raised eyebrows arching above those brown eyes, and asked, "Did you reach him?"

"Yeah." I slid into the booth. "But the jerk hung up on me. Says he broke up with Liz a month before she died and doesn't know a thing."

"What?" Toni stared out the windows for a moment, then turned back to me, saying, "Come on."

That's what I'd always liked about Toni. She had guts and

was determined. Resourceful, too. I was sure she was an incredible physician, too. It all added up to that, her intelligence and everything.

So we paid, leaving a generous tip because the waitress truly did remind me of my grandmother, and although I would never have flung change at my Nanna for fear of insulting her, I certainly didn't want this one to go uncared for. Which might have been the whole point. Maybe Peter's used grandmother waitresses the way the gypsies used kids to beg. The sympathy-pity factor soared.

We proceeded back to the phone by the rest rooms, where we fished up a phone book. There were three Robert Tylers in Minneapolis, but only one that matched the number I'd already called. So there was his name, his number, and the one thing that we wanted: his address.

"Harriet Avenue South," I said. "That makes sense—not too far from the College of Art and Design and really close to Liz's, too."

"Great. Let's go—he's there now."

With a renewed sense of purpose and mission, we traveled quickly back to the car, down the spiral ramp, out onto the sunny street. It didn't take long. Less than twenty minutes after I'd spoken to Rob Tyler and he'd hung up on me, we were there.

The house, an older, clapboard thing with a porch, looked rather dead. Toni and I crossed the small weedy front yard and climbed the steps. We found the place oddly quiet. I'd been expecting a stereo, big and loud, or perhaps drums, loud and stupid. But instead there was nothing, no reply to the bell, which I pushed long and hard.

"Hey, look at this," said Toni, peering at the mailbox, a beat-up black one hanging on the other side of the door.

Taped and retaped, then taped again to the mailbox was a photo of six people. Two women and four guys. All with shaved heads. All piled there on some ratty couch, a mass of legs and arms, shoes and leather coats. And, à la The Monkees of the sixties, there was a lettered banner above that read HEY, HEY WE'RE THE SKINHEADS!

Great, I thought. Was our Rob a neo-Nazi, too?

"This one," said Liz, her finger tapping the picture. "That's him."

I looked closer, saw a thin guy, gangly, shaved head, both ears pierced, and said, "He's a real looker."

Studying the photo, a sense of déjà vu clouded my mind. Then again, didn't all these guys look alike? Weren't punkers as conformist as suburban housewives, both trapped in a ridiculous mind-set and equally strict dress code?

I leaned on the bell, this time as long and as hard as a meter reader, and finally we heard something. Footsteps. Someone moving, albeit not fast at all. At last the door opened, and she stood there, a very pale woman, late twenties, her hair shoe-polish black and about an inch long, and four or maybe five noserings piercing her right nostril.

I smiled, asked, "Is Rob Tyler here?"

"What, Rob?"

All groggy as if she'd been woken from a deep sleep, she studied us with little eyes, shrugged, turned away, and shut the door. I looked at Toni; Who is this lady? I asked silently.

Toni said, "What are we supposed to do, wait?"

"Beats me."

We stood there maybe a minute longer. I was all set to ring the bell again when I heard steps once more, and the door was opened a second time. Rob Tyler. Just like he was in the photo, just like I pictured him in my mind. Thin face, completely shaven head, round and smooth. His beard was a bit bristly, coarse black hairs piercing from his chin and cheeks. He wore a rumpled black shirt that had a skeleton painted on the right sleeve, tight black jeans, and black, worn-out canvas shoes. He stared at us, and the pale woman, who'd answered the door moved up right behind, wrapping her arms around him.

Toni said, "Hi, Rob."

Tyler looked totally lost, and he half-turned back to the woman. "Sandra, who're these people?"

Toni didn't miss a beat. "I'm Toni Domingo, Liz's sister. We met once."

"Oh. Oh, yeah." Tyler looked at me. "Let me guess, and you're the guy that called and woke me from my nap."

"Sorry."

"Well, like I told you, I don't know nothing about Liz."
Tyler put a flat hand to his chest. "Excuse me, I don't mean no
offense to the dead, but me and Liz busted up. She kind of
bugged me and she was just too boring, you know? Sandra,
here, well, she's my girl now."

He reached back, put his arm around the woman, and
pulled her tight against him. She yawned, scratched her short,
black hair, then started kissing him on the back.

"Listen," began Toni, "I know you talked with Liz after you
broke up. I know you called her a few times. Did you see her,
too? Do you remember if you saw her that week she died?"

Sandra pulled back, made a sour face, and hit Tyler with
the back of her fist, saying, "Aw, Rob, have you been cheatin'
on me again?"

He turned, rubbed his bristly beard over her bristly head.
"No, baby, not at all. I don't know what these people are talkin'
about. Now you go back inside. I'll be right there." He turned
her around, pushed her. "Go on, get!"

I said, "Rob, we're just trying to—"

"Wait." He lifted a finger at me, took a deep breath. "Sandra and me, we got something good going. We do good art
together—I sculpt, she sculpts. Metal stuff, you know. Welded
stuff. I don't want to mess it up, you dig?"

"Sure."

"So I got to tell you, I really don't know diddly about Liz.
Sure we talked after we broke up. But I didn't call her, oh, no.
She called me, and she kept calling, you know, wanting to go
out for coffee."

Toni was quick to ask, "Why? What did she want? What
did she sound like on the phone?"

"Oh, man." Tyler shook his head, stepped back, started to
close the door. "I don't need this. Got it? I don't need no more
trouble. I had enough shit with Liz poking around here."

Toni glanced at me, then at Tyler, and demanded, "What
in hell's that mean?"

"Nothing. Nothing at all."

I saw Toni clench her hands, saw her try and stay cool.
"Rob, I'm not trying to blame anyone, I'm just trying to piece
it all together. Liz is dead and I just want to find out why it

happened. Maybe you can't talk now, I don't know, but if you think of anything, call me. Would you do that, please? I'm at the Holiday Inn at Seven Corners."

"Yeah, right, maybe we can do lunch." He bared his teeth, stepped back, closed the door, and called out, "Good-bye!"

"Hey, wait!" I called as I reached out, ready to push the door back open.

Toni grabbed me by the arm, said, "Let's get out of here."

"But—"

"He doesn't want to talk. Come on!"

Toni broke away, hurrying off the porch of that dump of a house. I descended, following after her, barely noticing the warm air, the bright sky. By the time I caught up with her, she was standing next to the car, rubbing her forehead, undoubtedly wishing she were anywhere but here.

"Toni, why the—"

"Alex, please. Just open the door."

I knew that tone of voice as well as I knew that chipped tooth of hers. She was saying, Don't Tread on Me. Did that also mean she was wishing she was with anyone but me? I was being paranoid, of course, but just to play it safe I shut up, silently unlocking her door, then going around to the driver's side and getting in. I slipped in the key, making no rush, half-expecting Toni to stop me, but she didn't. Within seconds we were heading down the street.

"What a jerk," I said.

"Really."

I slowly pulled to a stop sign, looked both ways, puttered on down a street where the diseased elms had been hacked down and spindly trees planted in their place. Liz hadn't killed herself over some idiot like Tyler, had she? She couldn't have been upset because of a breakup with that turkey, could she have? Shouldn't she have been relieved?

There was something else, though. Something itching at the back of my mind. What was it? What was the other ninety percent of my mind trying to tell the ten percent?

"Take a breath, a deep one, and let it float from your subconscious to your conscious mind. Just imagine a gate opening and letting that information out."

Lungs full, lungs empty, and what came to my mind's eye?

The image of Rob Tyler standing in the doorway. Hey, hey, I'm a skinhead. Blackness. The color black. That's what my mind kept pushing up. But black what? Hair? Shirt? Jeans? Yes, all of Tyler's clothing was black, right down to his shoes.

Shoes.

I pulled over, glided into a parking space on the quiet street.

"What's the matter?" asked Toni.

"I was just thinking of Tyler and that picture of him."

"So?"

"So his shoes were the same as that guy's, the one who broke into Liz's apartment. They were both black canvas high-tops."

There were lots of shoes in the world like that. Millions, perhaps billions. Sure. But why did it all seem to make such perfect sense?

"Another thing, I was thinking the guy at Liz's might've been bald, and maybe that's right. Maybe I didn't notice the color of his hair because his head was shaved."

"Oh, shit," said Toni, staring out the windshield at a big Oldsmobile parked in front of us. "He could've had a key."

"What?"

"A key—Tyler's probably got a key to Liz's apartment." Toni looked at me. "Turn around."

Which I did, cutting the wheel of my Honda as sharply left as I could, spinning us around, heading us back. So I'd been right. No one had actually broken into Liz's apartment the other night. Someone had had a key and just let himself in, and that more than likely was Liz's former boyfriend, Rob Tyler. I had a new hatred for him. Stealing from your dead girlfriend. How disgusting. What had he been after? Just a notebook or perhaps more? Money? Stereo? Camera? Sure, whatever would have offered quick cash.

I raced up to the stop sign, slowed, then pressed down on the gas. As soon as we were zooming forward, however, Toni's hand was on my arm.

"Wait!" she ordered. "Pull over, quick!"

Up ahead and through some budding bushes I saw movement. Rob Tyler movement? I swerved over, zipped us behind a Jeep. We peered up, around, through. A guy was descending from the porch of the house, making his way across the street, heading for a vehicle.

"That's him," I said, pressing against the side window.

I saw him fully, now wearing a black leather coat—all studded and hanging with chains—black jeans, those black shoes. The very same ones that had danced around me as the intruder swung the lamp at me? I'd certainly never be one hundred percent positive, but the lanky shape, the dark jeans and shoes . . . they all looked so familiar.

I reached for the door handle, envisioned myself pinning him up against a car, and said, "Come on, he can't get away from us now."

"No!" replied Toni. "Just sit still."

"What do you mean?"

"We're going to follow the asshole."

"What?"

"If he had a key to Liz's before, he's still got it." She smiled, ran her hand through her thick hair. "And if that's where he's going now, we can call the cops and nail him."

Of course. Right. Always clever, that Toni. So we let our man, Rob Tyler, start up an old beater, a midnight-blue Duster that was riddled with rust holes, and let him pull out. When he was halfway down the block, I pulled out. This wasn't going to be hard, tailing him. No, not at all.

Chapter 10

Tyler's old Duster was as easy to keep in sight as an American in Moscow. Of course, he probably didn't suspect that he was being followed, but I did nothing to announce it, either. Careful to remain far behind, I didn't pull out of our parking place until Tyler was down the block and hanging a right.

"He's heading north," I said, "which would put him in the direction of Liz's."

I punched the gas, and the Honda bolted forward. Harriet Avenue ran north and south—all avenues, for that matter, in Minneapolis ran north and south, all streets east and west; such was life on a grid in the plains—and, careful to keep my distance, I followed Tyler as he headed west on Twenty-fifth Street. Liz's place was actually only a couple more blocks over and one farther south, and I thought, could this guy really have the gall to return there?

But he didn't. He kept going west until he reached Lyndale and then he turned north. Where was he going, to the grocery store? Was that where this great mission would lead? No. That was what I feared, but I knew it wouldn't. Deep in my soul I knew that following Tyler would lead to a heart, a core, a kernel of truth. This was a dangerous path, I sensed, but an important one that would lead us to an intimate, even hidden part of Rob Tyler.

"Where the hell's he going?" asked Toni.

"Who knows," I answered, my curiosity sharpening, pulse thumping, aware that something of concern lay in the immediate future.

I stayed a couple of cars behind him, flowing with the midafternoon traffic down the broad avenue, which was dotted here and there with original elms now struggling to come into leaf. Tyler continued past the rude tangle of roads above and around Highway 94, past the Walker Art Center and the Guthrie Theater, the Sculpture Garden, too. Then straight past the Basilica, a huge copper-roofed structure of stone that looked as if it could belong in Europe except for the freeway that nearly ran in its back door. On Tyler went, not speeding or racing, just continuing toward the Farmers' Market. I lingered a bit in this broad stretch of road, let him gain some distance, and soon he was turning right. Way up ahead. Yes, turning right toward downtown and its sprouting towers of concrete. This was interesting. All roads in Minneapolis, I always said, led to Dayton's, the mammoth department store that anchored the city in both fashion and urbanity, and so I couldn't help wonder if this was where he was going. To get a Mother's Day gift? Somehow I doubted it, and then to prove me correct, he veered left, avoiding the downtown jumble of modern buildings, and going toward the collection of shorter, squarer buildings on the fringe.

"There, he's turning." Toni motioned with her hand.

"I get it. He's going into the Warehouse District." My mind whirled, settled on a logical possibility. "Maybe he has a studio. Or a friend who has a studio here."

The area was filled with a collection of dark brick buildings, many of which had housed machinery and equipment that had serviced the flour mills along the river and the almost endless expanse of farmland surrounding the Twin Cities. Endless numbers of farmers with endless supplies of hard winter wheat that they had brought to Minneapolis to be processed in the huge mills along the Mississippi. And these enormous buildings with high ceilings and huge beams and broad windows had been abuzz with activity until the waterfall that powered them all was no longer needed; gas-powered mills took over. So now these turn-of-the-century warehouses were struggling to find new life. And they had. The first to come were the artists, turning the vast spaces into studios and lofts. The second to come along were the trendy entrepreneurs, converting the atmosphere-rich environments into packed bars where hormones raged.

These warehouses, however, the farthest from downtown—past the Timberwolves arena, past the New French Bar, past the new parking ramps, and across a set of train tracks—had yet to have much new life. Some were just short of derelict, several totally so. Rob Tyler drove to the one that looked the most abandoned. When I saw him turning into an alley, I steered down another street.

"Come on," I said, pulling over and having no trouble parking in the nearly empty area. "Let's walk."

Toni was the first one out. I hurried alongside her, and we rounded the corner, came to a brick alley that was lined with wobbly-looking train tracks where freight cars had once lumbered. There were large puddles of blackish water, weeds sprouting around them. And Rob Tyler's rusty Duster. The car was empty.

Toni didn't hesitate. She sensed it, too. This truth that lay ahead. I knew there wasn't going to be a studio back here. It was too dark, too musty, too dead. You couldn't create art in a place like this. It wasn't a positive enough environment. Reaching the back of the warehouse, we climbed up a broad set of rotting wooden steps, crossed a loading platform, came to a huge sliding metal door that was cracked open. Toni looked at me, raised her brows. I agreed. We had to go in and we had to be quiet about it.

We stepped out of the near-perfect spring day and into darkness that swirled around us in great cool clouds. There was a staircase that didn't go up, only descended into a black hole. Another door straight ahead. Wanting to avoid the steps and some pit below us, I first pulled on the door handle, but it budged only a couple of inches before a chain and padlock on the other side caught it. Locked from the inside. Shit, I thought. That meant Tyler had in fact submerged beneath the building.

"You want to?" I whispered to Toni as I pointed down the black staircase.

"Sure."

I started down, Toni right behind me. The banister was cool, wet, rusty, the cement stairs gritty. It seemed as if we were making an immense amount of noise, the soles of our shoes scraping over the sandpaper-like steps. I could hear every movement of ours bouncing off every wall. The light faded with each step, gray to near blackness, as we descended down a half-flight, doubled back, and then sank deeper. What were we crawling into? Digging into? Could it be something as innocuous as a rock band's rehearsal space? I'd heard of a lot of bands practicing in the subterranean guts of the Warehouse District. So was our Rob a musician as well? A drummer seeking privacy to beat his brains out? Of course not. Our Rob couldn't be so talented, so diverse.

The stairs stopped and we came to another door. I was ready to reach for it when I heard steps above. I raised my head. Someone else was coming down.

Toni pulled on my elbow. Pulled as she backed into utter blackness. The two of us slithered over a small pile of wood and beneath the staircase, hid like two rats from the humans who were clumsily moving down. There were two of them as well. Toni clutched my arm and I reached over and grabbed her arm. Yes, clearly, two of them. They weren't speaking, whoever they were, but the strangers' steps were quite distinct as they walked down upon us. When they were on the last flight, I reached out with my other hand, felt for Toni, grabbed her. Then they were there, only feet away. I hadn't realized there was actually any light, but there was because I could see two black shapes. Massive ones, broad and heavy. Men.

Toni and I were barely breathing as we watched, sensed, the two of them open the heavy door and melt into the oblivion that lay beyond. Some unseen hinge or spring pulled the door shut and then we flinched, moved for the first time. I stepped over the pile of wood, moved out, Toni and I still holding hands, clutching for something warm and known in this cold, odd place. We should have turned around, ascended into light and safety. But my hand went right for the handle. Follow them. Pursue this truth. This was connected to Liz, tied to her fate. We both knew that, Toni and I.

I pulled that heavy door open just wide enough for the two

of us to slither in, felt a breeze of coolness, a great cloud of it, and as we entered I sensed that this was a much larger space. A huge one. From another doorway straight ahead I saw a hint of yellowish light. We moved to the side and then forward, not straight across that big barren space, but along a wall. I reached out with one hand, felt rough brick, took one careful step at a time. I kept my other hand back, wrapped around Toni's soft doctorly hand. She was just as scared as I was; her sweaty palm gave evidence of that. Just as determined as well. Perhaps more so, for I was only curious, Toni adamant. Liz had been her sister, a very loved one.

My hand felt nothing. I groped, realized this was a doorway. A room off to the right. One more step, and I felt the wall again. Now the light ahead of us was brighter, and dancing, swaying, and pulsing. Candlelight. No electricity down here. There were voices, too, rhythmic and pulsing. Chanting, that was it. Deep, hard voices grunting and pushing sounds that didn't make any sense. Throbbing, just like my own heart. So was this some sort of men's group, a ritualistic gathering to explore the male psyche? No, I sensed it wasn't anything so benign. Dr. Dawson had said Rob was involved with a group or gang, and this was it. A cult. Of course it was. I could sense that alone by my growing fear. A cult that might have been responsible for Liz's death? Quite possibly. Suddenly I knew in the pit of my sensibilities that Liz hadn't committed suicide. Not at all. Quite probably she had stumbled upon this group—perhaps Rob Tyler had even brought her down here—but she hadn't liked it. She'd hated it, in fact. Or maybe she'd just been amazed and supremely interested in it all. So interested that she knew this was the journalistic break she'd been craving. But then this cult had found out about her plans to make their secret group quite public, so they'd hurled her off the Hennepin Avenue Bridge and into the dark, swirling waters of the Mississippi.

Yes, that was what had happened, how Liz had gone down into death, and my heart was racing as fast as my mind. I knew we had to get out of there lest we fall into the same murky Mississippi waters. This was no place for Toni and me.

My outstretched hand hit nothing again—a doorway into another side room—and the warning bells were tolling, heart banging against my ribs. Far enough. Time to retreat, turn this matter over to the police and Detective Jenkins before Toni and I became fish bait as well. I turned, stopped Toni, leaned forward to whisper we should retreat. But the door behind us creaked and shrieked.

Oh shit, oh shit, oh shit.

Someone else was coming down, passing through this room. Who now? What next? We'd be spotted here, huddled against the wall, so I ducked into the side room, pulling on Toni's hand, and the two of us stepped into a dungeon of a hiding place. I pressed myself up against the inside wall as I peered back into the large main chamber, and Toni pulled away, let go of my hand. Another guy. I couldn't see his face, but he had long hair that hung all scraggly. Kind of fat, too, and tall. What was this? What were this guy and all these other men doing down here?

I turned around in the blackness, groped for Toni but couldn't find her, feel her. There was nothing to greet my touch, only emptiness. My heart flipped. Toni? Toni! Inside me I screamed: Toni, we've got to get the hell out of here but I can't see you, so where the hell are you?

In a far corner I saw a small button of light, noticed a shape right in front of it. Toni? I started toward the shape, thinking that if it wasn't her, we were in deeper shit than I'd ever been in my life. I walked carefully, trying not to trip over anything and lifting my feet high, almost prancing, and holding my hands out, groping, pushing at the emptiness in front of me to make sure it was just that, empty space. Then I saw a bunch of hair sweep down over that bit of light. So it was Toni, peering through, looking into another chamber. Spying. That's what she was doing. Eyeing the group of men, this cult on the other side of the wall.

I slowly moved close by, just behind her, and she grabbed my arm, pulled me forward, pulled me down to the hole of light. Bending over, I peered through, looked from our black chamber into the next one, where all those guys were gathered. A whole bunch of them circled around a table, a dais of some sort with silvery stars and moons dangling from it and on top of which something was lying. All of the men were shirtless, all of them wearing black masks that covered their eyes and rode down over their cheeks. They looked like a bunch of bikers, mostly chunky bodies, hairy ones, all sweaty. Dear Lord, oh Jesus, we gotta get outta here or we're dead meat.

But I kept staring, couldn't pry myself away because I was looking, checking to see if Rob Tyler was actually in there. I leaned to one side, looked into a far corner of the murky room, saw a shaved head behind one of those masks. The guy was lanky, wearing jeans and no shirt, and I saw the tattoo right there on the arm. Dragon roaring, tail drooping and curling down and around. The same tattoo I'd seen on the assailant back at Liz's apartment last night. So it had been Tyler back there. Tyler who'd attacked me. Proof positive.

Then, however, another lanky figure moved across the room, a masked, shirtless guy who looked like he, in fact, might be the real Tyler. From what I could discern, his head was shaven and he wore black jeans, too. I saw his arm, studied it because I didn't quite get it. It was the same tattoo. The dragon. My eyes started darting from right shoulder to right shoulder, all of them. They all had it. The identical dragon. Obviously it was their code, their brand, which meant that whoever had been in Liz's apartment could have been Rob Tyler, who had to be one of those two lanky guys, or it might have been someone else in this group. Maybe Liz had become involved here. Or maybe she had dumped Tyler and gone off with another of these masked wonders, for which Tyler had extracted the ultimate price, her life. Or maybe someone had snuffed Liz because . . . because . . . ?

Toni and I stood there, taking all this in, trying to believe it, comprehend it. We were too shock-struck to move. It was then that I saw what was lying on that dais in the middle of the room, the platform around which they were all moving. An animal of some sort. Oh Lord. It was a goat, quite dead, and quite split open, cut right up its gut. Something was pouring out of it. A mound of guts? No, nothing so fluid and messy. Right, there was no blood. One of the men moved aside, and I could clearly see the mass. What was tumbling out of the dead goat was big mounds of cooked rice.

A wave of disgust rolled from my stomach and snaked and tickled up the back of my throat, into my mouth, around my tongue. I would have cried out if I could. Instead I started to sweat, felt chilling drops of perspiration roll down my sides. I grabbed Toni by the arm, clenched her as tight as I could. She saw it then, didn't say anything, only clapped one hand over her mouth. A split-open dead goat stuffed with rice. Devil worship. Satan's followers. That's what they were, weren't they, what they had to be, this group? Was Liz the victim of this group's bizarre activities? Oh Lord, could they have cut her open, too, then drowned her? Oh my God, oh my God, that poor girl . . .

From somewhere in a back room came a rhythmic banging, and Toni and I leaned to one side, saw a man come out of a back room. He wore a mask, of course, was naked from the waist up, his chest covered with thick gray hair. The same dragon tattoo on his arm. The whole works. Only he wore some feathers, red and yellow ones poked in his mask, and he carried a staff topped with a large full moon. Of medium height, he appeared not as young as the others. One of their top guys? Yes, someone high up. He came into the room, banged his staff twice. All of the others backed into a corner, and I understood. This was it. The ritual for which they had gathered was about to begin. Toni and I couldn't leave because we had to see just what they were up to, how far they would go, how awful they were.

The guy with the staff banged two more times, and a man in a long black cape decorated with stars and moons entered the room. The obvious leader. All the others focused on him, watched his moves, and behind him came a figure, bouncing and swaying. A human being led into the room by two other men. My heart nearly exploded. It was a woman, pale and white, blond hair, figure full and bound in a plain white sheet, and she was twisting and kicking, trying to get away. Eyes huge, screaming fright, a gag drawn and tied tightly across her mouth. Oh, God, I didn't want to see anyone killed. I didn't want to see this woman sliced open like the goat. They wouldn't, would they? Could they? Yes, absolutely, because just then one of them stepped forward with a long knife and pressed it against her chin. Dark, rich blood immediately emerged from the woman's skin, then began quickly dripping down on the pure white sheet wrapped around her virginal body. There was a deep, guttural groan of approval from the crowd of men, and I understood that they meant to shove aside the rice-stuffed goat, draw the woman up on the dais, perhaps gang rape her, and then maybe quarter her, either leaving bits of her down here in this abandoned building or throwing her into the great Mississippi.

There was nothing Toni and I could do, not alone, not so outnumbered. We had to get help. We had to slip out of there, get to the car, to a phone, call 911. If we acted quickly we could stop all this, save this blond woman.

I leaned forward, whispered as lightly and faintly as I could, my breath not much more than a wisp of air, "We have to get help—now!"

She nodded quickly, and we pushed ourselves away from the wall, back toward the door and that big room. If only we could get out, escape this pit of darkness. I moved fast, too fast, for sure. I could have stumbled over a board, alerted the whole room of devil worshipers. But all I could think of was getting out of there, running back up those stairs, charging back into light and safety, finding a phone, notifying the authorities.

We made it to the door of the large chamber. I glanced to the right, toward the doorway that led into the ritual room. Only glowing light. No person standing guard. Toni and I pushed on, hand clutching hand. They were chanting back there behind us, loudly now. Grunts and groans rising and beating in rhythm, beckoning the forces of blackness. We were about halfway across the large chamber and to the stairs up. Almost there. I could see the faint outline of the door to safety. That was when they did it, tore off that woman's gag. Or maybe she chewed through it in desperation. Whatever—we heard it, were stabbed by it, a piercing, knife-sharp scream.

"No!" the woman shrieked and begged. "Please, no!"

Toni stopped. What was wrong with her? We should have been flying out of there by then, soaring to the surface for help. But instead she froze. Were images of her sister grabbing her, holding her? Was Toni certain that Liz had perished thus and was determined now to stop this blond woman's death? Perhaps that was what gripped Toni and held her, what caused her to scream out herself, shout back at that room where they were about to do God knows what to an innocent person. She did it without even thinking, acting quickly, like a doctor trying something, anything, to save someone's life, pull them back from the brink of death.

Through the darkness, Toni yelled, "Don't hurt her!"

Her message was like electric shock pads, the paddlelike things applied to a heart attack victim, now zapping this scene, because for a moment everything was still. No chants. No voices. Toni and I . . . just stood there. I didn't know what to expect, but was surprised by the momentary peace. Then, of course, one of the guys moved out of the room, stepped out into the chamber, and stood there staring at us. He was as shocked as we were terrified, just stood there, naked chest, black mask.

He screamed, "Intruders!"

A great whoop went up from the back room, a collective roar that rose and threatened with its animalish power. They started stampeding, pouring out of that room, and Toni and I tore for the door behind us. Lunged for it. Flew against it as the herd charged after us. I heard screams and hoots, knew that if we were caught we would be trampled upon, beaten and mauled. My heart soared out of my body, right out of my chest, up my throat, ahead of me.

Toni and I ran, came crashing against the door, hurled it out before us. I looked up, saw a faint light above. Two flights up. Then the alley, the deserted one. Oh, shit. We'd never make it. No way we could outrun this herd of wild men barreling after us. Just as soon as we were through the door, I pushed it shut, leaned into it with my shoulder. God, there was no way I could hold them back.

"Get a piece of wood!" I screamed at Toni.

I saw the panic butterfly across her face. Wood?

"Something to pin this shut!" Pointing to where we'd earlier hidden beneath the stairs, I shouted, "Over there!"

She dove into action, scooping up one, then two boards, bringing them over. We crammed one of them into place, wedging it up against the door, beneath the handle, then down against the bottom of the staircase. It was just the right length. Then we took the second board, a longer one, and jammed that between the door and the second step. That one was in place when we heard them come rolling across that room and against the door, banging against it. There was a great thud, a collective groan from inside, and a chorus of screams and curses. I looked down, saw the door swell and bulge toward us, saw the wood bend like simple chopsticks under all that force.

Toni and I turned, bolted up the stairs one and two at a time, feet clawing, climbing, leaving the screaming horde down there behind us. Toni tore ahead of me, bounded like the star marathon runner that she was. We flew up those gritty stairs, bobbed to the surface of light, into the small landing with the chained door, then out onto the loading platform, down the wooden steps, into the alley. Fading light, loose bricks, raggedy train tracks, and no thugs.

I glanced back. Had we escaped? Was it possible?

"Alex, don't stop!" hollered Toni. "They might have another way out!"

Which was highly possible, so we kept running, right out of that alley, down the street and to my car. The Honda. Hands shaking, I unlocked it and we scrambled in, huffing, sweating, and then I brought the engine to a roar and, tires spitting gravel, we were off, out of there, away from them and toward freedom.

So, I wondered as we skidded out onto Washington Avenue, were we okay? Safe? Was that possible?

"We've got to find a phone," said Toni, staring out the back.

I'd almost forgotten in that first moment of relief, but of course we had to. I sped down the broad street, raced like a dragster some five blocks, then slammed on the brakes in front of one of the Warehouse District's trendy restaurants. The one in the short blue building, J. D. Hoyt's. Toni and I jumped out, abandoning the car in the street, rushed inside, and every diner stopped and stared from the dark booths. There was a TV up in the corner with a game on it. But everyone was looking at us, thinking: This wasn't what we ordered. Wondering fearfully what had happened because we looked like hell and were pale and panicky-demanding.

I lunged at the bar, yelled, "Give me a phone, quick!"

It was an emergency, obviously, and I was hurled a phone, and I dialed 911 and screamed into the receiver. Screamed I don't know what, something about a cult and them attacking a woman, holding her, tying her up. Rape, too. I screamed all that to get them to come quick before they killed her. Where?

Where? asked the calm voice on the other end. Of course I didn't know, so I said we were where?—at J. D. Hoyt's—to meet us out front. The cops. Hurry!

Toni and I then ducked back outside. I pulled the car over, got it off the street and in front of a fire hydrant. By the time I was out of the car, I heard the swirling sirens, and seconds later, they were there, one and then two cop cars. Toni and I rushed to the first one, jumped in the backseat, then pointed down the street, blathering and shouting the way, the story, what we'd seen. Fifteen, twenty men down in a basement, we'd said, and the cops called for other cars, more help.

But by the time we got there, of course, it was empty. The whole goddamned warehouse. The cops made us wait in the squad cars, and they went down, guns at the ready. There was no one, though. They checked the entire building, up and down, and the only thing they found to confirm our story was a little spilled rice on the stairs.

Chapter 11

The cops questioned us in the backseat of the squad car, right there in the alley, and we went over and over the story as the sun faded away and an evening chill took a bite. When we'd told it the third time, I leaned back, looked out the rear window, saw a nearly full moon rising over the warehouses, and I couldn't help but wonder if we'd be there all night.

Toni briefly went into her sister's death—the cops were familiar with it, the suicide they said, the jumper—and she said she thought it was all related, this cult and all. No, she was sure of it. After Tyler's avoiding us, our following him, this cult, the blond woman with the gag, not to mention the rice-stuffed goat, Toni was positive. Well, that may be, said one cop, but how did this warehouse with the so-called devil worshipers, empty out so fast? How come the only thing they could find was a little bit of rice? We had no idea, but it pissed Toni off, being questioned and doubted like that, like maybe we'd made the whole thing up. She asked for Detective Jenkins, so they called into the station for him, but he wasn't immediately available. In a few hours, they said. He was out, but he'd be back soon.

That's when Toni and I went back to my place, and by the time we did, it was after nine. It had been the strangest of days.

I made some decaf coffee, got out some bread and cheese and mustard, and Toni and I sat in my kitchen, a small room with white walls and a tiny counter. We sat there, relaxing, the tension finally leaving us, but the questions mounting evermore. Tyler, the cult, Liz. How did it all tie together, and just what had we seen tonight? Was the blond woman still alive? Or hacked to pieces and bobbing about in the Mississippi?

Just before eleven, Jenkins called. He'd heard about the incident at the warehouse and wanted to talk to us both. I said sure, and about twenty minutes later the intercom screamed, then screamed again, which wasn't surprising because nothing was more than twenty minutes away except a treeless suburb called Coon Rapids. He came up dressed in a brown polyester sport coat, tan pants, open shirt, and clutching a messy yellow legal pad. He looked tired, as if he'd been on duty too long. All three of us went to the living room, Toni and I sat on the couch. Jenkins faced us, and then we went through the entire story again, from my having called Rob Tyler from Peter's Grill, to propping those boards against the door, to our rushing into J. D. Hoyt's.

First thing, Jenkins said, "Christ, are you two lucky you weren't chopped to pieces."

Toni barely paid him attention; instead, following a thought of her own, she said, "Tyler's trying to hide something. He knows something about Liz's death—maybe he even killed her. I'm sure of it. And it has something to do with this cult. That's what she wanted to write about and what she wanted me to photograph. It has to be."

"Probably," said Jenkins. "But let me put it this way, you two were really stupid to go into that warehouse. It was dangerous and you're lucky nothing happened to you. That's a very mean group."

I asked, "Are you saying you know something about them?"

He looked at me, apparently wondering how much he should divulge, then said, "Yes, I am." He rubbed his brow. "This group—the Dragons—is under investigation. We don't know that much about them, except that they are a very dangerous bunch. You know about the killings, right? The four women? Well, they've all been murdered since January, all of them killed in the same bizarre way, and it's possible this might be connected. More than that, I can't tell you, but this isn't something you should go poking around in."

Toni was shocked. "What?"

"Stay away from them, and stay away from Rob Tyler. Avoid him altogether."

"I don't get it," said Toni, the anger coloring her face. "Why the hell didn't you tell me? Why didn't you tell me my sister's death could be cult-related?"

"Because I didn't think it was and because we're trying to keep it out of the papers."

"But—"

"I didn't tell you because those other four women were all killed in the same ritualistic manner, and your sister wasn't."

"Yeah, but Liz dated a member of that cult, for God's sake!"

"Look, the other women were raped, carved up, and nailed to trees. Your sister had a history of depression, she'd already attempted suicide once, she was on medication, and she was found in the Mississippi."

Things weren't right here. Something else was going on, and it was wrong. But what?

"Alex, hold it there for a second. It's all right to let out whatever your subconscious knows. Just step back and imagine you're looking at a picture of all this. What's going on?"

I caught my breath, held it, and that seemed to capture time, hold it still for a moment. All of a sudden I was no longer sitting there on the couch, but I was up higher, looking down at them, Toni and Detective Jenkins and, oddly, at myself, too. Studying us all from a different perspective, as if I were gazing down on a photograph. Yes, there was something going on. But what?

"You've come back via hypnosis to that meeting with Jenkins. So now as you retell this you have more knowledge and better insights than you had back then."

Right then and there, back in my apartment after the episode in the warehouse, Jenkins knew quite a bit more about this cult and about Liz's death, too. I didn't know then why he wouldn't tell us, why we were going to have to hunt this all out for ourselves. We did, of course. By the end, we understood it all.

"What are you saying?"

That there was a whole other level to this, that we had only scratched the surface, that Jenkins wasn't . . .

I ran out of air. My lungs screamed, and I took a deep gulp, which sucked me back to that late night in my condo. There was a lot to find out here, an entirely different reality beneath the surface of Jenkin's sparse words, and we could only get to that reality by going through everything step by step. Logically and slowly.

Jenkins looked up, and said, "Listen, I'm just trying to conduct an investigation the best way I know how. I didn't think your sister's death was related to the Dragons, but maybe I was wrong. Obviously there are some things I need to check into, and if I turn up anything, you'll be the first to know."

Toni nodded.

"Good. Just trust me, I'm doing everything I can." He lifted up his pad of paper. "I need your help. Can you describe this woman, the one you saw in the warehouse?"

Toni bent her head, pinched the bridge of her nose with her right hand, and said, "Tall, about five ten. And not slender—real full body. Blond hair."

"Very blond—yellowy," I added.

"And round face."

"Definitely in her thirties."

Jenkins frowned, scratched the back of his head, then from the pages of his yellow pad pulled out a picture.

"This her?"

I took the photograph, a five-by-seven glossy, black and white, that showed a smiling woman, very Germanic or Northern European-looking, with big cheeks, big smile. White teeth, light hair. All of which made her look like half the population in Minnesota. The picture was taken outside, and she was on a sidewalk, looking back over her left shoulder. A soft-looking woman, attractive, someone I might have been friends with.

"God, I don't know," said Toni, obviously perplexed. "It might be. What do you think, Alex?"

The broad characteristics were the same. A full-bodied attractive woman. Light hair. The face we'd seen in the warehouse had been one of fear and rage. This one was happy and smiling, younger-looking. Think, I told myself, bring back her image.

That image came winging out of my memory, and I quickly said, "Yes, that's her."

"Are you sure?" asked Jenkins.

"Yeah, absolutely. I remember the eyes—I looked right at them because she was so afraid. And the chin—that's where they cut her. It's the same chin."

Seated next to me, Toni pursed her lips, hesitant to agree with me. After a moment, however, she nodded. I was right. This woman in the photo was the one we'd seen bound in that sheet, her mouth gagged.

"I agree, that's her." Looking up, Toni said, "Why do you ask?"

"Because this woman," said Jenkins, taking back the photograph, "disappeared last week from the U. No trace, no nothing. She went to the library and just vanished."

I thought, Oh, God, where would they finally find her? Tacked to which tree? In which field? I didn't like this, any of it. The insanity was creeping up here now, bleeding our way. What had happened to the United States when students couldn't cross a campus? When had we become the land of the fearful? Of course they'd never find her alive. Jenkins must have known, as must her parents.

Detective Jenkins slid the photo back into the yellow pad, said, "Well, I'm going to be checking in with our Mr. Tyler. Tomorrow I'll go over to his place, and if he's not there, I'll try the College of Art and Design." He ran his hand back over his receding hair. "I'm telling you this because I don't want him to know he was seen at one of these Dragon get-togethers. At least I don't want him to know yet. That's sort of an ace I want to hold on to, and I'm afraid that if you look him up, that might be a topic, shall we say, for conversation."

"Yeah," said Toni, shaking her head, "it was pretty disgusting what we saw, and I've never been very good at holding my tongue."

"So you'll keep away from him?" asked Jenkins, looking first at me, then Toni, then me again.

"Sure," I ventured.

Toni nodded.

"Good." Jenkins rose. "And keep away from the Dragons,

for God's sake. Just let me do some work here. I'll keep you posted, but call me anytime, especially if you think of anything else."

It was late, he was tired, Toni and I were exhausted. Jenkins muttered some more things, Toni muttered her gratitude. I escorted Jenkins to the door, where I shook his hand, and it seemed to me that he must have been a phys ed teacher once. That was what he reminded me of. A tired PE teacher who'd left education for a more glamorous job. If you could call this glamorous.

"Thanks a lot for coming over so late," I said to him through the doorway. "I know Toni really appreciates it. This has been very hard on her."

"I'm sure."

He lumbered off, and I shut the door, twisting the deadbolt and checking to make sure it was tight, just as I did every night before I went to bed. Then I turned around and realized I still had a guest. Toni. Why did it seem so natural, why did I just assume, that she was going to stay the night?

I started back toward the living room, wondering if indeed that would come to pass. Toni and me, once again.

Chapter 12

I returned to the living room, stood there on the edge of it, wondering what this day and night had been leading up to. My relationship with Toni had never been resolved, at least not from my point of view. Things had only been broken off. I'd never really understood why, and still didn't, of course, and so I now sensed that all of it was coming to a head. That was next on the day's agenda. The next chapter of Us.

Was it just sexual tension, residual tension, accumulated all these years? Was that what I was feeling? Certainly that was a great part of it. From me, anyway. I stood on the threshold of the living room, wondering what I should do, how I should handle this, whether we'd have sex and sleep together, and if so did that mean we'd do it again and again? Hoping we would. Oh, God, could we, would we be back together?

I didn't want to frighten her, to rush things and thereby push her away. Yes, I was conniving, trying to figure out how I could win her back, as they said. So what could I do to precipitate my greatest wishes? I was motionless, watching, thinking, and Toni, perhaps unaware of my presence, bowed her head into her hands and started to cry.

That's when I started moving. Of course I wanted to comfort her—she was exhausted, her sister was dead, we could have been killed tonight—but I also recognized a great opportunity. Her defenses were weakened, perhaps they could easily be breached. Yes, I knew that was taking advantage of her at that moment, but I didn't care. I had loved, and probably always would love, Toni. If only I could kiss her and tell her all that and more right here, right there on that couch.

"Alex, you can skip to the next part if you want. You don't have to go into this if—"

I couldn't stop myself. More than important, this was necessary. I knew I'd learn things about Toni I hadn't known, only suspected, and I knew that perhaps I'd learn things about myself as well. The driving force was lust, of course, but the altruistic reason was honesty and clarity.

I circled around the end of my big green couch, sat down next to Toni, who sat huddled over, sobbing. I began my seduction by reaching over, slowly, hesitantly, and putting my arms around her, the right one around her back, the left reaching across her front. I encircled her, pulled her into me. A good start.

I said, "It's okay, Toni. You're okay."

She folded herself and her pain into me, gave herself willingly, abandoned any pretext. I cradled her, hugged her, as she shook gently with her tears, and I mumbled again and again how it was okay, that it was good to let go, that it was late and had been a long day, and that she was exhausted. She pressed against me, and I pulled her as close as I could and marveled at her warmth, her freshness. I ran my hand through her hair and held her head against my chest, and we just sat there, the two of us clutching one another. From me Toni took comfort and security. From her I took hope, which in turn fueled my desire.

It wasn't odd, then, that I started nuzzling my face into her thick hair, which conjured up so many wonderful memories. It was sweet-smelling, as she was, as she had always been. I started kissing her. At first it was like a comfort kiss. Just a quick peck on the side of the head. Then I stole another one, kissing her hair, really, just above the ear. The third was longer, more full. It was as if I were testing the ice, wondering when and if it would crack. But it didn't. Or it was like a dance, a game, trying to find out exactly how much I could get away with. When I kissed her the fourth time, I found out. She reached up, wrapped her hand around my neck, held my lips against the side of her head, clutched me tightly.

Toni, Toni, Toni, rolled my heart. That was all the encouragement I needed, and I swelled with hope, kissed her ear lightly, three or four times. Definitely not kisses of comfort. I'd certainly transgressed that boundary of the past, and I wondered if now I'd be repelled, pushed away. But it didn't happen. Instead she brought herself closer, sitting up, lifting her face. I touched her cheeks with one hand, ran my fingers over her soft, tear-soaked skin, which made me smile and shiver.

She stared at me, looked into my eyes, lifted her fingers to my lips, caressed my mouth, and finally past fused with present: Toni lifted her head, our lips met. I clutched her to me, kissed her hard, perhaps too hard, but I couldn't help myself. Everything dialed up, got cranked right to high. Toni twisted around so that she was on her back, her head in my lap, and she lay there lingering and looking up at me. The impossible had happened. She was here, in my arms. I couldn't believe it; it felt almost as if I were observing the scene rather than participating in it.

"You are."

What? No, I was there, cradling Toni, and she wasn't crying anymore. That was gone. I bent forward, pressed my lips to her mouth, her face, over and over again, and then I reached down, caressed her waist, ran my fingers up her arms. Yes, it was the same Toni. I'd forgotten the bits and pieces of her—how firm her stomach felt against my hand, how buttery soft the underside of her wrists. But there was so much that was familiar— the arch of her back against my hand, the firmness of her breasts. I trembled with desire, wanted to dive into her, enter her, consume her, never leave her again. I tugged her shirt from her jeans, spread my fingers wide, ran them over her skin, up and around. Then, my fingertips flowing over her belt, over the outside of her pants, I reached down. Her legs spread, and I reached, ran my hand all the way down and around, then back up again.

Then I clutched her, wrapping my arms around her waist and her shoulders, and it was my turn to cry. My eyes reddened;

I could feel it. And they misted. A huge swell of pain rose from within me. This hurt. It was partly because of Toni, I supposed, and her dumping me some ten years ago. But it was also from loneliness. Yes, being with her now made me realize how utterly alone I'd been for so long, how I had three very expensive and rather redundant bicycles but had no mate or family, and how much more I wanted the latter.

I sighed, laid my head against her neck. "Toni . . ."

She ran her fingers through my hair, massaged my back, said, "I've missed you."

Thank you, I thought. Thank you for acknowledging that there had been something between us, something even profound. So it wasn't my imagination. I had meant something to her as well; she hadn't just dumped me and waltzed on. God, that first year after our breakup, I'd thought about her nearly every day.

"What happened?" I asked, not to cast blame, not to fuel anger, but to understand or, rather, to have it said once and for all, for I did have my suspicions.

She pushed me up, then stared at me, her head still cradled in my lap. Reaching for my face, she stroked my stubbly cheeks with the back of her hand.

"You never understood, did you?"

Was I so dumb, so dense? No, not at all. Somewhere inside me I'd known the moment she'd moved out.

Still, I wanted to force the words from her—she, after all, was the one who'd left—and I said, "No."

The desire and lust rushed out of us both. She pulled away, grabbed a bunch of her hair, swung it around and back over her shoulder. Sat back. Toni curled one foot underneath her, then reached out and took my hand in both of hers.

"Alex, I'm sorry. I should have made it clear back then."

I nodded. She should have. Instead she'd just packed up her things, went on her way, and shut me out of her life, leaving me to piece things together as best I could.

She cleared her throat. "Back then, when we were still living together, I met someone else." She paused, looked away, bit her lip. Of course she was uncomfortable. "It was while I was an intern."

"That's what I thought." I knew that much. Actually now I was sure I'd known the whole thing. "And you fell in love?"

She nodded.

I started mumbling, "What did I do? What didn't I . . . ?" It was useless, though, rehashing all that. "Why didn't you just say so?"

"Alex, I couldn't. Not back then."

"Was it another doctor?"

"No."

It had to be someone else at the hospital, for that's where she spent all her time. Someone from high up?

"Someone in administration?" I probed.

"No, Alex." She bowed her head, gulped, looked up at me. "It was a nurse."

I stared at her, tried to give her the benefit of the doubt, saying, "It wasn't that guy—what was his name? Phil? It wasn't him, was it?"

I wanted to be right. I wanted it to be him or one of those other big, brawny guys who were so gentle in their work, lifting ailing people from bed to wheelchair and so on. I'd met a handful of them, played softball with them on two Fourths, and I hoped it was one of them who'd stolen Toni.

But that wasn't the way it was.

"No," said Toni, shaking her head.

Now I cleared my throat, managed what I'd known to be the core truth. "You're gay, aren't you?"

She nodded, squeezed my hand. "I'm a lesbian, yes."

"Oh." I glanced away. "That's what I thought."

"Do you remember a friend of mine, Laura Cole?"

My voice was faint. "She helped you move out."

"Right. We fell in love and we've been together almost ever since."

I'd suspected as much, had grown to believe it, too, especially when I recalled little things Toni had done and said about her, Laura, the nurse. I'd met her on several occasions before Toni had left me; in fact, I remembered the three of us going out for dinner once. Someplace Italian. Laura had a sort of Slavic face, broad and warm, small eyes. Light hair, very long and straight. She wasn't heavy but not thin, either. And she had a bawdy sense of humor. I remembered that because I could never recall jokes, yet I still knew the one Laura had told that night.

"Did you hear about the nurse," Laura had said when we were well into our second bottle of wine, "who was walking around with a thermometer above her ear?"

No, Toni had said. No, I'd echoed, shaking my head.

"When one of the doctors asked her about it, she pulled it down, and screamed, 'Oh, my God, some asshole's got my pencil!' "

Sure. She'd kept us laughing all night long, particularly Toni. The two of them had gone into hysterics a number of times, while I'd tried to follow with a big laugh. I distinctly remembered, even then, feeling the odd man out. So that was the start of it. It all made sense, too. Now it did, anyway.

Antoinette Domingo a lesbian? Yes, it was said now, verbalized. She'd confirmed an unspoken reality, a truth that was hard to accept, but one that I could and would accept. Still, we'd been so good together, had had such great sex.

She said, "I loved you very much, Alex. I really did. But I couldn't stay with you because I couldn't go on pretending to be someone I wasn't. I couldn't be with you and be dishonest. So I had to leave. I know I didn't do a very good job at it. Lousy, in fact. And I regret that."

I stared at the big oak fireplace. My mind sifted incidents, latched on to facts.

"I wish you'd told me—it would have hurt, but I would have understood." I lifted her hand, pressed it against my lips because I knew that I would always love her, although now I would have to do so in a much different way. "I do feel like a fool. I mean, it's like trying and trying to put on a shoe and getting angry and upset because it won't fit, even though it's supposed to. Then finally, ten years later someone just says, 'Hey, buddy, that's a great shoe but it's the left one and you're trying to put it on your right foot.' "

"I know, Alex, and I'm sorry. All I can say is that choosing a same-sex relationship is the hardest thing I ever had to do. To face up to, I mean. It wasn't a choice of being straight or gay—I didn't get to make that one. It was just a choice of whether or not I was going to be honest."

"I'm sure." I looked at her, seeing her differently, the pain and the peace, now fully for the first time. "Are you happy?"

"I've been through some rough times lately—there's more than Liz's death, but I can't get into that right now—so I won't say it hasn't been hard. And I won't say that if it had been solely my choice I wouldn't rather have been married and had a house full of kids, but . . . but I know I made the right decision."

I reached out, touched her on the arm, asked, "Can I hold you?"

"I wish you would."

The two of us stretched out on that green sofa, lay there side by side, my front to her back like a couple of old spoons nestled together. I kissed her on the neck, and Toni pulled my arms around her, snuggled against me.

"Can we be friends again?" she asked. "I mean, real friends this time."

"I'm a little in shock," I began, clutching her. "But I guess if I can't have you as a lover, then I'll take you how I can get you . . . as a friend."

We lay there in silence, the hurt—hurt because it was impossible, we would never have made it, we both saw that now—pulling us into drowsiness, the drowsiness washing us with sleep.

Chapter 13

Somewhere toward early morning, I did in fact slip away, found a blanket to spread over Toni, then—

"That's right, it's time to get some rest."

What? What was that? Who was that?

"It's me, Alex, and we're going to pause here a bit."

I cringed, twisted. Someone was talking to me, kicking me out of that time. But I didn't want to be. I wanted to stay just where I was. Besides, there was something I had to explore and find out about.

"And you will, Alex. You will. Trust me. We need to rest a bit, though, and get something to eat. I'm starved, aren't you? Don't worry, we'll just take a short break."

I felt as if I were being slapped out of a dream, forced awake when it was the very last thing I wanted. Who cared about food? No, I should go back to the couch. Toni was there, asleep. I had to go back to her, lie down, cuddle up and hold her and all the dreams that might have been. Couldn't I make her love me and want me again? Wasn't there any way?

"Alex, now come on."

I just wanted . . . I just wanted . . . what? To know that

I hadn't been a fool? To know that I hadn't done anything wrong?

"You've done nothing wrong, Alex. Nothing."

Yes, I did. I waited too long before moving on. I was stuck on this one person when I should have let go years ago because it was an impossibility, Toni and me.

"I'm going to count backward from ten to one, and when I reach one you'll—"

Do I have to?

"Yes. My stomach's growling."

So she started counting, Sorceress-Sister Maddy, and I reluctantly began to surface, returning from my evening with Toni when the truth about her and our relationship was finally put on the table. As Maddy counted, I began to feel less and less like I was back in my apartment in Minneapolis, and more and more like I was on a leather recliner on Madeline's island. In fact, just before Maddy reached the bottom of her countdown, I opened one eye, saw the bright evening light, and realized how depressed I was. Not because I'd lost Toni, but because what I wanted could never be. And it was no one's fault.

Maddy took a long breath, whispered, *"And one."*

Both eyes opened, and I lay there quite still as if the blanket of reality that now covered me were too heavy to push off. How dramatic. That was how I felt, though. A little ashamed, too, for until now I hadn't told anyone about Toni and me—why things really didn't work out between us.

I heard Maddy next to me, looked over, saw her groping for her wheelchair. I hated to see her struggle, so I quickly got up and went around.

"Thank you," said Maddy, ever gracious, as I lifted her into the wheelchair.

She reached down, felt her legs from thigh to foot, and ascertained that, yes, all of her was there in the chair and properly positioned, too. Nothing to get caught or pinched. Then she put her hands on the wheels, twirled around, and started to roll herself onward. What, no comment, no word or reaction to what I'd just revealed? No opinion on Toni and me? I knew my sister well enough to know the answer to that one. She had a reaction, of course, probably a strong one. She was just holding it in. The only question was why and how long she could hold it. I gave her less than a half hour.

She was escaping quickly, and I called, "You really must be hungry."

"I am, aren't you? Come on."

She was off and rolling, and I half-jogged after her, through the big empty attic with its soaring ceiling. As we passed around the Tiffany dome that capped the stairwell, I glanced up and out the skylight above the dome. Outside a blue, blue sky. It would be clear tonight, and I was just about to ask Maddy if she'd ever seen any northern lights up here, but then I caught myself. As she whizzed to the back of the room and through a door to the rear of the attic, I realized what a good job she did at deceiving people.

Some twenty minutes later we were seated at the dining room table; we'd both washed and used the bathroom, Maddy with a bit of Solange's help. And now we were seated at this big plank of yellow oak, Maddy at the head of the table, me on her left, and actually it was kind of lonely, just the two of us at a table that could easily seat sixteen. The ceilings were twelve feet tall, maybe more, and there was a huge built-in buffet, an all-oak affair that must have once displayed pricey china but was now totally empty. All of this and only us.

"Do you ever get lonely out here?" I asked.

"Nope." She turned toward me. "How's the soup?"

Solange had served us each a large bowl of some summery concoction with lots of chunks of tomatoes and fresh herbs. We had bread, too, and more iced tea with more lemons.

"Good," I replied.

It was then that I tried my first real taste—I'd just sort of been playing around with it before—and it was good. Fresh and spicy and healthy-tasting. So the soup was fine; I had only told a white lie of sorts, a blip of a thing. I wasn't sure, however, if I believed what Maddy had said about not being lonely or, thinking back on it, just about anything else. And that in itself was a terrible realization. I'd always implicitly trusted my big sister, worshiped her, but I was just beginning to understand how much Maddy lied, even if only by omission. She insisted on doing things herself—moving around blindly on the paths of this island and through this huge house—so that you forgot she was both blind and paraplegic. Simply, she worked hard at pretending to be who she was not.

"You're awfully quiet," said Maddy.

"Just thinking."

"About what?"

"I don't know."

Maddy felt for the bread on the edge of her saucer, found it, said, " 'I don't know' usually means 'I don't want to say.' "

"I guess that's right." I stirred my soup. "Are you're egging me on?"

"I suppose so. I suppose I want to know what's going on in your head."

"I'm thinking that I felt bad for you when you lost your sight and I felt awful when you were hit by that bus, and I've felt sorry for you at times, guilty, too. But . . . but I've never really felt pity for you until today. Until just now, really."

She calmly lifted a spoon to her mouth. "Oh?"

"You hold back so much, Maddy. I pity you that. You always pull out another person's pain, and you're great at soothing that and healing it. You're a wonderful listener. But you're terrible at revealing yourself." How odd, I thought, I was beginning to see my big sister not as the mythical older sibling, but as just another person, an ordinary slob like me. "I mean, why didn't you ever tell me about this guy you were so madly in love with? It must have hurt like hell when he dumped you."

"I can't show my weaknesses, Alex. Not me. I have several handicaps, obviously, and I have to work doubly hard so people will see that I'm strong."

"I think you're overcompensating."

"You're probably right. I probably do hide things I don't need to."

Suddenly I was there. Without having planned it, I had her right where I wanted, in a corner.

"Then tell me," I challenged, "what you think of Toni. What you think of her and me and our relationship. You've been so quiet, but you're a shrink, so you must have an opinion. Am I a sicko?"

"Are you sure you want to hear?"

"Yeah, and be blunt."

"This might hurt," said my sister. "And you might be mad."

"No, I won't," I replied, at the same time thinking, Go ahead, judge me.

"Okay, if you're sure. Actually, it's something I've been meaning to tell you for a long time." She put her hands on the edge of the table, turned toward me, and said, "First of all, I don't think you're a sicko. And second, I knew."

"Knew what?"

"That Toni was a lesbian."

I looked at her, unable to hide my puzzlement. "So what's that make you, a good guesser?"

"No." Maddy hesitated, and when she spoke again, her voice was lower, softer, calmer. Unmistakably. "That makes me a good friend."

"What do you mean?"

"I mean, Toni and I were friends. Close friends, actually, and she told me about Laura and her."

This didn't make any sense except, of course, they'd both lived in Chicago. I hesitated, then asked, "What are you saying?"

"I'm saying that a while ago—"

"How long?"

"Well, six years maybe."

"Six years?" I gasped.

"Yes, about that long ago we ran into each other. I was at Water Tower Place, tapping along with my cane, when all of a sudden I literally bumped into someone, and who was it but Toni. We knew each other at once, of course. I mean, I used to see a lot of her when you two were together, and so we—"

Stunned, I said softly, "Oh, shit, Maddy."

Maddy's chin started to tremble, and she bit her lower lip. Then she turned away from me, pushed up those big Beverly Hills sunglasses that hid her darkened eyes, took her napkin and blotted her eyes.

"So . . . so you see, we went out for coffee," continued Maddy in her deeper, lower voice, tears now rolling down her cheeks. "Only it wasn't just Toni and me. Laura was there, too. It was obvious they were together. I knew within the first few minutes by the way they were hedging, the way they talked about their lives. So I just went along with it, and when I acknowledged it—I can't remember what I said, something about them living together—Toni acknowledged it, too, openly so." Maddy broke off, then forced herself on, her voice still low and deep. "And after that we just got to be friends, the three of us. They were really very nice to me—we'd get together maybe five or six times a year. After the accident, while I was still in Chicago, they'd come and get me, take me out to dinner and . . . oh, God, Alex, I'm sorry."

This was just great. "Jesus Christ, why didn't you tell me?"

"Because she made me promise not to!" Maddy spun toward me, her face wrinkled and red and wet, and she reached out, bumped her bowl, spilled some soup, groped for my hand. "I'm sorry, really I am. I didn't mean to keep it secret, but Toni made me promise. She said she was the one who had to tell you about Laura and her. It was her job, and she was right. It was. So I never said anything to you. Toni went up to the Twin Cities maybe once a year to see Liz, and every time I asked, Did you see Alex? You know, he'd love to see you. You have to call him, I told her, but of course she never did until after Liz's death. Oh, Alex, she cared so much for you, she really did!"

I clutched my sister's hands, and then I was pulling on the edge of her wheelchair, moving her closer, rolling her right up next to me because I was crying then, too. I hugged Maddy, and she clung to me because I loved Toni as a lover and Maddy loved Toni as a friend, and now she was dead.

"I understand," I muttered. "I do." And I really did.

"Why would someone want to kill her?" asked my sister. "Why? She was so lovely and so talented and . . . and so kind."

"I don't know," I mumbled.

I ran my hand through my hair, thought back to Toni's funeral in Chicago. Toni's mother and father had been white with shock, speechless, too, at having lost both daughters; actually her father looked and acted heavily sedated. There'd been a huge number of people, the church overflowing, but noticeably absent was Laura Cole. I'd searched the crowd, even asked about her, but unless she'd snuck in and out, she hadn't been there.

"I wonder what ever happened to Laura," I said. "I wrote

her about a month after Toni died, but didn't get a reply. A couple of months ago I wrote her again, and that letter came back unopened."

Lost in thought, Maddy was silent, and I understood why she'd been so insistent about my coming here and doing this trance and this age regression. The whole bit. Maddy was just as determined as I to find Toni's killer, find justice, revenge, punishment. All that. And since Laura had disappeared, it was evident that if we didn't pursue this, no one else would.

"You told Toni again, didn't you?" I asked. "After Liz died you told Toni to come and see me, right?"

"Not really." Maddy nodded, pulled away a bit, cleared her throat and wiped her eyes. "Liz was buried in Chicago. I went to the funeral, and I decided that I had to tell you about being friends with Toni and about Liz, too, of course. But then after the funeral there was a small wake or reception—whatever you call those things—and Toni came up to me. She was alone—Laura and she were having some problems—and Toni told me she was going to Minneapolis to clear out her sister's apartment. She promised she was going to look you up. I think she was just afraid to see you because you were the life she could have had."

Yes, I was, but it would never have worked.

"And she did look me up," I said, recalling that fateful afternoon when the doorbell had screamed *wheeeeeee!* and she had stood there, the person I'd lost so many years earlier.

The pantry door swung open just then and Solange stepped in, but stopped upon seeing the two of us there, holding hands, eyes puffy and wet, soup barely touched. She froze in her discomfort, unsure whether to retreat in respect or proceed as if nothing were wrong.

"I think we're all right, Solange," said Maddy, her voice higher again, as she blotted away the last of her tears. "Alex, do you need anything? More soup?"

I'd only had a couple of spoonfuls. "I'm fine, thanks."

I'd never noticed, at least not until just then, that Maddy had two voices, the higher, tighter one she'd just used with Solange and the deeper, slower, no-shit one with which she'd spoken about Toni. The first voice was the tenser of the two, one that wanted the world to be a certain way, that was determined to rise above it all and pretend that all was well. The second was her inner voice, her real one, the naked, unprotected voice of her soul that betrayed how she really felt about things. Unfortunately, I knew too well that the first voice was her normal, everyday one, the one she almost always used.

"Just let me know," said Solange, quickly slipping away.

Maddy continued in her high voice, now turning to me, asking, "Alex, would you mind if I gave both Solange and Alfred the day off tomorrow? They never get to go to shore together, you see. One of them is always with me. So since you're here, I'd like to let them spend the night away from here. They could go to Petoskey or up to Mackinac Island, though they're probably wanting land more than anything else, so it'd probably be Petoskey."

Of course we'd be fine out here, Maddy and I. What could happen? Now, however, that I'd discovered her high voice, the one that wasn't genuine and grounded, I couldn't help but be irritated by it. Why was she using it with me, her brother, of all people? Maybe the reason was as simple as Maddy having already promised them the day and night off, saying it was fine with me without checking first, so she was nervous.

"That'd be fine," I said. "Obviously, I'm not going anywhere."

"You're wonderful."

Even as Maddy leaned over and smooched me on the cheek, however, I knew from the higher pitch of her voice that dear Sister wasn't leveling with me, that she was holding something back. But what? And why?

"Did you get enough to eat?" she asked. "Are you finished?"

"Yes," I lied, quite easily, knowing that Maddy couldn't see how little I'd eaten. "Shall we go back up? We could still get in another hour or two."

"If you're up for a trance, yes, let's. The sooner we get this over, the better."

"Absolutely."

So, as we abandoned our meals and headed back to the elevator that would lift us to that magical room and carry me toward another age regression, I could only speculate what Maddy was hiding from me. That's when it struck me, hard and most unpleasantly, like when you hit your head going down some stairs. What more did Maddy know about Toni? Or Liz for that matter? Was there something Maddy knew—perhaps something she'd learned at Liz's funeral—that she was keeping from me and I had yet to discover?

Yes, quite possibly so.

Chapter 14

The trance descended on me quickly, probably because I was so eager to return to the past. As soon as I lay down on that recliner up on the third floor, I took a deep breath, rolled my eyes, and the trance started again. Slid right through me. I was that anxious to slip away from what Maddy had told me, and that keen on getting back to the last few days of Toni's life. Maddy went through her whole hypnotic spiel, her song-and-dance of breathing in and out, getting lighter, counting to ten. But I didn't need any of it. None of that blast-off stuff, the prep work. I was already there, which I finally told her, interrupting her routine, telling her that she had to hush, I had things to tell her and things to discover.

"Wonderful," she cooed from back there, from that pitifully small, self-conscious world, while I'd blasted into the dark universe beyond. *"Then go on. It was early morning."*

Yes, I knew. This was my story, and late at night or toward early morning, I slipped away, found a blanket to spread over Toni, then made my way back to my bedroom, where I crawled into bed. I was depressed, even then, in the middle of the night.

I told Toni that and more the next morning. We were in the kitchen; I was making coffee, my back was to her.

"I keep coming back to one thing: I just wish you'd told me back then," I said as I poured water into the machine.

"I should have, I know, come out back then, but I was having so much trouble handling it that I didn't think you could."

I turned around to see her sitting on a stool, that wild hair thrown back, face hopeful, mouth gentle. Just as beautiful and as warm-looking as ever. It was hard to be mad.

"I might not have been able to," I began, "not then, not right away. But that would have been my problem."

"Yeah, you're right. It's just that . . ." She glanced away, stared at the white walls, turned back to me. "I was still trying to come to terms with who I was, trying to deal with all my self-loathing, and it's just that it was easier to reject you, Alex, than to tell you and have you reject me." She added, "It may sound silly, but your love was that important to me."

I grabbed a sponge from the sink, started wiping a counter that was perfectly clean. No, there were crumbs by the toaster, a bit of spilled water by the coffeemaker, not to mention a stain that might disappear if only I scrubbed long enough, hard enough.

Behind me, Toni said, "Look, Alex, I need to get back to my hotel, then go over to Liz's." There was a pained pause. "It was nice to see you again."

"Goddamit, Toni, don't walk out on me a second time. We're not finished." I spun around, face red, said, "I spent all these years thinking about you, wondering what had happened to us, to you. You've no idea how much I thought about you. No idea. I thought I'd never get over you, that I'd never forget anything about you, and now . . . now . . ." I bowed my head and shook it. There was nothing else to be done. Nowhere else to go. "Shit, I spent all that time thinking about you and now I don't remember if you drink your coffee black or not."

She looked at me, hopeful. "Black, actually."

"Right, black."

I opened a cupboard, reached for a mug, took a long, deep breath, said, "You can go back to your hotel to get your things, Toni, but I want you to stay here for the rest of your time in Minneapolis. In fact, I'll be pissed if you don't. The guest bed-room is full of my bikes and junk, but you can put your stuff in there and sleep on the living room couch. I think it would be good for both of us to spend time together." I poured the coffee, handed it to her. "Is it a deal, Dr. Domingo?"

Touching me on my hand as she accepted the coffee, she said simply, "Deal."

That was the beginning of our new friendship, one that was based on how the cards really lay, not on how we wished they did. We had eggs, runny ones, of course, because I did remember Toni liked them that way. All was going fine, getting even cheerful, until I asked about Laura. From the way Toni had talked, I'd just assumed they were still together.

"How is she?" I asked. "Still as funny?"

"Actually . . ." Toni looked at the floor, sighed. "Actually we've had a hard year. Laura has a CD problem she has to work out."

"CD?"

"Chemical dependency. It's pretty common among nurses—at least that's what they say. You know, all the drugs they're around, all the stress. She was working on an AIDS ward for the past couple of years, and it finally got to her."

I sensed this was the tip of the iceberg, and asked, "What do you mean? What happened? Are you two still together?"

"No, not at the moment, anyway." She frowned, looked at me. "Do you really want to hear this?"

"Yeah, I do." All of it, I thought. I wanted to fill in all the blanks.

"Well . . ." Toni let out a long breath. "It started getting bad a couple of years ago. Laura has always been a heavy drinker, but then, you know, working with the AIDS patients and everything. All the deaths—she couldn't handle it. Who could? She started sneaking tranquilizers, I'm not sure which, and then she went downhill from there. I think, to be shrinky-dinky about it, the AIDS stuff really made her take a hard look at her own sexuality. Anyway, about a year ago I tried to get her help but she fought it. I started getting pushy about it—she really did get pretty bad, coming home either high or drunk almost every night. I'd only seen bits of it before, but then she developed this awful temper. And then . . ."

"Then?"

"I finished up early at the hospital one day, got home, and there she was sitting in the living room, about to shoot up some heroin. I hit the roof—I grabbed the syringe and smashed it, and she came after me. We had a terrible fight, you know, with fists and everything. It was awful." Toni hung her head, shook it. "All this anger came flying out of her. This rage. And she hit me. I mean, she knocked me out."

"Oh, no."

"Yeah, what a year, huh? My lipstick-lez girlfriend has a personality split, turns into the dyke from hell, I kick her out, and then my kid sister dies. God."

"I'm sorry."

"That's why it was so wonderful to see you, to feel your arms around me." She smiled and reached out for my hand. "I've never forgotten you either, Alex. I mean, you were a good friend once."

I took her hand, squeezed it, let go. "So you and Laura have split up?"

"I guess so, for now anyway. I hope it's not permanent. I still really love her, but she's got to get straightened out. Things went really downhill for her—I had to tell the hospital where she worked, of course, and they suspended her immediately. Then she moved back to her folks'. Actually she's here now, in Minnesota, at The North Center. It's about an hour out of town, and a month ago her parents got her into their chemical dependency program."

"Minnesota," I laughed. "Land of ten thousand treatment centers. Hazelden really started something."

"Well, you guys are famous for them. I know Laura's not out of the woods yet—I just hope it works."

"Have you seen her since you've been up here?"

"No. She wrote me after Liz died—a short card—but we haven't spoken at all, and she doesn't want to see me. That's her decision. She's really angry at me, both for blowing the whistle on her at work and, I think, because I represent all of her own homophobia. She has a lot of self-hatred, and I'm at the vortex of all that right now. I did talk with her counselor the other day, though, and she's going to ask Laura if I can come out to visit. I really want to see her, so I hope she'll agree.

I'm supposed to check back tomorrow for the verdict. If Laura says okay, I'll drive out there."

"Good luck."

"God, life's hard, you know? I mean, Laura's so wonderful. They loved her on the AIDS ward. Let me tell you, she kept them pretty cheery. Actually it got pretty campy in there—I swear to God, one of the patients laughed himself to death last fall."

"You're kidding?"

"Well, the guy had one foot in the grave, but . . ."

I shook my head, didn't know what to say, asked, "Did your sister know about you and Laura?"

"Yeah. She was fine about it. I mean, she was glad I was out. You remember her; she liked things up front."

"Right."

We finished our coffee pretty much in silence, and before I showered I called into work, told them I was okay but not great, and that I needed to take the rest of the week off to heal from the bike accident I'd never had. I could talk to my boss and the others about the software our company was producing, about garage door openers, too. Even answering machines. But never, I suspected, could I broach a subject like Toni and me and hope for any insights. Then again, perhaps that was where I erred.

After a while I drove Toni back to her hotel, where she packed up and checked out.

"Oh," said Toni to the desk clerk, "and if anyone wants to reach me, be sure to give them this number—that's where I'll be." She wrote my name and number on a slip of paper, then turned to me and rolled her eyes. "When you're a physician you've always got to be reachable."

I laughed. "No escaping, huh?"

She followed me back to my place in her rental car, and it was a relief having that time apart from each other. I got depressed, glanced at her in my rearview mirror, realized I'd always be attracted to her beauty and assuredness.

It was kind of funny. After we dropped her things at my place and headed over to Liz's apartment, we just got back on track, like there wasn't anything weird about hanging out

together. We stopped talking about us, about sexual prefer-
ences. We pushed away from all that, gladly, and started talking
about the doctoring biz, my sister who'd been slammed by the
bus, the terribly exciting world of technical writing. My bicycle
obsession. Just sort of catching up on stuff, as if we'd been
around the corner from each other and now it was gossip time.

"Let's hope we'll have clear sailing today," I said as I parked
in front of Liz's apartment.

We went in. We entered the dark apartment, and Toni
shook her head, looked around.

"Oh, God, what do you think happened to her?"

"I don't know, but regardless," I said, walking into the
kitchen, "I'm dumping that sandwich."

Which was still parked on the counter. I poured out the
coffee, too. It was then that I noticed the handful of photos on
the refrigerator, held by magnets in the best suburban fashion.
There was a picture of Toni, one of a group of women.

I called out to Toni, "Have you talked with any of Liz's
friends?"

"Not really. I suppose I should—she didn't have that many,
though."

I tilted my head to the side, saw that one of the things on
the refrigerator wasn't a picture at all but the business card of
Dr. Edward Dawson. There were two numbers given, one
printed with a downtown prefix, and then a second number,
handwritten, with the same prefix as mine. So Dawson lived in
Kenwood, too. I stood staring at the card, realized how important this must have been to Liz, this card, these numbers, her
shrink and the medication he prescribed. Then again, Dawson
didn't seem hard to get hold of, so help must always have been
at hand. I couldn't help but wonder if Liz were depressed
enough to kill herself, wouldn't she have called him first, wanted
to talk to him, instead of just dropping him a note?

Turning around, I strode out of the kitchen, down the hall,
into the bedroom where I'd been bashed with that lamp, which
still lay on the floor along with a variety of other objects that
had been thrown around. I flicked up the shades, opened a
window, went back into the living room, where Toni was doing
the same. Letting life back in.

Then Toni planted herself in the middle of the room,

looked around, moaned, "What am I going to do with all this stuff?"

It was mostly junky furniture, true, but there obviously had to be a number of things that either Toni or her family would want to keep. Photos, memorabilia, some old family mementos. Right. There was a silver box on a coffee table—family scrap, I thought.

"I guess you pick what you want, then give the rest to the Salvation Army," I said, offering the obvious.

"Just what I need, more stuff."

Toni went to the brick-and-board bookcase, which held a row of books, some CDs, a camera, and at one end a pile of papers. Bills? No, bills would have been smaller.

"What's all that?" I asked, nodding toward the pile.

Picking up a notebook, she said, "One of her poetry manuscripts."

I moved closer, peered over Toni's shoulder. "If she wanted to do an article on this cult, do you think she'd have already done any work?"

"What do you mean?"

"You know, taken some notes, done an outline. Maybe even started it."

Toni eyed me, brow raised. "Yeah, she probably did. She could have started it, realized she had something. But she wouldn't have written anything in here. Not about that, not journalistic kind of stuff in here with her poetry. Maybe in her journal, but I kind of doubt that, too."

"Well, did she have a computer?"

"No."

"Then if she had started something, it should be around . . . maybe something even typewritten."

I turned around, scanned the room. A legal pad? A folder? Was there anything?

"*Alex,*" called a distant voice, "*what about the intruder—the guy you surprised the other night in the bedroom?*"

I stood still, hit with the obvious. "So that's what that guy took—not any of her poetry, but her notes."

Yes. The guy who'd whacked me with the lamp. Rob Tyler or perhaps someone else had broken in here and gone through Liz's things, not looking for money or valuables but what she had written about this cult. Of course. The intruder was trying to prevent anyone from learning about the group and stop anyone from linking Liz's death to them.

"You're right, Alex. You've got to be. You saw that guy carrying a notebook and nothing else was missing. Nothing of obvious value, anyway." Toni picked up the entire pile of papers, searched the bookcase for more. "He could have missed something, though. I'll go through this—why don't you check the bedroom. I think she has a desk back there."

"Sure."

I started toward the rear of the apartment, hadn't gone more than a couple of steps when I heard heavy pounding on the door. I stopped, glanced back at Toni, who looked at me and shrugged. We hadn't told anyone we were coming over here. I was a little concerned, but I doubted someone like Rob Tyler would have knocked.

"Who's there?" I called.

A deep voice called, "It's the caretaker. Who the hell are you?"

Toni instantly started for the door, saying, "Oh, John, hi. It's Toni, Liz's sister."

Papers in hand, Toni opened the door, exposing the guy who'd helped Toni kick in the bedroom door the other night. He didn't look happy, and he didn't look like he'd changed clothes since then, either. Blue plaid shirt that was dingy and wrinkled, old blue jeans that were struggling to contain his waist, and the same brown shoes that were all cracked. The reddish hair just as messy, too.

"Hi," repeated Toni. "I'm just here with my friend Alex. I have to go through all of Liz's things, you know, and—"

"Yeah, well, I heard some noise, you know, and I wanted to make sure no one was busting in again."

"Thanks, I appreciate that."

Without asking, he strode right into the apartment, looked around, said, "So, ah, everything okay?"

Toni glanced back at me, shrugged, then turned back to John. "Everything's fine."

"What about the police? Did they say anything?"

"They're working on it."

"Oh." He cleared his throat. "Did you tell them about me, that I was down here?"

"Actually, no, I don't think we did."

"No, we didn't," I seconded, wondering why it mattered.

"Good. Good. It's the landlady—she don't want any more problems. Wants to get this place rented real quick." He eyed all the CDs. "When you going to get all this stuff out of here?"

"By the first, don't worry."

He turned back to Toni, said, "So, ah, you're from Chicago, right? Me, too— grew up in one of those brick apartment buildings right across the street from Wrigley Field. Used to sit up on the roof and watch the games. It was great. How do you think the Bears are going to do?"

Toni took a deep breath, ran a hand through that hair. "Listen, John, I've got a lot to do."

"Oh. Oh, sure." He pointed across the room. "Say, you want to sell the stereo?" He laughed. "I know it works 'cause your sister, she played it so loud."

Across the hall a door opened. I stepped around, peered out, saw a smallish woman locking up the other first-floor apartment. John grunted a couple of more things, then turned and stared at the woman as she came over.

Tapping hesitantly on the open door, she said, "Hi, I'm Chris. You're . . . you're Liz's sister, aren't you? The doctor?"

"Yeah," replied Toni. "I think we met when I was up last year."

Chris was a small, pale woman, early thirties. A bookish sort. Mousy brown hair, glasses, small, hesitant mouth. Blue T-shirt, plain khaki pants. Very ordinary. Probably an English major, a lonely one at that.

Chris glanced briefly and uncomfortably at the caretaker, said, "Hi, John. I . . . I just wanted to talk to Toni for a minute."

An awkward moment passed in which it became abundantly clear that John didn't get it and that he wasn't going anywhere. Toni seized control, motioning Chris in.

"Come on in, Chris. John was just leaving." She turned to the caretaker. "Thanks again for checking. It's great of you to keep an eye on the place. I'll let you know about the stereo."

John stared at Toni, then Chris, and finally began to move,

a bothered, even angry look on his face. Toni paid no attention and waved as the caretaker made his way out.

"Oh, okay," stammered John. "Well, I guess I gotta get going."

" 'Bye." Closing the door behind him, Toni shook her head, muttered, "Oh, brother."

Chris leaned forward, whispered, "Don't mind him. He's smart—I mean, he must be, he's a telephone repairman—but he's a little slow, too." Then Chris looked at the floor, shuffled from side to side, mustered up her purpose of coming over, and said, "I just wanted to say I was really sorry about your sister. We were friends, kind of."

"Oh, thank you."

"She was really nice to me. Sometimes we'd just stand in the hall here and talk and talk—once last winter for almost an hour. I liked her poetry—she let me read some of it a couple of times and we talked about it, too. She was a good writer." Then again, "I was really sad to hear the news."

Toni said, "I miss her, too."

Something uncomfortable seemed to float downward, through the room, around us. Maybe it was Liz passing by.

I cleared my throat, asked, "You didn't happen to see Liz before she died, did you? That week, perhaps?"

"Oh . . ." Chris shifted from foot to foot. "Didn't the police tell you? Like I told that detective guy, I saw her the night before she died."

Toni eyed me briefly, managed a small "Oh?"

"We didn't really talk or anything—it was late. I was coming home. I was parking and she waved at me."

I looked at Toni. Why hadn't Jenkins mentioned this?

"I have tickets to a dance series, and I went with a friend," continued Chris. "It was the American Ballet Theater. Yeah, that's right. Normally I'm not out so late."

"Was she was all right?" Toni added, "Could you see if she was happy or if she might've been crying or anything?"

Chris walked over to the large front window, and we followed. Out front I spotted John climbing into a dark brown van, starting it up, and driving off.

"Well, I don't know. I couldn't really tell," began Chris.

"See, I was down there on the street and they were way up here at the front door. She seemed fine, though."

I peered down the street, asked, "They? Was she with Rob, her boyfriend?" But she'd broken up with Tyler almost a month earlier, hadn't she? "Did you know him—kind of a punker type?"

"No, she was with the other one."

Toni couldn't hide her shock. "Other one? What other one?" Toni moved close to the window, right next to Chris. "You don't mean she was dating two guys, do you?"

Chris glanced from Toni to me and nodded. Nodded just a bit as if she was telling a secret, a deep secret or a dirty one. Had she, her expression said, just betrayed her dead friend Liz?

"It's all right," I said quickly. "We're just trying to piece a few things together." I sensed I shouldn't broach the issue that Liz might not have committed suicide; Chris didn't look the sort that would handle murder well. "Toni just wants to understand what happened and why. She just wants to talk to anyone who might have seen Liz that last day or so, you know, to find out how she was doing, what was going through her head, what might have upset her."

"Oh."

"So did you know this other guy?"

Chris shook her head. "I never met him—that was the only time I ever saw him."

Toni asked, "What did he look like?"

"He was older."

"Like how old?"

"I don't know. Maybe fifty. I don't think he was real tall or anything."

"What color hair?" I asked.

Chris shrugged. "I don't know. Gray, I think, but I'm not sure." She turned back to the window, gazed out. "Like I said, I was way down there and I couldn't tell much. But it was still kind of cold and I think he was wearing a hat."

Toni looked at me and her eyes said; Liz dating an older man, someone she never, ever mentioned to me? What was this?

I asked, "You don't know his name, do you?"

"No, she never told me. She just told me she was falling in

love with this older guy. She was really crazy about him and she didn't know what to do."

My mind careened back to our venture down in the Warehouse District. Most of the guys seemed younger, but there were several older men. The one with the feathers—wasn't the hair on his chest all gray? And the leader, what about him? I'd speculated on something like that earlier, the possibility that Liz had become involved with someone else in that cult and that Rob Tyler had killed her out of jealousy. Could that be so very far off? Perhaps not. Whoever this older boyfriend was, whatever part he had or hadn't played in Liz's death, he'd certainly have some insights into Liz Domingo's emotional stability in the final days of her life.

"Do you think you'd recognize him?" I asked.

She shrugged, looked sheepish. "I don't know, I didn't get a close look at him, but maybe."

She probably could, though. Someone like her; an observant person sensitive to literature and the finer details of life. But how were we going to do that? Bring her to one of those cult meetings? Hardly.

Toni eyed me, clearly wondering what I was scheming, then said, "Let me do some checking around. It'd be great if you could help us, Chris. I . . . I just want to talk to someone about Liz who knew what was troubling her. It'd help me a lot."

"Okay, good." Chris shrugged again, smiled, and said, "Well, I gotta go or I'm going to be late for work. Just let me know if I can do anything. I'll be around—mornings or after eight or nine at night are best. I work afternoons and evenings."

So Chris the neighbor lifted her hand in a small wave and left. I watched as Toni shut the door after her, then I heard Chris's steps in the hall, heard the front door. I went to the large front window where all three of us had just been standing and watched Chris as she descended the concrete steps out front and walked across the street to a small yellow car. A tiny one, a little rusty. From the living room window I kept my eyes on Chris, and as I did so, an awful dread started growing inside me. A cold sense that swept through me, entangled me.

Toni came up to me, put a hand on my shoulder as I stood peering out, and asked, "What is it, what's the matter?"

I couldn't voice it, of course, not back then, but I started trembling because inside me I knew. There was someone out there, someone who'd seen the three of us standing in the window and who was now watching Chris, the quiet, bookish neighbor, climb into her car.

"Alex, what are you saying?"

I didn't know it back then, when all of this was really happening. I only pieced it together later, in the end. It was the only way it could have happened. Liz's killer had to have been out there.

My God, I thought, we had no idea of the trouble lurking so close by.

Chapter 15

But as far as any kind of cult stuff, Toni and I didn't find anything. We searched the apartment, clawing through drawers and shelves, and came up with nothing, which meant that either we were way off or that the intruder had in fact ripped off Liz's journalistic endeavors about Rob Tyler's cult. Both of which were depressing thoughts.

Almost an hour later we left discouraged and returned to my apartment a little after noon, not sure what to pursue next. Boxes, Toni suggested as we drove. We should hit the liquor store and start collecting boxes so that she could start packing up Liz's things. It was close to the end of the month; only another week of April left. John was obviously eager to have the apartment emptied, and if Toni didn't have all of Liz's things out of there, she'd have to pay another month's rent. What fun, new moon, new month. Packing up a dead person's things.

I parked in front of my building on Humboldt, and we got out, headed up the sidewalk.

"I think you'd better give Jenkins a call," I said, as we climbed the three outside steps. "Ask him about this second boyfriend."

"I can't believe he didn't even mention it."

"Just call him, Toni. Besides, you need to let him know you're not at the hotel anymore."

"I suppose."

When I opened the outer door and ushered Toni into the vestibule, we discovered a man, bent over and his back to us. The postman, I assumed, getting ready to sort the mail. But on second glance, when did postal workers start looking so scruffy? Where was this guy's uniform? Why the black jeans, let alone the black leather coat?

When he failed to move, I said, "Excuse me, can we get by?"

The guy laughed, rose, and a bald head emerged. Oh, shit. This wasn't any mail carrier.

"Hello," said Rob Tyler, smiling as he turned around. "How are you two today?"

At the sight of the long, shiny knife in his hand, my whole body stiffened. Both Toni and I edged back as this creep with the smooth-as-silk shaven head stood before us. It was a fresh shave, too, for his head was nicked here and there. Little dots of dark, crusty blood. He grinned, his eyes small and dark, and I wanted to ask, The girl, the blonde, what did you guys do to her? Where is she? Still alive or already hacked to pieces?

I knew I'd be lucky to get that far, though, so I asked, "What are you doing here?"

"Well . . ." He pointed the long knife—a large hunting one—right at Toni. "The doctor here said if I wanted to talk, I should go to that Holiday Inn. So I go there and then they tell me you split, Doc, and that you're shacked up with this guy. Only one thing, I thought you were a dyke. Didn't Liz say something like that?"

I blurted: "Tyler, why don't you get the—"

Just as quickly, Toni's hand was on my arm, and she cut in, her voice measured and heavy, saying, "What do you want, Rob?"

My heart was on high, beating with anger, but Toni was right. She was obviously more experienced in these situations— her femininity as well as her homosexuality undoubtedly having been harassed over the years—and she knew the wise course. Dial it down.

Tyler replied, "Some cop came to see me this morning." He ran one finger down the long blade. "You know anything about that? You know what's up his butt?"

"No, Rob, I don't," replied Toni.

"You been talkin' with the cops at all? Sayin' anything about me?"

"No," lied Toni.

"Good. That's good." He shrugged, turned to the woodwork by the door, and pressed in the knife. "I told them what I told them before: Liz didn't mean shit to me. Nothing. We busted up because she was a drag and a half."

The asshole was starting to carve something in the woodwork of my building. My God, he was carving a letter. Starting on his initials.

"Tyler, quit fucking with my building."

He laughed, blew the sawdust away from his handiwork, grinned, and said, "Then quit fucking with me . . . unless, of course, you two want to end up like Liz." He wiped the blade of his knife on his leather coat, admired his work one last time, and said, "Guess I'll finish up later. 'Bye."

He plunged his knife into a sheath that hung from a chain around his waist, then swung open the outer door. As carefree as a diabolical Peter Pan, he bounded out and down the steps.

As the door hissed shut, I swore. "Oh, Jesus!"

Before I could say anything more, do anything else, Toni was lunging for the door, swinging it back open, going after him.

"Toni!" I hollered.

But I couldn't stop her, and in a second she was outside at the top of the steps and calling to him.

"Hey, Rob! Rob!"

Tyler stopped on the street, turned and looked at her, and snapped, "What?"

"Was my sister dating anyone else?"

"When we were together?" He laughed like it was a bad joke. "No way!"

"What about later, an older guy?"

"Like I told you, I know zip!"

With that, he was off, darting down the street. Toni stood there, frozen on the steps. I went out, took her gently by the arm.

"Come on."

"That guy's such an asshole," she muttered.

"Absolutely. You all right?"

"Yeah." As we went in, I saw the damaged woodwork and shook my head. "Can you believe it?"

We ascended to my apartment in silence, both of us trying to comprehend what had just happened, what it'd all been about. Toni went into the living room, dropped onto the couch, and I disappeared into the kitchen, where I busied myself with frenetic thoughts as I made fresh coffee. When I came out a few minutes later with the pot and two mugs, Toni was sitting cross-legged on the couch, the phone squirreled in her lap.

"Yeah," she was saying into the receiver, "and after that the jerk just darts out the door."

Toni eyed me, mouthed the name, "Jenkins," and finished up the story of our skinhead visitor. She listened to his response, was obviously not pleased.

Then said, "There's another thing. My friend Alex and I were just over at Liz's apartment. We talked with one of the neighbors, Chris something—I don't know her last name—and she said Liz had talked about a second boyfriend, an older guy. Chris said she'd even seen him once, though it was from a distance. She told you about this, didn't she?"

He said something, after which she methodically went through it all, all the stuff about the second boyfriend, the night Chris had seen him, the approximate time. A relatively short conversation. Very few questions from his end. Lastly, she told him she'd checked out of the hotel, gave him my number, and then hung up, dropping the receiver loudly in its cradle.

Toni shrugged, reached for her coffee. "Jenkins said he talked with Tyler this morning but he had an alibi for yesterday—ol' Morticia-face, his girlfriend, said they were home together, all snuggly, cuddly in bed. I told him Tyler had just threatened us, and Jenkins wants us to be real careful. He said he's doing what he can, that he's working on it."

I asked, "What did he say about Liz's other boyfriend?"

"He apologized, says he forgot to tell me, said earlier he didn't think it was important. Obviously that's not the case."

"What else?"

"They're real busy, he promised we'd talk soon." She took a sip from her mug. "They think that blond girl we saw in the warehouse might still be alive, so they're doing everything they can to find her. That's their top priority right now." Toni shook her head, glanced out toward the sunporch. "I guess Liz's case is going to have to wait a bit." She took a deep breath, blew it out. "Dammit."

What were we to do next? Sit around and wait? But for what? Probably nothing. We had to proceed, couldn't let this drop, which probably meant it was up to us to get an ID on the second boyfriend, the older guy. Perhaps he'd be willing to talk to us, either confirming that Liz had jumped into the Mississippi of her own volition or maybe even incriminating himself.

Searching the pages of her calendar, Toni said, "I've got to call Dr. Dawson and give him the number here, too."

"Good idea," I agreed, thinking also that Liz had probably been more open with her shrink than anyone else. "He didn't mention anything about the second boyfriend, did he?"

"No," said Toni, dialing. And then, "Hi, is Dr. Dawson in?"

It turned out that Dawson was in session and his phone had been picked up by his answering service. Toni left a message, saying she had a couple of questions for the doctor and asking him to call back at my number.

Toni hung up, and I sat there, thinking, pondering. What we needed was a photograph of the two older men in that cult. If Chris was able to identify one of them as the second boyfriend, then that would hurl us in a whole new direction. But a photograph—how were we going to get it? Ask Rob Tyler for a group photo? No way.

"Toni, how far do you think Jenkins is going to push this?" I asked, staring at the ceiling.

"Good question. He's obviously swamped right now. But later, I don't know. Why?"

"Don't you think it would stir up police interest if we talked with the guy Liz was with the night before she died?"

"What are you saying?"

"Well, someone should find him."

"Of course."

"And I kind of doubt that Jenkins is going to pull through on this. At least not anytime soon."

"So?"

"So . . . so maybe we're going to have to find him on our own."

She shook her head, rolled her eyes. "Yeah, right."

"There's got to be a way, Toni."

I slumped back in the armchair, sipped some coffee. Stared up at the ceiling. Chances were that this guy was one of the cult members. He might not be, but that had to be our first angle.

"We have to get ourselves to another cult meeting," I mumbled. "The guy Chris saw Liz with might be one of those older Dragons."

"Alex, you saw Tyler. You heard him. What are we going to do? Pop in at their little get-together, introduce ourselves, ask them a few questions, mainly which one of them killed my sister?"

"No, you're going to bring your camera—you have it with you, don't you?" I asked, recalling she'd never been without it before.

"Yeah."

"Telephoto?"

"Sure."

"Well, there we go. We'll only get close enough for you to use the telephoto, you snap a picture of those two older guys, then we see if Chris can identify one of them."

Toni stretched out on the couch. "Okay, so I might be able to get a couple of pictures, but don't you think the cops would be around, too? Don't you think they'll have them under surveillance?"

"Maybe, but they weren't yesterday. Besides, we can just disappear if we sense that Jenkins or whoever is around."

"Yeah, but how are we going to actually get to another one of these meetings? You can be sure as hell the Dragons aren't going to post their hours anywhere and that they're not going to use that warehouse again."

"We'll just have to follow Tyler again."

She gazed at me like I was nuts. "You're telling me we're just going to sit outside his house and tail him everywhere until he leads us back to the cult? Great idea, Alex. That might not be for another week or another month or . . . or God knows how long."

"I'm working on that."

I closed my eyes. Cults usually had to do with the devil or paganism, worship of some kind that went beyond the everyday encounters of my life. I thought of Celts and Druids, witches and warlocks. Sacrifices, too.

That's right. There'd been the woman they were about to do God knew what to, and there had been a goat in the warehouse, too. A sacrificial goat, split wide and filled with ceremonial food. A sacrifice to what, a mythical dragon? Some fire-breathing creature from the other world? Perhaps. But why would they have been doing it that night? What was their schedule, their calendar?

"Toni, if a cult had a calendar of some sort, what do you suppose it would be?"

"Um, I imagine they'd be on some sort of cycle. A solar one, maybe. Then again, I think they'd be on a dark cycle, something occultish, I suppose, so I guess they'd be on a lunar cycle."

My eyes opened wide. The other night after we'd been chased out of the warehouse. After we'd called the cops. When we were sitting in the cop car. Yes. That was it. When the cops were going through the warehouse and we were sitting there waiting; I had leaned back. Stared up and out the rear window. And what had I seen? A big white orb rising in the sky. A big, solid circle of pale light rising in the dark blue sky.

"Toni, maybe you're right. Maybe they're on a lunar calendar, and they were meeting specifically that night because it was a full moon. Maybe it's all part of some spring ritual."

She stared at me, latched on to my logic, and said, "Of course." Pause, then, "But if the moon was full, it'd be waning now."

My balloon of excitement immediately began to deflate. She could be right, and if so there wouldn't be another full moon for another twenty-seven days.

"Where's the newspaper?" I said.

I jumped to my feet, glanced about the living room, saw no sign of the *Tribune*. I hurried down the hall, past the bedrooms, through the dining room, and into the kitchen. There it was, lying next to the coffee maker. Snatching it up, I scanned it, quickly flipped to the only part I regularly saw mention of the moon.

Walking as I read, I returned to the living room, said, "Maybe there's something here in the horoscopes. Some shifting of planets."

"Good idea," said Toni.

However, there was nothing of the sort mentioned in today's predictions. Only advice, sometimes sage, often banal. No reference to any kind of lunar activity that might spur a cult into action.

"Damm it," I moaned. "Nothing at all."

Toni wasn't so easily defeated. "What about the weather? Sometimes they list solar and lunar activities, don't they?"

Almost madly, I threw the paper down on the coffee table, sat down on the couch next to Toni, and flipped through the pages. In a state where the temperature fluctuated some 130 degrees or more from summer to winter, in a region of unending soybeans and corn, Minnesotans were obsessed about weather and anything that might affect it. It took up almost a whole back page of one of the sections. Big color weather map, the whole bit. Even a weather column, which I had never read because war and famine, politics and crime were what absorbed me over my cereal. Besides, what kind of paper, I had always wondered, had a weather column full of nerdy drivel about highs and lows and pressure systems, and what kind of people read about weather rather than experienced it? I understood that talking weather up here was a compulsive pastime, but . . .

I spread the paper flat, Toni and I leaned forward, and we both searched the temperatures, the forecasts, the average lows and highs. If there were anything, it would be here on this page.

Toni's finger went right to one box. "Look."

It was a section simply marked "Sun and Moon," offering how many hours of daylight there were would be, time of sunrise, sunset, as well as a diagram of today's moon. My heart jumped. The moon had not been full last night but it would be tomorrow.

"Look." Toni had leaped ahead, gone beyond the Sun and Moon box. "Read this."

With a long, thin finger, she was pointing to the weather

column. Chatty. Very much so. Nice system coming in. Clear skies. Pleasant spring temperatures. Beautiful skies. Beautiful nights. All will maintain. Perfect for tomorrow evening's lunar eclipse.

"That's it. Absolutely," I said, glancing up, reaching out, touching Toni on the knee. "What kind of cult would miss not only a full moon but an eclipse on a beautiful spring night?"

Toni bit her bottom lip, ran a hand through her hair. "Alex, do we want to do this? Tyler's obviously not a very stable sort. This could be really stupid, not to mention dangerous."

"I know, but . . . but . . ." I kept seeing Tyler's knife, the light glinting off the blade. "I don't want the dregs of the world to dictate my life."

"Oh, cut it out, this isn't the time for any kind of cowboy-macho shit."

I nodded. "You're right, I know, but if Jenkins is off chasing around on some other case, how else are you going to find out what really happened to Liz?"

A question to which Toni had no response.

Chapter 16

That afternoon and evening, Toni and I talked about it over and over again, coming at it from all different angles, trying to find a different, less dangerous way, but always ending up with the same conclusion. There just didn't seem to be any other course of action, at least not in the immediate future. If Jenkins was busy trying to find that abducted young woman, who else was going to follow up on the issue of Liz's second boyfriend? And how else were we going to follow up on it except to snap some photos of a few of the Dragons, photos that we could then show Chris?

The only wild card, of course, was the police. We had no way of knowing or finding out what they were doing. Jenkins certainly wasn't going to tell us. It was fairly clear that they wouldn't be tracking the Dragons for Liz's sake, but they might be doing so in an attempt to locate the blond woman before she was killed. In that case, if the police were around, Toni and I would back off, be sure to keep out of the way. But if they weren't there, well, then . . . then we certainly would have chosen the right course.

All of that, for sure, was presuming that we were correct, that the Dragons would hold a meeting the following evening, the night of the lunar eclipse. We didn't know where their meeting would be, though, and Toni and I quickly realized that meant we would have to follow Rob Tyler once again. We also surmised that we would have to be smarter about it, too. In the little vestibule of my building, Tyler had said nothing about our following him the other day, so apparently he was unaware it was he who had led us to the Dragons. Regardless, he'd certainly be taking stricter precautions. Employing a trick I'd read about in a spy novel, however, I figured we had a reasonable chance of avoiding his detection.

Which was how we were going to handle it, the double method, the two of us working semi-independently. A rotating car tail was very difficult to detect, and between my Honda and Toni's small rental car, we felt confident, even certain, that we'd be able to follow Tyler successfully. This was America, after all, and this was Minneapolis, the city that had wiped out its six-hundred-mile streetcar system for ribbons of freeway, so we were fairly sure all this would transpire via auto. The following morning around ten, Toni went out and bought a set of walkie-talkies.

"Oh, very nice," I said as I started to fix lunch at my place. "A his and hers."

She was fitting her walkie-talkie into her camera bag, and sniped, "Just you wait."

While I made us each a turkey sandwich, Toni disappeared into the living room. I peered through my dining room and down the long hall, and discerned that she was on the phone. I figured she was checking in with her office, perhaps advising on a few patients, but when she returned a few minutes later she was clearly distressed.

"I just called The North Center and spoke with Laura's counselor." She groaned as she dropped onto one of the kitchen stools. "Laura's not sure she wants to see me. Can you believe it? I left my number and asked her to at least call me." Toni eyed the sandwich. "Give me lots of mayo. Got any chips?"

"What, are you going for calories or carbohydrates?"

"Both. The more the better. How about cookies? Any around?"

We had a leisurely if rather quiet meal, Toni lost in thought most of the time. I tried to talk a bit about Laura, but Toni quickly changed the subject.

By three o'clock we were in our respective cars. When we didn't find Rob Tyler at home, we went directly to the Minneapolis College of Art and Design, which was our second and perhaps only other chance at finding Tyler. The lunar eclipse wasn't until well after sunset, so he still had to be around, and Toni followed me to the sprawling arts complex, which included the museum, the Children's Theater, and, of course, MCAD. The surrounding streets were lined with cars, and I drove the north and south avenues, Toni the east and west streets, as we searched for an old blue Duster.

I saw nothing like it, though. Lots of other studenty cars, trashed-out old ones riddled with rust holes. Some Cadillacs, fancy foreign cars, too, which certainly belonged to patrons of the Institute of Arts. But no near-moldy Duster.

Nothing until Toni came over the walkie-talkie, simply saying, "Found it."

I braked, pulled to the side of First Avenue South, and into my transmitter said, "Great, where are you?"

"By the dorms. There's a student parking lot back here."

I pulled around, found Toni parked in a corner. I squeezed my car next to hers, and we spoke through rolled-down car windows.

"Up front there," said Toni. "See?"

I saw it, nodded. It was a car you couldn't miss. A Duster well into its teens if not beyond. Toni volunteered to scope the campus, see if she could spot him. She stuffed her walkie-talkie back into her camera bag, climbed out of her car, and started for a gathering of whitish buildings clumped in the shadows of the Institute of Arts.

"Just call me," she said, patting her bag and heading off, "if anything comes up."

I watched her go, Toni whom I'd always wanted, probably always would. Toni with the lithe figure and energetic spirit. Spiraling downward in a vortex of worry, I slumped into a depressing and very boring twenty or thirty minutes.

Finally my walkie-talkie came alive with her voice, now low and hushed, saying, "Alex, he's here."

I grabbed the little black box from the seat beside me, pressed the button, and asked, Dick Tracy-like, "Where?"

"In the student lounge." Then urgently, "He's getting up. I mean, he's leaving. He's talking to a couple of—wait. Yeah, he's leaving, heading toward the door on the parking-lot side of the room."

Pulse quickening, I said, "Great, just stay back. Don't let him see you. I'm in my car, so we're covered up here."

Within several minutes I saw him, his fleshy scalp making him nearly impossible to miss. He wore the same black leather coat, a few shiny chains hanging from it, and pants that were purposely torn around the knees and ass. I slid down in my seat, peered through the steering wheel, spotted him there, across and behind another car. I glanced at all the other cars as well. Any cops? Anyone following him undercover? Not that I could tell.

Tyler went directly for the Duster, got in, revved it up to full growl, and quickly slammed it into reverse. This could be it, I thought. The meeting, the chance for the photos we wanted and needed. Or could he be heading home or off to a friend's to get high?

"Toni?" I said into the transmitter. "Where are you?"

"Across the lawn."

"He's pulling out. I'll follow him and give you directions."

"Great."

As soon as Tyler backed out and headed out of the lot, I had my Honda going. As soon as he turned onto the street, I was in gear. I checked one last time, saw no sign of any cops, and so I went flying out of there. We weren't going to lose him.

"Toni, no sign of Jenkins or anyone else. Looks like we've got him on our own. Turn left out of the lot," I walkied-talkied back to her. "I can see him. He's turning left on First Avenue."

"Okay, I'll be right behind you."

Her breath was heavy and fast. So I imagined her running to her car and jumping in. Soon she was radioing back that she was on her way and racing after us. Which was good, because I wasn't really sure how far these walkie-talkie transmitted, and Tyler wasn't wasting any time driving wherever he was going, which wasn't back home. His house was the other way, and he was bombing up First Avenue, right on Franklin, across the freeway, then left at my favorite Dairy Queen.

"Toni," I called, checking in the rearview mirror and pressing on the accelerator pedal, "he's heading onto the freeway. I think this is it."

First Tyler, then me, next Toni. We all went whizzing down the freeway ramp, onto the wide Highway 94, on toward St. Paul, going faster and faster. Soon I was absolutely certain no one else was tailing Tyler, so I knew we'd made the right choice. This was it, and after we crossed the Mississippi and entered St. Paul, I wondered if the Dragons had given up on the warehouse district of Minneapolis and were now gathering in the old warehouses on the edge of downtown St. Paul. But no, Tyler and his Duster went zooming along the curls of concrete, past the Cathedral of St. Paul, past the imposing state capitol, and on east.

When we emerged on the other side of the city, Toni and her white rental leapfrogged past me.

"How you doin'?" I said into my intercom.

She flashed a thumbs-up, went zooming on, soon radioed back that she had Tyler in sight, not to worry. I dropped back and kept her in good view as we passed through dribbling suburbs and mind-numbing exurbs, as we went speeding past shopping malls and parking lots and cheap discount stores, which were reproducing on hill after hill. Finally, there were fields that were turning from mud brown to spring green with the first of the year's growth. I looked to the south, knew that in a few months it would be a near-unending sea of corn and soy. And I wondered, where was he leading us—to Wisconsin, which was less than twenty miles ahead, to a cabin on some remote lake nestled in the pines?

About fifteen miles later, when we were just short of the broad St. Croix River that divided Minnesota and Wisconsin, Toni's voice came over the speaker.

"He's getting off at this exit."

I snatched the walkie-talkie from the seat, said, "Okay. After he exits, whichever way he turns, you go the opposite. I'll pick him up then."

"Very good."

Way in the distance I saw Toni slow and steer her car up the long exit, up the lane that led to a road that crossed via a bridge over the highway. I couldn't, however, see Tyler's car, so I pressed on the accelerator, readied myself to leap into position.

"He's turning right," relayed Toni, "so I'm going left. Still no sign of Jenkins or anyone?"

"Nope. They must be hot in pursuit of something else."

I sped up the exit ramp, then turned south, hurried now for fear that I might lose Tyler. But I didn't. In about a quarter of a mile I saw his car emerge from a dip in the road and follow the swell of a hill.

"Got him in sight," I radioed back.

"Good. I just turned around, so I'll catch up with you in a second."

I drove on, closing in on Tyler only slightly. I didn't want to get too close, so I let him disappear around the corners, over the ridges, watched him reappear around the bends, after the hills. We sailed on, past immaculate farms with close-cropped grass and red barns, past plaster deer in front yards and shiny silos. Tony bleeped in, told me she had me in sight. I looked back, spotted her only for a moment. And wasn't all this, she continued, beautiful? Yeah, it was. This was the real heartland. Rich soil, plenty of sun and water. A quarter of the world's grain was produced within an expansive radius around the Twin Cities, from Illinois on up into Canada, and it was easy to see how and why.

Suddenly a vision hit me like a powerful wave that knocked me off my feet, and I saw trees, thick bunches of them, and a line of water. I caught my breath, tried to keep focused on the blue Duster. Yes, there it was. Rising over a hill, up past another farm. Several miles later he slowed and turned off this larger road, headed east toward the St. Croix River. According to plan, I drove straight on, leaving him behind as if I weren't the least bit interested.

As she turned after him, Toni advised, "I think I'm pretty easy for him to spot back here. I'm taking it slow."

About a quarter of a mile past the road Tyler and Toni were now going down, I spun the car around, raced after them.

It wasn't long before I was heading east behind them, before I caught a glimpse of Toni's white car. And it wasn't long before Tyler made another move.

"He's turning south again," came Toni's voice.

"Careful," I countered. "He's got to be getting close."

The St. Croix was just up ahead, which meant he couldn't go much farther. So the river was his destination, which made a lot of sense. The St. Croix was a national scenic waterway, development along it extremely restricted. Purposely frozen in time to protect the environment, it was fairly desolate along the banks, dotted here and there with small cabins built fifty and more years earlier. A deserted spot along the St. Croix, then, would be the logical meeting place for the Dragons. A near-ideal spot for lunar-eclipse festivities, a heavily wooded area where they could conduct their activities without notice.

Proving my premonitions correct, Toni's voice suddenly broke over the receiver. "Alex, he's turning down a dirt lane. I can't go down it, he'll notice me, so I'm going right on past."

Up ahead I saw a cloud of dust rise from a field. Tyler. I couldn't see the car, but the jet of grime he left in his trail rose thick and high. As my Honda roared past the road, I glanced down it, saw a lone mailbox. So this wasn't a public road but a private drive, one that likely led down to a cabin.

Toni relayed, "Alex, I turned down the next road—it's by a big oak."

"Be right there."

I glanced in my rearview mirror, saw a speck of a car emerge behind me. Another of the Dragons, or had we been set up, had we been followed? And by whom, the police? My heart fluttered at the possibility, but then as I drove on, the car disappeared. I slowed, glanced back, saw another cloud of dust rise from the fields. Yes, it was another Dragon driving down there. So we had been right. This would be a full-blown meeting.

Up ahead I saw the large oak, the white car, Toni. She was standing beneath the tree, by her car, peering through her lens, a long one, back at the road Tyler had cut down. I turned in and pulled up behind Toni.

"Can you see anything?" I asked, climbing out.

"It looks like they're parking their cars right before that line of trees," she said, unmoving. "At least that's where all the dirt stops flying."

I peered across the field, saw a blackish-green band of trees. That made sense, their parking up there.

"It's a really sharp drop-off down to the river," I said.

I'd been to a party once on the Wisconsin side of the St. Croix, and I remembered parking above, then hiking down the steep bluffs to a cabin. So Tyler and his fellow Dragons were leaving their vehicles in some clearing and descending into their black nirvana.

Suddenly my head began to pound and my vision crackled with flashes of light. I leaned against Toni's car, put my hand to my forehead. Shit. I closed my eyes. What was it, the start of a mega migraine? A sense of things soon to come?

"Alex, perhaps we should break here. We can—"

No, there was no going back, no stopping. We'd pushed too far, were too close. Had to go all the way. I shook my head, beat back the sensation of fear and pain, opened my eyes.

Toni turned to me, said, "So what do we do, sneak down there somehow?"

"Yeah," I replied, "I think if we go down this road, then we can cut across—probably on foot."

Yes, that was how we'd do it, I thought, staring past Toni and down this dirt road. All the way to the end, then to the left. There'd be a place there where we could leave the car. Then the woods. In my mind's eye I already saw the place waiting, lurking down there. I knew we shouldn't do it, press on like this, that we'd be better off turning back. But I couldn't stop the inevitable, and besides there was much too much to learn.

Chapter 17

We left my car parked up on the road, pulled it off to the side by the burgeoning cornfield, got into Toni's rental car, and headed down toward the river. Down the dirt road, which was slightly pitted and grew narrower and narrower.

Farther along, surrounded by a bunch of huge oaks and pines, was farm central. Nice white house—clapboard, of course. Nice barn—red, of course. And a shiny aluminum silo. Very prosperous with a clean green yard, no visible trash or dumpy, abandoned cars.

"Is this the end?" asked Toni as the road turned into a single lane.

"Just keep driving," I said.

We came alongside the farmhouse, a dog barked, came running out. A woman was hanging sheets out on a line. She turned. I waved. She nodded.

Just when it seemed the road would end in a wall of lilacs, there was a break. A small lane that led on and probably serviced a row of cabins down on the river. Toni steered toward the opening, and the small road dipped out of the light, leading us down through more cornfields, along some old fences, and toward a wall of trees. That would be the top of the bluff, I thought.

And it was. When we reached the trees, the dirt drive led to the left and continued on through a dense forest. Soon the road went across a small clearing—a place for cars—and to the right there was a little shed with two narrow rails leading downhill.

"The bluff's too steep for a road," I said, "so a lot of these cabins have trams leading down."

"Sounds romantic."

I nodded. Probably was. Little cabins and little trams. We passed two or three more until the road ended in a circular clearing of sorts. A turnaround. From here we'd have to continue on foot. Toni brought the car to a stop; we got out.

I pointed to some electrical wires that continued into the woods and said, "Those should lead us where we want to go. Tyler probably parked over there in the next clearing."

Toni swung her camera bag over her shoulder, and we started off, tromping through tall grass, around small bushes. As we progressed, the woods thickened and became even more tangled, and the late spring light slipped fainter. It was approaching the end of the day. I glanced at my watch. The moon would soon rise, the eclipse soon occur, and we needed to find this group and take pictures while there was still enough light.

We passed down and through a small ravine, up into a grove of birches, by some pines. That was when I first heard them, the Dragons. One or two of them, anyway. Talking deeply, not loudly. I couldn't tell what they were saying, and slowing, I held out my hand and hunkered down, then made my way behind a bush. Toni, the camera now hanging by a strap around her neck, moved in right next to me.

She whispered, raised her hand, said, "There."

Yes. Two figures. No, three. All of them guys. Youngish. Tallish. They wore jeans, black and torn, and T-shirts, equally worn. One was a skinhead, the other two were scruffy. Or, rather, hard. Guys who went to biker bars—or maybe that was a stereotype. Whatever. I just knew they weren't the kind I'd associate with in the city, let alone out here in some deserted forest.

Click. Click, click, click. Toni's camera whirled and snapped, freeze-framing these guys on film. None of them could have been Liz's mysterious second boyfriend—they were all too young—but I understood what Toni was doing. Getting them all down on film. Or as many as possible. Photos of these three guys could turn out to be proof of some sort. Especially if she could get their faces. Last time we'd seen them, they'd all had masks on, but for now at least their faces were bare and exposed.

They came to the edge of the bluff and slipped over the top. Toni and I scanned the woods, trying to see if there were others on their way, if we could see Rob Tyler, and most important, if there were any guards stationed about. That was what concerned me the most. Dragons posted throughout the woods, ready to warn of intruders. But there were none, at least none that we could see, and Toni nudged me, nodded downhill.

As we slid and scrambled downward—bracing ourselves on tree trunks, grabbing on to bushes to keep from slipping— I kept checking, and we pushed on. We'd gone about a hundred feet, and then all of a sudden, beyond the trees and fresh greenery of the woods, there was this big dark band of river about a half-mile wide. The St. Croix. I caught a glimpse of the Wisconsin side, saw that over there the bluffs were still washed with the last of the setting sun.

In front of me, Toni held out her hand. I quietly moved up behind her, peered into the woods, through the gray light, and saw tongues of flames licking at the intruding darkness. A bonfire.

I whispered, "Is there still enough light for pictures?"

Toni nodded. "Just barely, but we need to get a little closer."

The blood that started rushing through my veins foretold of impending problems. I paid this future sense or trance sense no attention, however, and Toni and I started creeping across, angling our way down and closer to the gathering. We hadn't gone far when I saw the first of them moving around the fire, shirts now off, faces now masked. There were two or three, then all of a sudden there were perhaps a couple of dozen. Certainly one of them was Tyler. Had to be. The question, though, was whether the older men were at this meeting, too.

I slid behind a tree, tried to imagine what it was they would do, how their cult would honor the lunar eclipse. A fire, obviously, but what else? Had they kept the young blond woman alive, would she perhaps be sacrificed tonight? Suddenly I realized how foolish we were. There was definitely no way to signal for help way out here.

A man's whoop split the silence of the woods. Toni crouched down and moved closer, slipping behind a tree, lifting her camera, focusing, and then snapping and clicking away. Employing the telephoto, she was within range to get good enough pictures, but that wasn't the problem. It was the trees. We had to get closer so that there wouldn't be so many branches and trunks blocking the way. And the nearer we got, the more of the Dragons we could see. Their activities, too. A bunch was pacing around the fire, circling the flames, grumbling and chanting, deep voices, words rolling in rhythm.

I inched downward, over, and that's when I first saw one of the older guys. Face masked, of course, and chest covered with gray hair. I glanced back, motioned to Toni, who strained to see, then spotted him, too. But she was uphill from me, and needed to be closer, so she kept down low and scurried nearer yet. The light was slipping fast now, there were only moments for Toni to snap the pictures.

I saw some movement down below the bonfire, right down on the river banks. Following my curiosity, I edged downhill, spotted a boat and a couple of guys standing by it. No, there weren't two but three men; one of them kind of heavy and of medium height. Could this be the second of the older men we'd seen the other night? Bent over, I moved forward, my feet silently treading the fallen leaves, and I saw that the boat was actually a canoe and that it seemed to be filled with wood. A pyre to be lighted and launched out on the river? If so, I only hoped there wouldn't be a corpse riding on top of it. And who was that on the bank above the canoe? That scraggly guy? Was that Tyler, now wearing a mask?

Toni had to get them all on film, but as I turned toward her, I froze. Shit, oh shit. There was one of them up there, a

Dragon, shirtless, face cloaked, making his way in an arch through the woods. So they were checking the area, and this guy was looping around and, yes, he'd spotted Toni. He was coming up behind her, stalking Toni, who was completely unaware because she was absorbed in taking pictures. I was watching him, he was watching her, she was snapping the Dragons. *Click, click, click.*

I stepped back, stood still, moved again. He hadn't seen me, not yet anyway. I crawled back, peering through the silvery light, watching the guy zero in on Toni, and soon I was far enough back. Next I started up the hill, scrambling quietly on all fours. I was behind them now, some thirty feet back. I searched the ground, spotted a meaty branch on the ground, picked it up, started forward.

The next instant the Dragon was lunging forward, seizing Toni from behind, wrapping his thick arms around her, and yanking her to her feet. Toni cried out, then started twisting and struggling. Her camera tumbled out of her hands, dangled and swung by the strap around her neck.

The guy shouted, "Hey, we got another fuckin' visitor!"

I burst forward, brought the branch back like a baseball bat, and swung. But the wood was partly rotten, and when I struck the guy's head the branch burst into a spray of pieces. It was enough to stun him, though, and Toni burst out of his arms, spun around, face red, chest heaving. The guy reached out for her with one hand, and she hesitated not an instant. Bringing her foot back, she kicked him in the crotch, connecting right where it would certainly hurt the most. The guy screamed and doubled over, grabbed his balls. Taking full advantage, Toni then raised her fist and clubbed him on the back of his head. In a moment the thug was on the ground. Toni clutched the camera, stood there in shock at her effective work.

I charged forward. "Toni, come on!"

As voices by the bonfire raised the alarm, we broke into a run, pushing and moving up the hill. I glanced back, saw a handful of guys tearing into the woods. Someone was calling, another yelling. So they didn't know quite what had happened yet.

"Did you get the pictures?" I gasped as we charged upward.

"I think so."

"What about the guy down by the boat—did you get him?"

"I don't know. I don't know if they'll come out—the light."

Sweat was pouring from my face, stinging my eyes. I searched the top of the hill, spotted the electrical wires that would lead us to our car and motorized escape. We were both heaving for air, and it seemed minutes upon minutes before we were pushing the crest, reaching the relatively flat ground above. As we did, I looked down one last time, saw the Dragons spread out and swarm up the hill commandolike. We still had a good lead, I realized as we ran. Just had to follow the wires. Another hundred yards or so to that turnaround and the little white car. It was easier traveling up here, too. No steep ridges. Just the forest, thick and gray.

I reached out, took Toni's hand in mine as we tore through the woods, hearts thumping, bodies sweating. Behind us I heard someone shout out, which spurred us on even more, drove us on as fast as our legs could carry us. Up ahead I saw the clearing. Within steps I spotted the white of the car there in the dark green forest, waiting to be revved up, waiting to whisk us to safety. Toni saw it, too, let go of my hand and reached into her pocket as we ran, and came up with a couple of jangling keys. As long as they didn't have a gun, we'd probably make it, we'd probably be all right.

We raced to the car, she jumped in, and I stood on the passenger side, heart pounding, sweat pouring, thinking she was never going to get the goddamned door open, those guys were closing in. When she did unlock my door, I dove in. Toni brought the car to a roaring blast, and looking out the rear window, I saw the first of the Dragons rushing into the clearing.

"Here they come!"

She slammed the car into drive, the car leaped forward some ten feet. There wasn't enough space to make a full turn, though, so she had to jam it into reverse, back up. We both stared out the rear, saw a big beefy guy lunging toward us, face red with anger, hands ready to rip and beat. Taking a huge leap, he jumped, hitting the trunk with a deep thud. Against the rear window I saw hands and a face, all swollen and red, and Toni and I shouted out. Then she heaved the gear shift back into drive, stomped on the accelerator, and we were off, swerving and fishtailing out of the turnaround, out of that clearing. The guy was still clutching the back, pounding on the trunk, the glass, and shouting at us. He was still there until Toni hit a big pothole and the whole car went flying upward.

And then he was gone.

Chapter 18

He was gone, that Dragon, flicked off the rear of Toni's car, and we left him back there, a blob of human flesh on a narrow dirt road. I looked behind us, saw him barely moving, saw the others running up to him. Toni kept her foot hard on the accelerator. We flew down the road, around the curve, past the farmhouse and the hanging laundry, leaving a huge plume of dust behind us. Once I'd reclaimed my car and had it going, we took a more circuitous route, looped around some of the roads rather than pass the drive the Dragons had used, and actually it wasn't until we were all the way back on Highway 94 that I began to relax. Then there weren't only a few odd head-lights on the country roads, but lots of cars and trucks, which seemed to offer some sort of protection.

It was evening and dark by the time we reached the limits of St. Paul, me leading the way, Toni close behind. Each mile made me feel safer and safer, as if we were burrowing into civilization, and by the time we crossed the Mississippi and into Minneapolis, it seemed as if all that had simply been an unpleas-ant dream, the nightmarish sort.

Picking up the walkie-talkie from the seat, I checked the

rearview mirror, saw her behind me on the highway, said, "Toni?"

A moment passed before she called back, "Yeah?"

"You all right?"

"I guess so. You?"

"I'm okay. Let's head back to my place and drop off one of the cars, then get the film developed."

"Sure."

We followed 94 around downtown Minneapolis and exited at Hennepin Avenue, then took that on down to Twenty-eighth, where we turned over to Humboldt. I pulled over, Toni parked, and then we were off again. If we hurried, we could still make it to the photo shop, so we drove the very few blocks to Calhoun Square, a small mall of sorts carved out of a series of old buildings. Uptown, the surrounding business district gone yuppie and trendy but always fun, was relatively quiet. Within minutes we'd parked in the ramp behind Calhoun Square and made it inside to one of those sixty-minute photo places. Just in time, too. The manager promised it to us in an hour, said to return at nine, right at closing.

We went upstairs to a restaurant in a corner on the second floor, a place that was designed to look like an old diner and actually kind of did. Lots of chrome, some stools at a counter. We got a booth by the window, took turns washing up, and then ordered. I hadn't realized I was hungry, but now that I was relaxing, my stomach was untying itself and I was actually pretty starved. As was Toni. We both had burgers with a pile of fries. Appropriate food for nerves.

"How much," I began as I stuffed my face, "did you get on film?"

"Well, the pictures aren't going to be all that bright, that's for sure, but I took a bunch." She shrugged, took another bite of her sandwich, chewed, then added, "I got some of the guy by the fire."

"What about the one by the boat?"

"I got a shot or two of him, too. The big question is whether it's going to be enough for Chris. They all had masks on."

I looked up at her, felt suddenly worried. In those few words she'd alluded to something of concern. But what?

"I mean," continued Toni, "Chris probably won't be able to tell a thing."

My head started pounding. That was it. Chris.

I muttered, "Maybe she'll be able to recognize the body type."

"Maybe, but if not, where are we, back at square one?"

"Perhaps."

It struck me that Chris wasn't going to be able to help us. God, no. Somewhere deep inside me I knew that.

"Alex, what is it that your unconscious is trying to say? What information would it like to release?"

That . . . that while we were sitting there discussing the pictures, what would come out, what Chris might be able to discern, all of that, well, it was pointless.

"If she can't, then what do we do?" asked Toni. "Go to Jenkins? Show him the pictures?"

I looked up at her, nodded numbly. "I guess so. Maybe there's something he'll be able to pick up on."

I wanted to stop eating, stop talking. Wanted to freeze that scene, put it on hold, and rush out of there. Just about then, just about while we were eating those stupid hamburgers, she needed our help.

"Are you saying Chris is in danger?"

Absolutely. And we'd put her there, squarely, clearly. An easy target. But there was nothing to be done.

"That's right. You can't control this, only interpret it."

So we went on eating, stuffing down the food, most of which was covered with ketchup. We ordered a chocolate malt and split it. Soon, right when it was the most inappropriate time if we'd had any sense about the danger to Chris, we started laughing.

Toni said, "God, I can't believe I kicked that guy in the balls."

"Yeah, you dropped him pretty quick."

Then we started talking about how scared shitless we were running out of there, those guys chasing after us, and how we hoped the pictures would turn out. The pictures, I exclaimed. It was already five to nine, so we quickly paid up and hurried out of there, dashing down the stairs, down to the fast-photo shop. Even as I wrote out a check, an eager Toni was ripping open the envelope.

"Here's those guys up on the bluff," I said, pointing to the first pictures she'd taken. "They didn't have those masks on yet, so maybe this'll help later."

Toni was going through them as fast as if she were dealing cards, finally hitting on one, muttering, "Dammit."

It showed one of the older men, the guy with the gray chest hair, but was very faint. His head was half-turned, too. And, of course, his face was masked.

"Let's see the next one," I asked.

Toni flipped to it. A little better, the body a little more in view. But the light—it was very weak.

"God, these aren't going to do us any good," said Toni, who let out a long, frustrated groan.

She shuffled through a few more photos, came to one of the Dragon down by the boat. She'd zoomed in well, everything was in focus, but again the mask and of course the light, so faint. And this time a tree that cut off part of the man.

"Look at this," I said, pointing to a large object strapped on the guy's left wrist.

"What is it?" asked Toni, squinting and holding the photo closer.

I leaned closer but couldn't tell, couldn't be sure. The picture just wasn't quite sharp enough.

I said, "It almost looks like a Soviet watch. You know, one of those things with huge faces and gargantuan bands."

"Sure." Still studying the image, Toni said, "I wonder if Chris will remember it. I mean, it's the kind of thing you'd notice and remember."

My heart began pounding. I quickly went through the last of the pictures. There were some of the other men, but nothing that interesting, that clear, that telling. Then I was struck with an overwhelming purpose, need, desire.

I started putting away the photos, said, "Let's go show these to Chris."

"Now?"

"Yeah, right now. She said she works afternoon and evenings. It's after nine—she should be home."

As soon as I said it, I knew, unfortunately, she would be. Toni agreed, said okay, let's go, so we stuffed the pictures back in the envelope and headed out. I drove quickly, almost as if one of the Dragons were behind us, and Toni said, What's going on, why are you driving so nutty? Relax, she told me. Everything's okay. But it wasn't. I just knew that it wasn't.

Chapter 19

From Uptown to Chris's was only about ten minutes, maybe even less. Just a quick swing up Hennepin, then a right on Twenty-fourth and a few more blocks. We were getting close, dangerously so, to piecing together Liz's death, but we didn't know it, not then. In fact, it didn't seem as if we had much at all. Just a few hunches and some dark photographs of men in the woods.

I parked behind John's dark brown van, a beat-up old thing, and glancing up, saw a figure in one of the upstairs apartments. Just as quickly, it was gone and an instant later the second-floor window fell dark. Had that been John looking out at us, perhaps checking on his vehicle? Was he now on his way out and would we run into him? I hoped not.

Toni and I got out of the car and started across the street, up the front concrete steps, right up to the old white wooden door. Chris's front window glowed with light, so she was home, reading a book perhaps. I wanted to hear a stereo, some sign of life. Voices. Anything. But the building and even the whole neighborhood seemed horribly quiet.

At the door, Toni paused, looked back at the street, said, "We're standing right where my sister did with that guy—who-

161

ever he was." She pointed to a small yellow vehicle parked below. "There's Chris's car. She would have been about that far, too, the night she saw Liz with the mystery man."

And whatever Chris saw, I sensed, was of grave concern to someone. Not wanting to waste any time, I reached over and pressed Chris's doorbell.

We stood there at the outer door, poised for Chris's voice to bleep over the intercom, poised for her to buzz us in. Ten seconds later there was not even a hint of a response. I stood perfectly still, tried to hear a chair shifting, footsteps hurrying across a hardwood floor. There was nothing but silence. Impatiently, I pressed the doorbell again, this time holding it in good and long, and there was no way she couldn't hear that. No way if she were in there and everything was all right.

"Come on, Chris," I muttered. "Come on."

"I've got Liz's key to the building." Toni reached into her small purse. "Maybe Chris is down doing laundry."

"Maybe."

But I didn't think so. I leaned on the doorbell again, pushing my body against it as if the force of my weight would bring Chris running. It didn't.

Toni stepped up to the door, said, "Here."

She unlocked the door, we stepped into the small vestibule lined on one side with mailboxes, through another door, and into the small, dark hallway. I quickly glanced to the left and at the door to Liz's apartment, which still looked securely locked, and we turned right, stepped up to Chris's door.

"Chris?" said Toni, raising her hand and knocking. "Chris, are you there? It's me, Toni Domingo, Liz's sister."

No answer, no voice calling, Hi, I'll be right there. Only silence. I pounded on the door, my fist hard, determined. Still nothing. Concern was bubbling in my stomach. The lights were on; she'd said she was almost always home at night. She had to be there. Impulsively I reached for the doorknob, twisted, and the door clicked open, just as I'd known it would. I pushed and it started to swing back.

"Chris?" I called. "It's us, Alex Phillips and Toni Domingo. Chris, are you here?"

I pushed the door wide, and it creaked the whole way. Toni and I stood there on the threshold, peering into an apartment that was identical to Liz's, only flipped in layout. The furniture and decoration were totally different, of course. This was the home of someone orderly. A nice couch, a framed print hanging squarely above it. A side chair and standing lamp, which must have been where Chris did her reading. And a couple of bookcases, both packed. I took a step in, saw a blond wood dining set, four chairs all neatly arranged around it in the dining alcove.

"Chris?" called Toni.

No voice, not a sound, came back to greet us, and I didn't like it, because who in this day and age, particularly a single woman, left their door unlocked in the evening? Something was terribly wrong. We entered Chris's apartment, leaving the door wide open behind us, and I felt the blood coursing through my veins and rushing, shoving, every worst fear into my imagination.

The living room was empty, as was the dining area. The kitchen light was on, and impulsively I was drawn to it, pulled to it, like a bug seeking light and warmth and death, too, all at the same time. Something creaked behind me. Toni. She was just several steps behind me. We were both silent as if we already knew.

"Chris?" Toni weakly called one last time.

Which is when I saw it. The blood on the kitchen floor, a long, winding red trail of it, slowly rolling over the whitish linoleum like spilled coffee or maybe maple syrup. Something dark and thick and hideously viscous.

"Oh, shit," I gasped.

I didn't want to go any farther, but I couldn't stop myself, of course. My breath started coming short and quick, as if I were jogging instead of eyeing a riverlike flow of blood. Oh, Chris. I reached back as I moved, reached back and took Toni's living hand in mine, and the two of us moved forward, stepped right up to the threshold of the kitchen. I closed my eyes for a half second, turned, gazed past the sink, past the old stove.

And there she was.

"Oh, Jesus!" I cried.

Toni screamed, I think, and crushed my hand in hers. We couldn't move, either of us. I felt my stomach flop over. Her skin a chalky gray, Chris was sitting in a chair by the sink. Her eyes were open and still, her mouth frozen wide. But there was so much blood, a veritable waterfall of it still slowly gurgling from her throat, over her chest and dripping onto the linoleum. My first impulse was to rush to her, that there must be some way of saving her, but then I saw the wound, a large, coarse gap cut across her neck.

I was caught by this death before me, unable to move or think, and then I heard a loud gasp from behind me. Toni. Too shocked to speak, she clutched the back of my arm, sank her fingers angrily into me. Yes, it was clear now. Absolutely. We'd been on the right track. Toni's sister Liz hadn't committed suicide. She'd been murdered, and Chris had been silenced into death for what she had seen and what she might have been able to tell us about Liz's other boyfriend.

Chapter 20

Toni had a brief, doctorly urge to go to Chris, to check her, but I pressed her back and out of there, and we stumbled out. It was no use. Nothing to be done. Chris was mutilated and dead, and so we retreated through the living room. As soon as we opened the door, a large figure rushed toward us. Toni screamed, I jumped. It was John, the caretaker.

"What happened?" he demanded, lumbering into us. "I heard someone yelling."

"It's Chris . . ." I gasped.

Saying nothing, he pushed past us, hurried into Chris's apartment. We crossed the hall, where Toni fumbled for the key to Liz's apartment and somehow got us in there.

I went on automatic, picked up the phone, and dialed 911, said, "I need to report a murder."

The trained voice on the other end was calm, cool, asked a series of questions, like was I hurt or was I in danger, was there a weapon present? And I blathered no, no, no. We'd just stopped by someone's apartment and the door was open and she was in the kitchen with her neck cut and, Jesus, there was blood everywhere. When the dispatcher asked me to confirm the address, I said I didn't know, we were in one apartment, had discovered the body across the hall but I didn't know where we were, somewhere in south Minneapolis, I thought. Shit, I couldn't even remember the name of the street. The woman on the other end said to calm down, it didn't matter, they had already traced the phone, help was on the way, don't worry. The police and an ambulance would be there within minutes.

"Ambulance?" I said. "It's too late. There's blood everywhere. She's already dead."

I hung up, turned around. As I did so, the door to Liz's apartment was hurled open. John stood there, his face long and red.

"I called the police," I said to him.

He looked at me, his eyes completely blank. "Someone killed her."

I nodded.

"Lots of blood."

"Yes, I know."

A couple of cops were the first to arrive, soon followed by an ambulance with two medics. John greeted them all silently in the vestibule, pointed the way, then followed them zombielike.

Toni and I sat on the old couch in Liz's place, held hands, and listened to all the commotion. There were radios crackling, people running, voices barking orders. Within minutes the place was swarming with officials—more cops, some plainclothes detectives. Neighbors, too. Out front the whole street sparkled with red lights, and I got up, glanced out, saw clumps of people gathered on the sidewalk, looking, muttering, whispering, and shaking their heads. Yes, someone had died in their midst. Horribly so.

Toni and I were at first barraged with questions—what happened, when, did we see anyone, notice anything? Then, naturally, the cops busied themselves with roping off the place, getting it ready for a crime detection squad that would study, test, and examine.

I was back on the couch again, sitting next to Toni, when I heard heavy steps and a familiar voice out in the hall.

A cop said, "They're in there."

"Okay. I'll be right with them. Let me take a look first."

It was Detective Jenkins, I recognized his voice, knew his step. He faded into the commotion in Chris's apartment, then a couple of minutes later I heard him again, telling someone what to do, what he wanted. Then he walked through the open door of Liz's apartment. Big and broad, face flat with seriousness, he wore the same wrinkled brown sport coat and a shirt without a tie. He headed for an old armchair on Toni's right.

"What happened?" he said, seating himself, rubbing his face.

It was as much a question as an order and, my voice shaky, I said, "We were coming to talk to her. We wanted to show her some pictures. Her door was unlocked, and so we went in and . . . and found her there, in the kitchen."

Toni's eyes were puffy and wet with tears, and she cleared her throat, said, "She was the one who told us she saw Liz the night before she died—it was Chris who said Liz had another boyfriend."

I bowed my head, stared down at the dingy green carpet. Would any of this had happened if we hadn't pushed things? Would Chris still be alive if we hadn't cornered her? We should have just left her alone with her books, not asked her any questions, not gone out to the river, either.

Jenkins scratching the back of his neck. "What did you want to talk to her about? What's this about pictures? What pictures?"

I glanced at Toni; she nodded. Of course we had to tell him.

"We followed Tyler," I said. "There was another Dragon meeting."

"Dammit." Jenkins shook his head in disgust. "I thought I told you to stay away from him, I thought I made that clear."

Toni's anger flared and, her voice full of sarcasm, she blurted, "Someone had to investigate my sister's death."

He glared at Toni, said, "I'm doing as much as I can," then turned back to me, simply saying, "Go on."

I did. I told him how we wanted to try to get a picture of a few of the gang members, how we wanted to see if Chris could recognize any of them. Eventually Toni spoke, telling about her camera and telephoto lens, and the trip out to the St. Croix River.

Flushed red with anger, Jenkins took it all in, then said, "Let's see these pictures."

Toni lifted the red and white envelope from her purse and handed it to Jenkins, who pulled out the pictures and went through a half dozen or so. Toni and I sat in silence.

"At first glance, I have to say that this murder across the hall doesn't resemble the other ones—there's nothing cultish or ritualistic about it. But these pictures will be helpful," said Jenkins, studying one photo in particular. "Can I keep them awhile?"

I didn't see why not. I looked at Toni, who was nodding very slightly. If we'd spurred the police into investigating Liz's death further, if these photos might actually help now in regard to Chris's murder, then good. They could keep the pictures as long as needed.

"Sure," I said.

He quickly folded up the envelope, negatives and all, stuffed it into his sport coat pocket, and said, "I'll get our lab to make copies from the negs."

I stared at him, figured he knew best, muttered, "Oh."

"Don't worry, I'll get 'em all back to you tomorrow or the day after." Jenkins ran a hand over the top of his head. "Okay, now tell me about coming over here—when you got here, what you saw, if you heard anything. I want it all."

"It was a little after nine, I guess. Like maybe quarter after. We picked up the pictures right at nine at the photo place in Calhoun Square . . . and then we came straight over here." I bowed my head, shook it. "We parked out front, came up to the building. Chris said she was almost always home at night, and her lights were on, so we rang the bell out front."

"But no one answered?"

"Right," said Toni.

"And then?"

As he sat there, Jenkins lifted his left arm. As he lifted his arm, his sleeve came back. As his sleeve came back, I caught sight of a large silvery thing on his left wrist. It was thick and metal, and I thought, Is that a large watch, an oversized one?

My eyes focused on the band on his wrist, I watched Jenkins massage his head again, and my heart tightened and seemed to gasp.

"And then?" repeated Jenkins, putting his left arm back in his lap.

I could barely respond. "Then . . . then she didn't answer and so Toni used Liz's key to let us in." I was staring at his arm, but whatever he was wearing was covered up by the sleeve of his sport coat. "And then we knocked on her door and . . ."

I was gawking, couldn't speak. Holy shit, was that the same watch we'd seen on one of the Dragons—the guy we'd photographed, the one who was kind of heavy just like Lieutenant Jenkins?

I glanced to my right. Toni was staring at me, obviously wondering what was wrong. What could I say? I turned away from her, got up, started pacing, steering myself behind Jenkins. I had to get another look at what he was wearing on his wrist.

Toni picked up where I left off, saying, "Then we tried the door and it was unlocked. We opened it and . . ." As she spoke, she was eyeing me. "And called out for her, but there was no answer."

"Did you hear anything?" asked Jenkins. "Any noises? The sound of anyone running out the back?"

Toni shook her head. "Nothing."

As he sat there, Jenkins touched the back of his left hand. Just a little higher, I thought. Just scratch up a bit. Push back the sport coat, expose whatever it is you're wearing on your wrist.

"That's when you went into the kitchen?" he asked.

Toni nodded. "Right."

Standing behind Jenkins, I looked over at Toni and my eyes widened. I touched my wrist, then pointed to his. A wave of puzzlement washed over her face, and Jenkins turned around, stared at me.

On impulse, I looked back at Jenkins and asked, "You don't know what time it is, do you?"

"Sure." He reached into his pants and pulled out a small silver pocket watch, said, "Nine-fifty."

I frowned, not seeing at all what I wanted to see. A pocket watch?

I said, "Nice watch."

"Thanks, it was my dad's—he worked on the Burlington-Northern."

Unable to stop myself, I asked, "But what's that on your wrist?"

Jenkins smiled proudly, lifted his left arm, pushed back his sleeve. "This? Something I picked up in Arizona a long time ago."

I froze. That was it. The exact same piece we'd photographed. But it wasn't a watch, after all. No, it was a Navajo bracelet or some such southwestern piece. A big silver thing. Massive. There were two little pieces of turquoise on each side, then on top there was a big, flat round piece, a face of the same stone, polished and shimmering. From a distance it could be mistaken for an oversized Soviet watch, but up close it was a beautiful turquoise-and-silver bracelet. Obviously, I didn't need the photo to identify it. I was certain.

I managed to mutter, "Oh."

I glanced at Toni who was staring at the thing, unable to speak, or move even. My mind careered ahead. I wanted to grab Jenkins's arm, shake it, and point to the silver bracelet, and demand to know exactly what he'd been doing down there by the St. Croix. But I knew. This meant that he was one of them, a Dragon, didn't it?

Toni was pale, full of thoughts but empty of words. What should we do? Tell him we had that picture of him standing there in the woods, chest naked, face masked, wrist exposed? A horrid thought punched me. We didn't have any of the photos. No negatives, either. We had none of them. How could I have been so stupid? I'd just given them all to him. Jenkins had them now. The whole envelope, negatives and all, stuffed right into the pocket of that old brown sport coat.

We had to leave. Now. Before I said something, before Toni did, before we put ourselves in as much danger as we had put Chris.

I looked at Toni, started for her, said, "Toni, you don't look so good. Are you going to be sick again?"

"But—"

Before she could say any more, I hurried to her side, took her by the arm, interjected, "Come on. You'll be all right."

Then she got it, and she rose and I held her and things happened fast, the two of us walking briskly, then charging toward the kitchen, me the whole time muttering to her to keep quiet, we couldn't expose our knowledge, not yet. I held her like she was going to vomit, and we darted into the kitchen, up to the white ceramic sink, where I turned on the faucet full blast and huddled right up next to her so that Jenkins couldn't hear.

Toni pressed a hand to her forehead. "Oh, my God. Did you see that, did you? He's a Dragon!"

"Yeah." What were we going to do? "Toni, you've got to get sick," I whispered. "We've got to get out of here."

She nodded. I could see the panic in her face, the fear that was now taking her over, driving her, and she bent into the sink, stuck a finger into her throat. She jammed it way in, wiggled it around, and her body tightened like one big muscle. She sobbed, groaned, and heaved.

I patted her on the back, said loudly, "You're okay. Everything's all right."

It came up, a big wave of something all biley. I rubbed her back, stroked her, as it came up, this fearful purge that emerged so easily. So easily that I wondered if she was indeed forcing it or if it was coming on its own.

A voice from the kitchen doorway said, "Want me to get one of the medics?"

It was Jenkins. Standing, staring, a look of concern on that nondescript face. A murderer? Was it he who had killed Liz as well as Chris? I didn't like being cornered here in the kitchen, him blocking the only escape, controlling our fates.

I managed to say, "I need to take her home."

He nodded, a big gruff kind of guy with a southwestern bracelet. It didn't make any difference if he was or wasn't a real Dragon. I hated him. He'd been leading us along, asking for our trust, pooh-poohing our worries.

Toni was still bent over the sink, her back to Jenkins, shaking with fear and anger as if it were hopeless. Maybe it was. Maybe there'd never be a way to prove it. Or maybe we'd be wiped out by the Dragons, too. Toni and me.

"It's going to be okay. That's it, everything's going to be all right." I massaged her back, wanted to fold my arms around her. Instead I turned to Jenkins, said, "Can we finish this tomorrow?"

He stood in the doorway, awkwardly shifting from foot to foot, and said, "Sure."

But he didn't move. He just stood there, staring at Toni, then looking at me. He pushed back his sport coat, scratched his chest, and that's when I saw the gun. Hanging there in a holster. A lightning bolt of fear zapped me: Maybe he wasn't alone in all this. Maybe there were a number of Dragons in the police force.

I grabbed Toni, wrapped one arm around her waist, and we started toward the kitchen door. Jenkins finally jumped aside, opening the way.

"Are you sure you don't want a medic?" he asked.

"No!"

Toni was moving fast, I was struggling to keep up with her, to keep my arms around her as if I were really supporting her. We whooshed out of the kitchen, down the short hall, into the living room, and toward the door. Then suddenly Toni stopped.

"My purse!"

I left her by the door, said, "I'll get it."

I hurried over to the couch, grabbed the small brown leather bag. Liz's keys, too, which were on one of the cushions. I snatched everything up, returned to Toni, and took her by the elbow and escorted her out. We rushed through the hallway, which was still bustling with police officers and detectives and now photographers, too. We went flying through them, out the vestibule, out the door, down the steps, to my car. When we were some twenty feet away, we broke into a run and darted around the squad cars now filling the street. There were people everywhere, gawkers and gossipers, and there were flashing lights, too. Red and yellow lights squawking and blinking maniacally. I opened the passenger door for Toni, hurried around, got in behind the wheel, rammed my keys into the ignition.

As I brought my car to a charging start, I looked up at the red brick apartment building where Liz had lived and Chris had died, and there he was. Jenkins. He was standing in the big front window of Liz's apartment, staring down at us, following our every move. A spasm of fear rippled through me, and I froze.

Toni was leaning against the dash, head in hands, and she said, "Just go, just get out of here. Go!"

I tromped on the accelerator.

Chapter 21

We raced out of there. I had to swerve around a couple of cop cars. I nearly ran over some kid who was rushing across the street to see what all the excitement was about. But within seconds we were down the street and around the corner.

"I can't believe it," muttered Toni. "It was him. That bracelet or whatever—it was the same one. That was Jenkins out there with the Dragons."

"I know."

I glanced in the rearview mirror, saw a pair of headlights swing around the corner after us. Dear God, were we being followed? Did Jenkins know we knew, and so someone was after us now to guarantee our silence in the same manner that Chris's had been assured? Quite possibly. It was a large car—I could tell by the width of the headlights—and a fast one, too, rapidly gaining on us.

Or was I being paranoid? At the next corner I turned right, then sped on to keep our distance at a maximum. But the other car didn't turn, just zoomed by. Which meant we were safe, for now. I slowed to a reasonable speed.

"Alex," said Toni, looking across the dark car to me, "what are we going to do? I mean, what in hell is Jenkins doing?"

"I don't know. I suppose he could be undercover, but you'd think he'd have said something, certainly by now, certainly after tonight. I mean, wouldn't he tell us if they had something like a sting operation going on?"

"I guess. How can we find out?"

"I don't know."

"There's got to be some way, someone to ask!" she shouted in frustration.

"Yeah, but . . ."

That was all I could say. Yeah, but . . . who? Certainly not the police. Not yet, anyway. We couldn't go to them about Jenkins and his involvement with the Dragons because what if there were more Dragons in the police? Simply, we didn't know who to trust among them. My God. Trying to make sense of it, I drove slowly through the dark neighborhoods of south Minneapolis. Liz and Chris both murdered by someone, a lieutenant, on the city police force?

"If Jenkins is really one of them, a Dragon, I mean," I speculated, "it's no wonder he didn't seem to be doing anything—he wasn't."

"Yeah, and no wonder he kept trying to get us to believe Liz killed herself." Toni took a deep breath, followed by a long sigh. "He just wanted us to stop asking questions and go away. Not now, though. No way."

"Thank God you didn't let any of this drop."

"I couldn't. I never believed she committed suicide."

It all made sense. The police detective who was eager to call it a suicide because that would eliminate totally and completely any hunt for a killer. The detective who was eager to be rid of the curious and persistent sister, namely Toni.

In view of all that we'd stirred up, Toni and I had to be very careful now. If Chris had been murdered for information she might have possessed, we could be killed for information we were aggressively seeking. Although we lacked any hard facts, we could still be just as great a threat as Chris, so I checked behind us a couple of more times and I took a rather indirect route across Lyndale, then across Hennepin and back to my apartment. When I parked in front of my building, I glanced around, saw no one lurking by any cars or trees, could detect no stranger hanging about in the depths of the night.

"Come on," I said, opening my car door.

Even as we got out and started across the quiet street, however, I couldn't help feeling we were being observed, as if in fact there was someone out there behind a bush or perhaps in a vehicle, watching, waiting. Down the street I saw a rusty old red van, imagined it filled with two, three, four, or perhaps many more Dragons, and realized how stupid we were to have returned to my place.

My distant directress broke in, calling, *"Alex, hold it there for a moment."*

Toni and I had made it across the street, up to the sidewalk in front of my building. There was a slight breeze overhead, the leaves rustled. And then everything was interrupted. In an instant it all slowed like a film grinding to a stop. All of it—us, the leaves, the distant sounds.

"Good. Now study that time. Is someone out there? Is there something your subconscious would like to make known? If so, this is a good time to release that information."

It was as if I were stepping out of myself, leaving my living body and moving ghostly out of it. I did that. I separated from that still-frozen part of me, and I looked around. There were houses, most of them stucco, most of them good-sized. Well-maintained, too. And two or three apartment buildings like mine, dark red brick, three stories, six units. Down the street, to the south, I saw someone walking a dog. To the north all was equally quiet, and—

Wait. That wasn't right. I'd seen something back there. We'd driven in from that direction and there was something odd. But what?

"Alex, your eyes and mind take in much more than you can actually notice. You're given a vast array of stimuli each time you open your eyes, but you can only absorb and focus on a small fraction of that. That's why this trance is beneficial. You can freeze a screen of your memory and take a closer look at it. Just imagine you're doing that— freeze-framing a film."

All of a sudden things were backing up. Time was reversing itself. Yes, I had noticed something, seen something odd. It really didn't strike me at the time, but looking back, something was off. Twenty-seventh Street, which ran east and west, was a narrow street, and there was no parking on one side, the south side, yet there was a vehicle there.

"What color?"

I squinted, couldn't tell.

"Light or dark?"

Dark. Definitely dark. Kind of boxy, too. A truck or something, and across the front were letters.

"What letters?"

It said something. I squinted, concentrated, saw: MIT-SUBISHI.

"Good. Now, can you tell if there's anyone in it?"

Yes. There was a dark figure, the shape of someone behind the driver's wheel. A Dragon? Tyler perhaps? Or was it Jenkins himself? Couldn't the detective have sped over, arrived before us? Quite possibly. It was apparent, too, that whoever was in that vehicle was in fact watching Toni and me. I could see movement, discern that the focus was upon us.

"Very good. What else?"

Nothing. Only that much was clear—we were being watched, someone was waiting to strike.

"Go back to where you were." A deep, luxurious breath. *"Continue from there."*

I zipped back ahead, found myself again on the sidewalk with Toni. I didn't like this, the two of us out on a dark street. No one else around. Breaking the odd silence, a car door slammed, then I heard footsteps, quick ones. Someone running. I turned, looked back toward Twenty-seventh. Was someone coming from back there, from that truck? Wait, no. Those hurried steps were coming from the alley behind my building, weren't they? Toni heard it, too, and I took her hand and we started running down the sidewalk, up the walk to my building, up those concrete steps. I heaved open the outer door and the two of us charged into the vestibule. With trembling hands, I lifted the key to the door.

And then froze.

Carved into the molding of the door was no longer just a faint letter, the one that Tyler had started the other night. No, now there were two, a set of initials deeply cut into the dark old oak: R.T.

"Toni, look."

She gasped, said nothing. My eyes fell to the floor. Chips of wood were lying there undisturbed, not swept out of the way by feet or an opened door. That meant this was freshly done. Rob Tyler had just been here. I had a horrible thought and turned around.

He was there, just emerging from behind a tree. That shaved head. That sick smile. I saw it all through the glass door. The big hunting knife, too, which he held in his hand.

"Oh, God," said Toni.

I fumbled to get the key into the lock, and as I struggled to open the door, I glanced over my shoulder. Tyler was coming up the walk. Oh, Jesus. Only twenty feet separated us.

"Hey, assholes," shouted Tyler from just outside. "Do you know what Dragons do to people who spy on 'em? Do you? Liz ever tell you? Huh? Well—"

The lock clicked and I heaved open the inner door, and as Toni and I rushed inside, I shouted, "Fuck you, Tyler!"

Once in, I turned, pushed the inside door shut, made sure it locked, and then looked out through its window. Toni came up next to me. We peered through the glass, through the vestibule, through the outer door, and outside. The walk out front was empty. Tyler was gone.

"Maybe he's going around back," I said. "Come on, let's get upstairs."

Toni and I didn't waste any time climbing to my apartment, and once we were inside my place, I locked both locks on my front door, then went back to the kitchen and checked the rear door. Nothing wrong there, nothing kicked in or even tampered with.

When I returned to the living room, I found Toni in the darkened sunroom, staring out the window and down at the street.

"No sign of him," she said. "Maybe he's gone."

"I sure as hell hope so."

I dropped down on the couch, and that's when I realized how exhausted I was. Everything seemed to ache. I checked my watch. It was after eleven. No wonder. Toni looked even more worn out. Her eyes were puffy, face red, and that wonderful hair was quite disheveled.

She came in and sat next to me, and said, "What a night." She rubbed her face with both hands. "I wonder how he did it. Jenkins, I mean. How he killed Liz."

I hated to say it, but I had to. "Or if he really did. We can't get too far ahead of this. There's still the chance that Jenkins might be undercover. And we can't rule out Bozo down there. Tyler, I mean. He could have killed both your sister and Chris."

"I suppose." She anxiously kneaded her hands. "But if Jenkins is really a Dragon he could be covering for Tyler. That could be Jenkins's role in the Dragons—keeping the police off their backs. Or maybe . . . maybe he had Tyler kill Liz. You know, Jenkins ordered him to do it."

It was a disgusting thought, but a viable possibility. One that made sense, too. Maybe the Dragons had learned of Liz's plans to write about them, and before she could do so, they ordered Tyler to kill her. What had Tyler just said, Did Liz ever tell you what Dragons do to people who spy on them? What the hell did that mean?

"On the other hand, if Jenkins is actually covering for Tyler or if he even ordered him to do it," I said, "then that would mean they actually knew each other. We know they're both members of the Dragons, and we also know that the identities of the members are probably guarded. After all, they're masked, so we can't really say they collaborated on killing Liz or Chris because we don't know if Tyler and Jenkins really know one another."

I thought of ways to connect the two, of ways to ascertain if in fact Jenkins and Tyler were in contact with each other after their Dragon duties. I shook my head, cursed myself. The damn photos we'd taken at the St. Croix. We'd given the pictures and negatives—everything—to Jenkins. Shit, that had been stupid. I'd been tired, freaked out by Chris's murder, only too willing to trust the police. Those pictures had been our only possible proof of his involvement in the Dragons. Was there anything else in them, anything we might have missed?

Toni flopped her head back on the couch, stared up at the ceiling, said, "Wait a minute." She rubbed her eyes, her forehead. "Does all this mean that Jenkins could have been Liz's other boyfriend, the second one Chris had seen her with? It does, doesn't it?"

This terrible sensation sank to the bottom of my stomach, started chewing at me. "Oh, God. We were the ones who told Jenkins that Chris had seen Liz with someone else. We told him Chris knew Liz had another boyfriend."

So Jenkins could have killed Chris to keep her from talking. It could easily have gone that way. All too easily. How else would someone know we'd spoken with Chris?

My mind was whirling, skipping around for thoughts, possibilities. I glanced across the room and my attention was caught by a blinking red light. The answering machine. The red light was flashing because I had a message. Instinctively, impulsively, I rose, crossed the room to the table by the phone, and pressed the button. The thing clattered and spun, and released a message from one of the Larses, three hang-ups, and then two more messages.

As the second-to-last message began to play, a voice said, "Hello, this is Ruth Harris at The North Center calling Toni Domingo. I gave your message and number to Laura, and I do believe she tried to call you."

I cut in, saying, "The hang-ups."

"Unfortunately, however," continued Laura's counselor on the machine, "Laura became quite upset late this afternoon and decided to leave the program. She left the campus a few hours ago. If she contacts you we hope you'll encourage her to return—her treatment was going quite well. Feel free to give me a call at 459–3186. Oh, area code 612—the same as the Twin Cities."

I leaned against the wall, watched Toni's shocked and annoyed expression. She stopped the machine, looked at me.

"Typical. Laura's got this uncanny way of getting into trouble at the worst possible time."

"I didn't know there was ever a good time."

"No, but I swear to God she has some sixth sense, this radar, that knows exactly when I'm stressed out the most. That's when she cries out for help. Just watch, she'll probably turn up here." Toni shook her head, ran her hand through her hair. "There's nothing I can do for her. Not now, not tonight."

Angrily she hit the button on the machine, and it played the last message.

"Hi, this is Ed Dawson returning a call from Toni Domingo," said the steady and polite voice. "I'll be in session the rest of the afternoon, but feel free to leave a message with my answering service and I'll call you back as soon as I can. Hope everything's okay."

He slowly gave his number, which quickly brought Toni to her feet and sent her charging toward me and the phone.

"What are you going to do, call him now?" I asked.

"Absolutely. Liz told Chris she was dating someone else, so you'd think Liz would have told her shrink, too. I know Dawson didn't say anything about it, but you never know. Play back his number, would you?"

"Sure," I said, picking up on her thought, and doing as she asked. "Maybe Liz just called this other guy a . . . a friend or something."

"Exactly."

Seconds later Toni was speaking with Dawson's answering service, telling them it was an emergency.

"Does Dr. Dawson have a beeper?" she demanded. "Good, then you've got to page him—now, tonight. Yes, right away."

The operator on the other end was obviously balking at the thought of bothering a client so late at night.

"Listen," commanded Toni, "tell him someone else was killed tonight. Murdered. Tell him that, would you? And tell him I need to speak to him as soon as possible."

As we waited for Dawson's return call, Toni went out on the dark sunporch, peered out several windows, still seeing no sign of Tyler. She then found a chair in a corner out there, lowered herself into it, and disappeared into sulky, lonely thought. She might have been pondering Chris's death and Jenkins's possible involvement—there was certainly plenty to think about—but I knew that wasn't the case. No, I was sure she was thinking of Laura, what to do, how to handle her, and I had the good sense to disappear into the back of the apartment.

About fifteen minutes later, as I was pouring myself a glass of red wine, the phone rang. It was Dr. Ed Dawson, returning Toni's call.

Chapter 22

"**A**lex, I'm going to count from ten down to one."

What? No, that was impossible, there wasn't time. Everything was happening so quickly and there was someone crazy out there and Toni was in danger. No, I couldn't possibly stop, not now. Liz was dead, Chris butchered, and I had to figure this out before anyone else met the same fate.

"*It's best if we break here. We can continue tomorrow, Alex. I'm exhausted and you're tired, too. I can hear it in your voice.*"

Sure I was tired. It was late. We'd been through a lot, but there was more to be learned and looked at.

"*Of course there is, and you'll do all of that. Trust me. But it's better to wait and do it when you're not so worn out. When we're both not so tired. If we keep going now, we might miss something.*"

Was she right?

"*Yes, I am. You're doing this regression to look for things you might have missed the first time. That's why you've got to be alert and sharp.*"

Which I certainly wasn't, not right then.

"*Exactly.*" She took a long, slow breath. "*Good. Now follow me as I count: ten . . .*"

Jarring me from my trance, the goddess who was watching

over me started her chant in reverse, voice soft and soothing. She went on and on, rhythmically, seductively, from ten down to nine to eight and so on, once again sucking me out of the past, counting down, pulling me up. No, she was hooking me like a fish and reeling me in. That's what it was like. I was the big fish being slowly cranked in, and I struggled, made her pull hard, because I was in it deep and heavy, the waters murky and obscure.

"... *and one.*"

My eyes popped open, saw nothing, only black, and then there was a click and a light behind us popped on. I was sitting up by then, and I looked at my hands, the recliner, then over at Maddy with those sunglasses. The big attic, too. I glanced out the window. Oh, it's night. It's dark. Nothing out there but blackness.

I said, "It must be late."

She touched the watch on her left wrist. "Just after midnight. No wonder I'm so tired."

I was, too. Exhausted. I felt like I had the beginnings of a hangover, my head dull and thick. I stood, went to the screen doors; I saw Lake Michigan out there, just a hint of moonlight bouncing on it, a huge black plane of water that stretched on forever.

"Is this making any sense to you?" I asked, my back to Maddy. "Am I just blathering or what?"

"No, you're being very clear. You're doing an excellent job."

"Then why doesn't it seem like I'm getting any closer? Why don't I understand what happened? I don't have any better idea who killed Toni, do you?"

In a low and calm voice, she said, "I can't talk about that now."

I spun around. "What? Why not? Listen, I don't want to have to go through this whole thing if I don't have to."

"I'm sure you don't. And neither do I. But I don't want to say anything because I don't want to influence you, not yet anyway. Right now I don't want to prejudice your trance in any way; that would only skew your memory. You're the best source of information, and I don't want to pollute that with any of my hunches." She reached over for her wheelchair. "Now come over here and give me a hand, would you?"

She was speaking in her calmer voice. Not the high one, but the inner one. The more honest of the two. Interesting, I thought as I went over to her and helped her from recliner to chair. Yes, we were both wiped out, our defense and pretenses totally down.

"But Maddy—"

"Alex, please, no," she snapped. "I can't talk about it with you. Not yet. It would hurt the process, not help it. Besides, I'm too tired."

Obviously so. I'd rarely seen her crabby, but she certainly was now. So was I. We'd pushed hard, too hard perhaps.

"We'll finish tomorrow, won't we?" I asked, not eager to relive Toni's murder yet anxious to be done with it.

"I hope so."

She spun her chair around and gave it a big push, hurling herself directly toward a wall.

"Maddy, the door's not over there!"

She braked quickly, then bent over, put her face in her hands. I saw her body sort of puff up, then deflate. It was a sob. A big, dry one. What was it, I wondered, that she knew? What had she gleaned from what I'd said?

"Alex, I'm too tired. Would you push me, please?"

"Sure."

I did, gladly so. I took the chair by the handles in back, pushed Maddy from the big room, back through the attic, past a couple of the old servants' rooms, and to the elevator. We rode down to the second floor, and I lifted the wooden gate and rolled Maddy into the back hall.

"Solange will take me from here," said my sister.

"Sure," I replied, and headed to the door that led back to the servants' quarters.

"Wait, Alex!" Maddy practically shouted. "Their sitting room's right there."

The stress was obviously getting to us both, and I said, "Don't worry, I'm just going to knock."

Before I had time to do even that, however, Solange stepped out, her body wrapped in a pink robe.

"Are you ready for bed?" asked the black woman.

Maddy bowed her head, quietly said, "Yes."

Solange smiled at me and took over, wheeling Maddy up another hall and toward the master bedroom. I followed as far as the bedroom door.

"Good night," I called.

"Night, Alex," she said, just raising one hand and waving. "Love you."

"Love you, too."

They went off, disappearing into their night ritual, where Solange helped my sister wash and undress and get comfortably settled. When, I wondered as Maddy faded into the night, would my sister divulge her thoughts? And what had she actually picked out of my story?

I circled the open staircase, looked over the railing and into the entrance hall below—they'd left one light on—then up at the dark Tiffany dome that hovered way above the third floor. I counted the bedrooms—one, two, three, four, five, and six, including the master bedroom. All of them branching out from this upstairs landing, all of them spacious, all of them actually much larger than my living room back home.

My bedroom was in front, the only one with a light on, and I saw my bags carefully laid out, a crystal carafe of water put by the bed, the bed itself turned down. I stopped at the threshold. Yes, I was tired, but I wasn't ready for sleep. Not yet. My mind was still whirling. While my body was obviously here, another part of me was still in Minneapolis, back there in April with Toni. I was jet-lagged, or rather trance-lagged, and my body had come back to Madeline's island faster than my aura or my karma. Part of me was still strung out between Minneapolis and Lake Michigan, my thoughts dusting the skies.

I turned around, went down the stairs, through the front hall, and out the front door. The porch, broad and painted gray, wrapped around the west side and the front of the house, and I followed it, breathed in the fresh air, which was moist and cool. I could hear the waves crashing below, could see the stars in that navy blue–black sky. I went up to the front, leaned against one of the columns, and stared at a rocky beach straight in front and the lake beyond. There was a bit of a moon, and as my eyes adjusted, I could see blackish clumps of trees, the beach, a short dock. How was all of this going to come together,

Toni's death and what I knew? How was I going to solve what the police had not been able to? Did we have any chance at—

"You shouldn't be out here."

I jumped, turned around, saw a thick black figure, a face that blended in with the night. "God, Alfred, you scared me."

"The dogs run free at night, so you shouldn't be out here without letting me know."

"Oh."

He just stood there, both thuglike and schoolmarmish. I was about to make small talk, realized it was pointless, that it was obvious what he wanted, so I took a last whiff of fresh air, stretched.

"Well, I guess I've had enough."

As soon as I moved, so did he, holding the front door open, ushering me inside as if indeed I were the delinquent, untrustworthy pupil. He then stepped in behind me and carefully locked the door.

"Good night, Alfred," I called as I started up the stairs.

" 'Night," he said and disappeared into the billiard room, where there was another door leading into the back of the house.

Well, so much for an evening stroll, I thought as I climbed up the stairs. Locked in. Lights out. It was odd, this house. A prison in a way, for I was beginning to feel less like a guest and more like a captive.

With the exception of my footsteps on the carpeted runner, it was perfectly quiet as I headed up the stairs and retreated to my room. No, I realized, that wasn't quite right. As I reached the second-floor landing, I could hear a voice, not two, but one. It was my sister's. It grew louder, and it was obvious she was angry, shouting at someone and going on and on, which didn't make any sense because Maddy never got riled, never lost it like that. She was the one in control. So what was she doing? Could she be possibly getting furious at Solange? For what? I stood quite still on the edge of an oriental rug, stared at the closed door of the master bedroom. I should have been able to see light seeping out the bottom, but it was black. Did that mean Solange wasn't in there? But if it wasn't her, then who was it? Could there possibly be someone else here on the island and in this house that I didn't know about?

Very clearly I heard Maddy shout, "God damn you!"

I shivered. This wasn't my sister, at least not a part of her I'd ever, ever seen, known, or even suspected. Then something slammed. A door? Slowly and quietly I edged closer. Inside I could hear my rock-solid sister crying not just little waves of sniffles but loud, deep sobs. Jesus Christ, what had happened? I took another step, listened in shock to Maddy's outburst. And then she shrieked, and the next instant I heard some glass object strike a wall or the floor and shatter into tinkling pieces.

I went up to the door, pounded, and asked, "Maddy? Maddy, are you all right?"

No response, nothing. Even the sobs were immediately corked.

"Maddy?"

I twisted the door handle, pushed open the door, took a half step into the dark room. I scanned the black space before me, but couldn't tell if she was straight ahead by the bow windows, to the right by the bed, or perhaps to the left in the bathroom.

"I heard a noise. Are you all right?" I asked.

There was some sniffling to the right, I glanced over, saw a glint of metal. So she was over there at the desk by her bed, still in her wheelchair.

"I'm fine," she said, voice trembling. "I'm sorry, did . . . did I wake you?"

"No. Who were you talking to?"

"No one."

"But I heard you," I pressed, looking toward her office door, seeing that it was shut. Was someone back there? "And I heard something slam."

"Alex, please—"

"What is it, Maddy? What happened?"

"Nothing."

"Maddy, is someone else here in the house?"

"What?" Then quickly she added, "No. No, I was on the phone."

"Oh," I replied, though I wasn't sure I believed her. "Who was it?"

She didn't reply, and I stood there in the darkness, realized she wouldn't turn on a light because she didn't want me to see her teary and puffy-eyed. Wasn't right for her big-sister, insightful-shrink image. And I of course couldn't turn on the lights because I had no idea where the fucking lights were; I was as blind in her world as she was in mine.

"Maddy, who were you talking to?"

"It was nothing, no one." Then realizing she had to do better, she mumbled, "It was just my broker . . . he made a horrendous mistake." Pause. "He was supposed to sell something and he didn't, and now I'm out a lot of money, something like . . . like six hundred thousand dollars."

"You were talking to him now, at this time of night?" I asked, thinking that she might have lost that much—it was a good story, she couldn't have made it up so fast—but not today, more likely last week.

"Alex," she said as condescendingly as possible, "when you have an account of over forty million, your broker will wash your underwear for you at four o'clock in the morning."

Get off it, I thought. Maddy never talked like that, not to me or anyone else. She was bullshitting me, trying to sidetrack me onto a different subject, keep me away from the real issue. Yesterday or even this morning I would have believed her. But not now. Earlier this evening I'd learned that Maddy had been friends with Toni and her lover, Laura. Close friends by her own admission, yet Maddy hadn't said a damn thing about it for fear of transgressing some boundary. Or some such thing.

Some such thing as? My mind danced, looped arm to arm, from idea to idea, possibility to possibility, and on down the line, each thought more awful than the next. This outburst of hers had nothing to do with her millions. Maddy didn't care that much about all those dollars. No, standing there in the dark, seeing the outline of my blind sister in that wheelchair, I kept circling and coming back to Toni and sensing that of course this had to do with her murder. Of course there was more that Maddy knew about Toni and perhaps about Liz as well. After all, Maddy had been friendly with Toni for at least six years, been in regular contact with her, in a way knew her better than I, so perhaps there was another angle to this whole thing that I was missing. Maybe Maddy knew that Toni had been involved in something. Or maybe Maddy knew of some scandalous aspect of Liz's life.

Shit. This was driving me crazy. The very idea of Toni, Laura, Maddy, and possibly even Liz all getting together made me twist inside with paranoia. Those four women gathering without the one link that tied them together: me. What had they talked about? What had they done? Something, anything, nothing? Still, there was the strong chance that Maddy had learned something at Liz's funeral. Toni could have taken Maddy aside, revealed some angle, some fact, some possibility that I was never privy to. So, if Maddy really had been on the phone just now, who could she have been talking to? Toni's surviving partner, Laura? Could Maddy be in touch with her? I hadn't been able to contact her, but perhaps it was simply that Laura hadn't wanted to talk to me, Toni's old boyfriend.

I stood there steaming with speculation, wondering if there was indeed anyone else on this island. Maddy wasn't going to brush me off so easily. Not anymore. She surely knew that now, could tell as much.

And so she laughed slightly, said, "I've never gotten mad at him like that—Steve, my broker, I mean. I'm just exhausted. I'll have to call him in the morning and apologize for hanging up on him."

"Yes, you will," I said, wanting to nail her on this one.

"I'm sorry I bothered you." Her voice was high and sweet. Very, very Audrey Hepburnish, as if there couldn't possibly be a problem in this God-forsaken world because after all there was still Tiffany's. "Now you go off to bed and get some rest. I'll see you in the morning."

"Are you sure you're all right?"

"Absolutely."

"Do you need help getting into bed?"

"No, I'm going to just sit here a bit longer."

"Okay," I said, turning, thinking again, bullshit.

"Good night."

I gave up, said nothing more as I left her world of darkness because I knew there was something she wasn't telling me, and I knew I wouldn't get it out of her. Either she'd continue to deny any problem or at best admit that there was something but that she wouldn't tell me because—how had she put it?—she didn't want to skew my trance. Pollute it, that was it. And once Maddy decided upon something, there was no swaying her. Of that I was still absolutely sure. Such resolve. My granite sister.

So I left without saying anything because I was so pissed and I knew that if I opened my mouth I wouldn't be able to shut it, the string of demands and questions would come gushing out, and she'd gun them down, one right after the other. I pulled Maddy's bedroom door shut behind me, but didn't move. No, I thought. She'll be listening. She could discern things through hearing that I missed like a dumb clod, so I stood in place, yet kept pacing, marching to make it sound like, yes, I was and always would be the dutiful little brother. I'll do as you say. I'll go to my room. I'll go to sleep. I'll believe your every goddamned word.

That's what she must have thought, anyway. That I'd left her alone and to her business, because a minute, perhaps two, later—I'd stopped pacing by then, stood there just outside her door absolutely silent—I heard her pick up the phone again. She bleeped in a bunch of numbers, and then she was talking, demanding, ordering. I couldn't hear anything besides a forceful yes, yes, yes, no. Now! Nothing more could I discern, except that she didn't make just one phone call. But two. Three. To whom? Steve the broker? Very doubtful. Laura? Quite possibly.

There might have been more calls, but I left after the third, in the end shamed by my spying. I stripped off all my clothes and crawled into bed, but I couldn't shed my thoughts and fears so easily, and I drowned in an ugly sleep.

Oh, shit, Maddy, what is it? What do you know that I don't?

Chapter 23

I woke up the next morning feeling like I'd been out with a bunch of Russians and had drunk too many of those godawful *koktaili*, a bizarre combination of one third cognac, one third vodka, and one third champagne; no olive, just a bloated prune. My limbs ached and my head felt thick and dull. I lay in bed, eyes open, body not moving, realizing only now how much energy I'd expended in trance yesterday. How drained I was this morning, and how much I didn't want to go through the rest of it.

But I had to. I knew that. I lay there, my thick curly hair buried into that feathery pillow, and a few minutes later I repeated the trick that I'd learned the first time I visited Maddy out here: I reached over and pressed a button on the wall. While I'd felt embarrassed before, amused, too, this time I was praying it worked. And it did. About five minutes later there was a gentle rap on my door and Solange stepped in, carrying a bamboo tray.

"Good morning," she said.

I smiled, managed to push myself up, prop a pillow behind my back, and Solange set the tray of coffee, juice, and muffin on my lap. There'd been a newspaper last time. None now, which meant either they were having difficulty with delivery out here—likely—or Maddy didn't want me distracted—more likely.

I cleared my throat, said in a toady voice, "Thank you."

As Solange went over to the three large windows and pulled back the curtains, she said, "Alfred and I will be leaving shortly, if that's all right."

"Absolutely."

"We'll be back in the morning. Is there anything you need before we leave?"

"No." I thought better of it, imagined taking a walk. "The dogs—what about them? Could Alfred pen them up somewhere?"

"They're already in the kennel, watered and fed, too. Would you let them out tonight, after dark?"

"Sure. Is my sister up?"

"Oh, yes. For hours. She's in her office, says she has about another hour's worth of work and asks not to be disturbed."

Absolutely, I thought. This is Madeline's island and Sister rules it. All commands to be obeyed.

"What time is it?" I asked.

"A little after eleven."

"My God . . ." I'd thought maybe nine at the latest.

Solange left and I downed my first cup of coffee in bed, the second while I stood in the shower. I had trouble getting dressed; putting on a sock seemed a real chore. As I stood at the windows buttoning my blue shirt, I stared out at the rocky point out front, then heard an engine. I leaned over, looked toward the eastern side of the island, saw Solange and Alfred motoring away from the boat house, and felt a stab of regret. No, don't leave us. Don't leave me here. I don't want to go through this. Take me away.

I wandered the house for at least an hour, shot a game of pool in the billiard room, ate two more muffins in the kitchen, then went back upstairs, passed through my sister's bedroom, and went to a heavy sliding door in one corner. I tapped once, didn't wait for a reply, then stepped into what had once been called the hay-fever room—apparently the owner had retreated here during his attacks—and was now Maddy's office. She wasn't at either of the two computers, not at her quote machine or the fax, either, but beyond all that high-tech gadgetry, lying on a Victorian fainting couch.

"Hi," I said. "It's after one."

She lifted a hand from the red upholstery, motioned for me to stop, and I did, knowing what she was doing. A trance. She was under. Self-hypnosis was undoubtedly her best and most rewarding escape, and I watched her chest rise up and down, her body begin to move, and then seconds later she rolled her head toward me.

"How'd you sleep?" she asked.

"As they say in Russian, like the dead."

"I bet. Age regressions are exhausting. It's all that channeling, it really burns you out."

"Were you just under?"

Maddy pushed herself up, then lifted and pushed her legs down to the floor. "Yep. I was just reliving some old memories . . . you know, seeing colors again and going for a walk. It sounds morose, maybe, but it really helps me from feeling so trapped inside myself."

I could understand that, appreciate it, yet I wondered exactly what old memories she'd chosen to revisit. Anything connected to her outburst last night?

"Shall we go up and get back to work?" she asked, her voice light.

"Okay."

"You don't sound too eager."

This was weird. I studied her, didn't get it. Why was she being so normal, why was she completely skipping over last night, pretending as if I hadn't heard or seen a thing?

"Maddy, what was that all about last night?"

"Alex, please, I just got all relaxed. Do I have to go into that now?"

"But—"

"I told you it had to do with my broker," she snapped.

Okay, I thought. If that was how she wanted to play, I was just going to have to sneak the truth out of her. I went over, helped her into her wheelchair, was struck by how readily she was now accepting my help.

I asked, "Do you think this is going to work, that we'll actually discover who killed Toni?"

"Sure. They say we only use ten percent of our minds, but I know hypnosis enables you to use more than that. Maybe it's only another two percent. Maybe it's twenty. I don't know, but I have a lot of faith in it, and yes, I do think you're going to get that answer."

"Do you already know who killed her?" I bluntly asked.

"Alex, I can't give you the truth, I can only help you find it."

I groaned at her response, I groaned as I lifted her into her wheelchair. Maddy the blind, paraplegic Zen master. Why was she going to make me work for the answer when I sensed she could just as easily hand it to me?

"Don't worry," she said, reaching for the edge of a desk, getting her bearings, then starting to wheel herself out. Her voice rose to that higher pitch, the fake one, and she added, "Everything's going to be all right."

My point exactly, I thought as we headed back up to the third floor and, I hoped, the final trance. We both wanted everything to work out, we both wanted to wrap this all up nice and neatly, but there were no guarantees, never had been. After witnessing Toni's murder, I knew that only too well.

Chapter 24

Neither Toni nor I slept very well the night of Chris's murder. As I lay in my bed, I kept thinking I heard someone fiddling with the locks, and when I closed my eyes, there wasn't darkness but Chris's face, her hideous final one. And all that blood. I'd seen only two dead bodies in my life, one at a funeral, the other being pulled from a terrible car wreck. Those were bad enough, but this was real, someone I had met. Was it also going to take months, perhaps years, to forget what I'd seen in Chris's apartment?

As I tried to block Chris's last image, I heard Toni tossing about in the living room, alone out there on the couch, later pacing, later yet taking a shower. My mind bubbled and popped. I wanted to go and hold her, and I probably should have, but I thought it might not be right.

What was truly inappropriate, though, was the two of us flung on our own, fretting and stewing so lonesomely. It seemed like hours before I drifted away, and only then I slipped into a dream that acted out my worries—something about the Dragons bursting down my door, charging in, and murdering us, too. Altogether awful, altogether a distinct possibility. After

that, my heart raced, and for the rest of the night I flinched at
every noise.

I was glad when it was time to get up the next morning,
even though I could feel the exhaustion puffing my eyes and
numbing my joints. I was glad to move into some sort of action,
resolve. I didn't like lying and waiting so passively. So it was a
relief when, a little before eight o'clock, Toni and I headed out
to meet Ed Dawson.

I locked both locks on my apartment door, double-checked
them, and then Toni and I started down the main staircase.
Her hand slipped easily into mine as we descended, and I took
it, held it.

"It's not even four blocks to Uptown," I said, "but we probably shouldn't walk it."

"Okay."

Her voice was low and calm. Exhausted. I studied her face,
noted her lack of color. Had she slept at all?

We paused in the vestibule, and through the glass door
checked the sidewalk and street. I was looking for a man, either
Jenkins or Tyler. Or a group of men from the Dragons. Everything, though, looked calm, just a normal morning, just a few
people with briefcases trudging off to work.

Toni and I, still holding hands, had almost reached the
sidewalk when I heard a car door open and reflexively scanned
the street, my eyes coming to rest on an Oldsmobile, a light
green one. A woman climbed out, stood alongside the worn
auto. The long, straight hair, the broad face. No, I thought, it
couldn't be. Toni clutched my hand tighter yet, gasped and
stopped still.

"I knew you'd go back to him," said the woman, her voice
accusing and deep as if she'd smoked far too many cigarettes,
drunk way too much coffee.

"Laura," said Toni, her voice barely audible.

I hadn't seen her in—what?—ten years, but even from a
distance I could see how much she'd aged. The hair, though
still long, had dulled from light to dark brown, then silvered.
Body a little heavier, perhaps. Face puffy, worn, as if she'd
partied too hard and too long. A little haggard. Yes, a person
in recovery, someone who was not only drying out, but being
forced to confront a myriad of personal and family issues.

"I knew you always wanted him," continued Laura, hanging on to the edge of the car as if it were an island and everything else a horrible sea.

Toni said, "What?" She eyed me, then quickly dropped my hand, threw it out of her grasp, took a half-step forward. "Wait, no, don't be—"

"I understood everything as soon as I called up and heard his voice on the answering machine. I thought it was him, and when I checked the phone book, sure enough, the name and number matched up." She shook her head in disgust, started climbing back into the Oldsmobile. "I've been sitting out here for a couple of hours praying I was wrong. But I guess I'm not. Hope you lovebirds are happy."

Toni jogged to the curb, called across the street, "Laura!"

But Laura paid no attention, and she brought the Oldsmobile to life with a huge roar, jammed the thing into gear, and burst out of the parking place. To no avail, Toni shouted out again.

Laura cracked her window, eyed Toni with contempt, and hollered, "Drop dead, Toni!"

And she was off, racing down the street, turning with a squeal at the first corner, then disappearing.

"Shit!" said Toni, standing in the street. "Do you see what I mean? Do you? She just drops out of the sky, assumes she knows everything about anything, and then storms off. I can't tell you how many times she's done this exact same thing. Damn her!"

"I can't believe she thinks we're back together."

"She believes exactly what she wants—that she's alone, that no one loves her, that she's a toad." Toni clenched both hands, hissed her frustration. "Well, she *is* a toad. God, and I wanted to go out and visit her." She shook her head, stomped to my car. "Let's get out of here."

We rode to Uptown in stormy silence, Toni muttering but not really saying anything. I parked in a lot, and as we walked to Sherman's Café, a popular spot on Hennepin just down from the Uptown Theater, Toni assertively took my hand.

"Are you all right?" I asked as I pulled open the door.

"Don't worry, I'll be okay." She took a deep breath, and added, "Just forget about Laura. I'm sure she won't be back."

Once inside, I looked across the café, a bright place buzzing with morning business, and said, "There he is."

Liz's therapist, Ed Dawson, was seated at a table in the middle of the room, and he raised his brow, opened his eyes wide, upon seeing us. We quickly went to him, and he stood, took Toni's hand first, then mine.

"Thanks for meeting us so early," I said.

"Absolutely."

I felt quickly relieved. Here was someone who could listen and on whom we could impose our worries and fears. Here was someone who could advise us on all of this. That was his glow anyway. The kind of safe-harbor feelings he seemed to give off. Yet he was worried. That much was obvious from the serious, even stern, look upon his face.

"I can't believe it." Dawson motioned toward a newspaper he'd placed on the empty fourth chair. "It's even in this morning's paper. And the brutality of it—that poor woman."

I shook my head as the recent incident with Laura was overshadowed by the memory of Chris's murder.

Toni said, "Well, there's certainly no question anymore that Liz was murdered."

"No, I suppose not," replied Dawson.

On the phone last night, Toni had told Dawson most of the story of finding Chris, and Dawson had listened, taken it all in, agreed with Toni's initial speculations.

"Did Liz ever mention Chris?" I asked as our waiter came over and poured coffee for us all.

He pursed his lips, shook his head. "Not much. She did say she liked the girl across the hall—I do remember that—but nothing else. And once she came in all upset because she was having trouble with the caretaker."

I glanced at Toni, then back to Dawson. "With John? What kind of trouble?"

"Oh, nothing major. He was just getting after her for playing her stereo too loud. As I understood, it was kind of a control thing with him, and Liz just needed some help on how to tell him to back off."

Dawson had two or three clients that morning, so we ordered right away. Pancakes sounded good. Something nice and grounding, food that was solid and not runny, food that would soak up the acidy sensation in my stomach.

Toni didn't waste a minute. She turned from the waiter, back to Jenkins and asked, "What about dating—did she mention anyone besides Tyler? Was she going out with anyone besides him?"

Dawson thought, took a sip of coffee. "No. She never mentioned anyone, that is. We spent quite a bit of time talking about her relationship with Rob. Before they broke up she was eager to go out with other people, but he didn't want her to."

"He was jealous?" I asked.

"Oh, yes. According to Liz, Rob had a real problem with even the thought of her seeing other men. With his temper, too." He thought for a moment, then added, "This was told to me in confidentiality, of course, but I suppose now it's in Liz's best interest. Rob Tyler's a violent man—he struck Liz on several different occasions and threatened her as well."

Toni closed her eyes and shook her head.

"That's why she wanted out of the relationship," continued Dawson. "She knew that it would be best for her to leave Tyler and find someone else, and I was encouraging this. She did say there were a couple of people she wouldn't mind going out with."

"So it's possible, then, that she might have started seeing someone else?" I asked.

"Well, maybe." Dawson seemed to withdraw in thought, looking out the front window, wrinkling his brow, then added, "Recently she talked about another fellow, someone she was beginning to like."

Toni asked, "An older man?"

"Well, as a matter of fact, yes, that's right. That's how it came up—she asked me what I thought about age differences in couples. I said if the relationship was good, then it didn't matter. She smiled and blushed a little bit and told me about an older guy who was really nice to her. She was wondering what it would be like to go out with him."

I turned to Toni. "That could have been Jenkins."

Our breakfasts came soon, and as we ate, Toni went into detail about yesterday—our following Tyler, going down to the

St. Croix River, taking pictures. And then, of course, finding Chris, and talking to Lieutenant Jenkins and seeing the thing on his wrist, that southwestern bracelet, the very same one we'd seen in the photograph. The more Toni explained, the slower Dawson ate, until finally he put down his fork and knife altogether, and just sat there, dumbfounded, pale even, in discomfort.

"You're sure about all this?" he asked.

Well, as sure as we could be, I said. The only truly stupid thing we'd done was hand over the pictures to him. We were both certain of one thing, though. The bracelet. We'd both recognized it right away.

Dawson shook his head. "Oh, my God."

Toni and I glanced at each other, both of us smugly pleased by Dawson's shock and concern. It was confirming, affirming— all of that stuff. So we weren't nuts. The ramifications were dreadful. If Jenkins wasn't undercover, it would mean that a police lieutenant was a member of a dark cult. It would send a blast all the way through the police force, right up to the mayor's office.

Speculating, I said, "If the Dragons are responsible for killing those four women, Liz, now Chris, and probably the blond woman we saw down in that warehouse, that would be seven."

"Dear God," muttered Dawson.

The waiter poured us fresh coffee, and we sat there stewing over the possibilities, venturing what might have happened, who might have killed Liz and why. Rob Tyler certainly could have murdered Liz and made it look like a suicide, either as part of a cult ritual or perhaps out of jealousy.

"You know," Toni commented, "Liz always wanted the truth out in the open. It would have been just like her to threaten to expose the Dragons."

"Yeah." As I thought about it, that fit, made sense. "After all, the night Liz died, Chris saw her with someone who matched Jenkins's description."

Toni said, "And don't forget we were the ones who told Jenkins—not Rob Tyler—about that. That Chris might be able to help, I mean."

Our thoughts fell into silence. All so logical. So complete.

It was like dominoes falling, one right after the other. Neat and clean. Poor Liz, poor Chris. If their deaths could be attributed to Jenkins, how many other deaths had he covered up? What other crimes had he forced to remain undetected?

Ed Dawson looked shaken. This obviously wasn't the kind of stuff he liked to be involved in. Divorces, self-esteem, parental problems. Those were his specialties.

He asked, "So what are you going to do?"

"I don't know." I rubbed my chin. "I just wish there was a way to get Rob Tyler to talk. That's what I thought about in the middle of the night—some way of forcing him to tell us what he knows."

"Yeah, but how?" said Toni.

"I don't know, but there must be a way of getting him to say something about the Dragons and Jenkins. If only we had some evidence, something to bribe him with."

"Wait, wait, wait." Dawson lifted his hands, palms out. "Just slow down. You don't want to go getting yourselves into any more trouble than necessary. I think it's best if you just back off a bit, let the proper authorities handle this."

"But who?" asked Toni. "What if there're other Dragons in the police?"

Dawson considered it, said, "I have a cousin in St. Paul who works for the FBI. Do you want me to call him and see what he can find out about Jenkins?"

"That'd be great," said Toni, smiling for the first time that morning.

Which was where we left it: Dawson was going to get hold of his cousin as soon as possible and we were to wait for his advice. That was probably the best way. It should have been, anyway. As we sat there finishing our meals, though, my mind kept going down another path, the one where we forced Tyler to tell us what he knew. To do that, though, we needed something—information, an object, something remotely incriminating. But what?

Ed Dawson soon excused himself, dashing off to his first session of the day, promising he'd be in touch with us soon, this morning probably. His idea seemed safe, a good way to be handling this. Turn it all over to some higher power: the FBI.

After he left, I took the last several bites of my pancakes, stared into my plate, felt oddly unsettled. What were we supposed to do for the rest of the day, go shopping? How were we supposed to bide our time so passively? That certainly wasn't my nature, and, turning to Toni, looking at her, seeing her eyes darting, hands fidgeting, I recognized that it wasn't hers, either.

"Toni, what do you think about going back to Liz's apartment and taking one more look?"

"I think that'd be a really good idea."

For it was fully possible that we'd missed something, that we might find something there to hold against Rob Tyler. And besides, we had to go back over to Liz's because when we'd left so quickly last night, we'd left the apartment wide open and Jenkins standing in there.

We had to claim it back.

Chapter 25

As we drove to Liz's, we fell into silence again, neither one of us talking about Liz or Chris or Jenkins. Or Laura, for that matter, wherever she was. Off binging perhaps?

When we parked in front of Liz's, we got out, came around the front of the car. It was rather daunting, looking up at the small apartment building. The two lower apartments were once occupied by young women, both now dead. It made me sick.

I checked the street, spotted John's brown van, but no cop car. Still, I was rather worried that we might find Jenkins here at Chris's or perhaps, God forbid, still in Liz's apartment. But he wasn't. No one was. When Toni opened the building's outer door, we were greeted first by total silence, and then by yellow and black tape on Chris's door stating this was a crime scene, keep out, police—all that kind of stuff. The door was pulled tightly shut, secured, and sealed with tape. So it really had happened. Someone had been killed here.

I turned to Liz's door, which was nicely closed, didn't look violated in any way, and I just stood there as Toni went up to it, key in hand. What was wrong here? What was calling out as not being right? I couldn't tell, but a queasy feeling rolled through my stomach, rocked my insides, as Toni unlocked the

203

door and pushed it open. I took a few steps, then stopped right on the threshold and checked the door. There was no tape here, nothing had been sealed. The lock was a dead bolt, which you had to lock from the outside.

"Wait a minute," I said. "We left this door wide open and Jenkins standing in here. How'd he lock it?"

Toni stopped in the living room, looked at the key in her hand. "Shit, you don't think he has a key, do you? You don't think Liz gave him one?"

"I don't know." But I didn't like it. "Come on, let's hurry. Look for anything that has to do with Tyler—clothing, writing, anything—then let's get out of here. I don't want to run into Jenkins."

"I just hope he didn't take anything last night."

Toni disappeared into the back, starting in the bedroom, shuffling through Liz's desk, her closet and dresser. I took the living room, starting with the bricks-and-board bookcase three levels tall, the exact kind I'd had for years until I moved so many times that the thought of lugging it all one more time made me abandon the whole setup. Lined up across the pine boards were CDs and lots of paperbacks. Just a few hardcovers. Most of the books were sci-fi novels, which I found interesting but not particularly useful. I checked all the books, hoping to find something on cults, perhaps something that would show an obsession with groups of a devious nature. But nothing. Her music was fairly standard, even mild. R.E.M. and a handful of New Age stuff, too.

I was down by the stereo when I glanced along the boards, saw that camera, the small black one, on the far end of the top shelf. I remembered having seen it before, of course, but I didn't remember seeing it open, as it was now, the back side open to the film cavity. I stepped over there, stood above the camera, gazing down. The lens was toward the wall, the back toward the living room. No, it hadn't been that way at all. I remembered seeing the lens, remembered wondering what Liz had last taken pictures of. Shit, I should have thought of it before, for if there had been any film it was now most definitely gone.

I turned around. Couch, dumpy chair. By the door a small table with a bowl. Attracted by a pile of papers that was climbing out of the bowl like rising bread dough, I went over and started sorting through discarded mail, bills that had been opened, half-pulled out, then ignored. Some flyers. Communications from two or three charitable organizations, too—I saw the envelope from the omnipresent Minnesota Public Radio and skipped right past it. At the bottom of the bowl there were some rubber bands, and a pair of sunglasses. A discarded battery. And then a jumbo-sized paper clip with two keys on it, one a very small one, the other more of a standard-issue house key. I picked it up, let it dangle from my fingers.

A voice down the hall called, "What's that?"

I turned, saw Toni standing outside the kitchen doorway, and said, "Keys—they were in this bowl."

I turned to the door, opened it, and tried the larger of the keys in the lock, but it wouldn't even begin to fit.

"It's not a duplicate," I said.

Toni came out, stood next to me, looked at the keys on the paper clip, and said, "This small one's got to be a mail key."

"Of course."

We looked out the front window for any sign of Jenkins, then hurried out of the apartment, through the hallway, into the vestibule. I'd forgotten all about Liz's mailbox; I'd noticed it that first time over, seen it all packed with stuff. Toni went directly to the bank of brass boxes mounted in the wall, slipped the key into the lock of Liz's box, and of course it worked. The small brass door opened and mail came flooding out, cascading onto the floor as if we'd hit the jackpot. I was sure we had.

Toni and I gathered everything, a whole pile of envelopes and catalogs and papers, and we wasted no time retreating into the apartment. I locked the door behind us, and we sat on the couch and tore through everything, ripping letters and bills open, dropping them on the floor, dashing through it all, hoping to find some incriminating letter, some bit of telling information. I was sure there was; we both were. I ripped open a manila envelope, tossed aside a Guthrie Theater schedule. Plowed on, into a Minnesota Public Radio pledge form. Them again. And more bills. One from Northern States Power. One from Visa.

Within a few minutes, however, there was a pile of papers at our feet and nothing in hand. Crap, all of it crap. I looked at Toni, shrugged.

I said, "I thought we were going to find something."

"So did I."

Motioning toward the bookshelf, I said, "I found the back of the camera open—you don't know if there was any film in it, do you?"

She shook her head, didn't say anything, the discouragement on her face like thick makeup. Toni had never been very good at hiding her emotions.

"What about that other key?" I asked. "What's that for? You don't think it's to Rob Tyler's house, do you?"

"Maybe. Then again, maybe it's to her storage room downstairs."

"She has more stuff in the basement?"

Toni nodded.

I said, "Come on."

I stood, grabbed Toni by the hand, pulled her up. Toni didn't seem too eager, but she came along. I led the way past the kitchen, past the hall closet, and then to the back door, which was on the right, just before the bedroom.

"We need to find something to corner Tyler," I said, as we exited the apartment and onto the back staircase.

"Yeah, but what?"

"Well, what if we'd found her journal and there was something in there or what if there'd been film in her camera that showed . . . showed, I don't know, Tyler dressed as a Dragon. Something like that."

"If only life were so convenient," she muttered, unable to hide her sarcasm.

The back hall was dingy, to say the least, an old staircase with grayish green paint and old wooden steps that had darkened and cracked with age. Toni hit a round button, a couple of bulbs came to life, and we descended into cool dankness and the forgotten, unseen part of the apartment building where things were stashed and then abandoned. I looked up. Hanging from the ceiling were pipe after pipe, most of them wrapped in asbestos and all of them leading spiderlike to a huge object in the corner, the original boiler, which had undoubtedly been converted from coal to gas.

Toni pushed aside an old curtain, and we walked around a pile of boxes, past an old washer and dryer sitting out in the middle of the floor—unhooked to water or electricity—and past some barbells and dumbbells on the floor. Off to the right I saw a large water heater, bicycles, some hoses, a rake, then another washer and dryer, those apparently hooked up. Not much more, at least what I could see. Off on one side was a small window, way up high at ground level and clearly nailed shut, but it had been painted over, gave off nothing more than a murky glow.

"I was down here once," said Toni. "Her storage room's back there, in the far corner."

I could barely make out a series of old doors, and I knew at once that, yes, this key would unlock the one labeled TWO, which was Liz's. And it did, of course. Toni and I skirted more piles of books and crud, the jetsam of years of tenants who'd moved on, and Toni went up to the storage door, slipped the key into the padlock, which popped open with a faint chink. She swung open the door, but we could barely see inside, it was so dark. A bicycle tire was about all I could make out. I reached for a string, tugged, and a light burst on, exposing a room that had only walls of chicken wire separating it from the other storage lockers. In front of me I saw not a lone bike tire, but a whole bike, plus a lawn chair, the foldout kind, a bag of charcoal, some old cross-country skis, and an assortment of other inconsequential junk.

"Doesn't look like much to me," said Toni.

"Me, neither."

Not knowing what to look for, I tried to imagine what could have been here, what might have been. A mask used by a Dragon. Something worn by Liz if she'd attended a Dragon function. Or?

I bit my bottom lip, stared at the sad pile of junk. I couldn't think of anything else. I was shaking my head, coming to the conclusion that this was hopeless, useless, a wild chase of the goose type, when it happened. The lights went out. I was looking at the red bike—an old Schwinn—when the lights snapped off and Toni and I were left in near-total darkness.

"Shit," I said. What a time for a power failure. "Toni?"

She grabbed me, suddenly and hard, fingers sinking through my shirt, into my skin.

"Hey," I began, "it's all—"

She whispered, "Someone's down here!"

Toni was pulling on me, leading me aside, out of the way, and my heart began to trot, then gallop. Someone down here? My eyes scanned the darkness, tried to probe this wickedly blackened basement for the sight of another human being. I turned. Was the boiler over there or the washing machines? And those weights? No, they were over there. So that meant the stairs were about—

I saw him. Definitely a man, a big guy, now pushing aside the curtain at the bottom of the stairs, then letting the curtain drop and closing off all but the faintest of light. I couldn't tell much, only a vague shape, but one thing was absolutely clear. The stranger held out his right hand and in that hand was a gunmetal gray shadow. A pistol. This wasn't one of the tenants down here searching for a lost sock. This guy knew we were down here and he was hunting for us. Oh, shit, and we were back by the lockers, cornered in the rear of the basement, no gun, no knife, no nothing.

Toni tugged on me, and I moved after her, fearful of saying anything, fearful of bumping into something. Either would give us away. So what could the two of us do, so weaponless? Nothing but hide.

She led the way, slow step by slow step, and I saw him, our hunter, stalking us equally slowly. No, he didn't know where we were because he was going the other way. He was sliding toward the boiler, while we were going off toward the washer and dryer and then another pile of junk. Perhaps we could slip around him, bolt for the stairs, break for safety, but then he turned into a shadow that slipped into blackness. Where the hell was he? Where were we?

In front of me I felt Toni stumble. Then I lost my balance, too, nearly fell as something wrapped around our feet, something long and coiled and hard. A hose. Dammit. I couldn't even kick it aside for fear of being heard, and Toni and I clung to one another, somehow kept our balance through this obstacle course of household refuse.

Finally I stepped beyond it, still held on to Toni, and I realized this wasn't going to work, our hiding or even trying to slip around him and bolt for the stairs. We'd never be as quick as a bullet. We had to separate. Toni could go one way, I another. We could lure him. Yes. Toni could lure him, then I could jump him from behind, whack him on the head, strangle him, whatever. It was our only chance, the only way.

I pulled on Toni's arm, brought her close to me, pressed my lips right into her thick hair, and said, "You go up that way and try to get him to follow. I'll jump him from behind."

She didn't risk a verbal response, and we squeezed hands, parted. This had to work. There was no other way, none that I could figure, and I watched Toni slip away from my touch and drown in the darkness. I bit my lip, turned back, reached out, tried to find my way back toward the locker. There was a column back there. Right. A post. I could go back up and wait there, then go around the other side of it, come up behind him and smash him. With what? I needed a baseball bat or something. Had I seen a rake, a shovel, any such thing? I had to do it quick and hard before he had a chance to fire.

I stepped back carefully over the hose, heard a noise behind and to my right, a thud of a person bumping into something metal. That was Toni. She'd either hit something unwittingly or banged on something, probably the side of the washing machine, to attract him. And it was working. Just over on the right I saw an arm, a black mass moving across a black plane. Yes. He was over there, inching now in Toni's direction, so he'd heard her, was tracking her, moving in, ready to kill.

I reached out and my hand hit the post. I was closer to it than I thought, but that was okay. Now I knew where I was. I turned slightly. He was just out there, straight in front of me. Or he should be. I heard a slight shuffling noise. Toni? Him? I wasn't totally sure, couldn't see a blessed thing, but I couldn't risk letting him get too close to Toni. So I moved out, putting one foot forward, shifting my weight, lifting—

Something hard and cold jabbed into the side of my head, and a voice said, "I wouldn't move if I was you, asshole!"

My body froze as if it were a total muscle. That was a gun sticking right in my temple. I could feel it round and hard, wanting to explode into me, splatter the better part of me all over this cellar. Oh, Jesus. Why wasn't I at work discussing the pros and cons of digital garage-door openers?

"What the fuck are you after?" demanded my would-be assassin, standing there in the darkness next to me.

"I. . . . I . . ."

I thought I knew that voice, but I didn't know what to do, what to say, because he was waiting for just the right moment to squelch my life, and I was sure that moment was going to come very soon. I closed my eyes, bit down on the bitter, acidic bile creeping up the back of my throat. Oh, God. Toni, I cried silently, Toni, where are you?

My assailant grabbed me, his big thick hand seizing my upper arm, squeezing, and he ordered, "Speak up, asshole!"

Suddenly there were other footsteps. Toni? No. Someone bounding down the stairs, shouting, and then hitting the switch. The lights came on suddenly, the curtain thrown back.

"What the hell's going on?" shouted Lieutenant Jenkins, now entering the basement.

I felt the gun jerked from my head, and I spun away, stared at John, the caretaker, shouted, "Jesus Christ!"

John turned away, stood there, arm flaccid, pistol now aimed at the cold floor. He wouldn't look me in the eye, just stared off, shaking his head as if he'd failed badly at something.

"Sorry, I . . . I . . ."

"Didn't know it was us?" Toni grabbed me, pulled me farther away from him, and demanded, "Didn't you hear us in Liz's? Or did you and that's why you came down here?"

John's face blossomed a deep red, and he spun toward us, waved his gun, and said, "What the hell are you talkin' about? I . . . I came down here 'cause I heard a noise and I thought it might be the person who killed Chris and . . . and maybe your sister, too!"

"Yeah, right," countered Toni, eyeing him with distrust.

"Hey," said Jenkins, suddenly our savior, moving in, easing himself right between John and Toni and me, "just calm down. Everything's fine. Nothing happened."

I saw Toni's doubts creeping to the surface. John, the caretaker, who'd had complete access to both Chris and Liz's apartments and who seemed aware of our every action in this building. What was his real intention of cornering us down here in the dark? Having just felt John's wild rage and the gun at my temple, nothing seemed too outrageous a possibility.

Jenkins turned to Toni and me, ordered, "You two go upstairs and wait there."

I didn't like any of this. Being trapped and caught by John, and particularly being down here with Jenkins. What was the police lieutenant doing here anyway? Yes, we had to get away. Not just upstairs. We had to leave here, this basement, this building.

I took Toni by the arm, my grasp weak, still trembling with fear. "Come on."

"Alex, no, he—"

"Dammit!" I yelled.

She stared at me, realized shouting wasn't going to prove anything, and so the two of us turned, left John and Jenkins standing there in the basement. We were hurrying now, past the weights and the rusty washer and dryer, making for the stairs, escaping to the surface and safety. Ahead of me Toni pulled aside the curtain, but then I stopped and looked back. I had to clear my throat because my memory was so fresh with that imprint of gun upon temple and my vocal cords were still stretched hard and tight with fear.

"There's only one thing," I began. "Who locked Liz's apartment last night?"

Jenkins didn't get it, asked, "What?"

"We left the door wide open and you in there," I said to Jenkins. "There's a deadbolt. How'd you lock the apartment?"

"With a key, of course."

"Did you get one from Liz?"

He looked at me blankly, clearly taken off guard. "What?"

"Where'd you get the key?"

The lieutenant motioned toward John. "From him, what do you think?"

I stared at Jenkins, speechless. Of course. That made sense. Too much sense, actually, and as I rushed up that dark staircase, I thought there had to be more to this. And I wondered, they couldn't be in this together, could they, Jenkins and John? Then again, was there any reason why John, too, couldn't be a Dragon?

Chapter 26

We flew out of there, up those basement stairs, back through Liz's apartment, and out the front door, right out to the street. We didn't stop. Jenkins wanted us to stick around, but no way. All we could think of was getting the hell away from that building, so we rushed to my car, climbed right in, and were off. Jesus Christ, what had that big, lumbering John been trying to do? What did he think he could get away with? It was ridiculous, him shutting off the lights, cornering us down there.

As I pulled out, I felt as if I were shedding a layer of fear, stepping out of it and leaving it behind. Aside from a few near car accidents, I'd never been so close to death before, never had it so purposely pressed right up against my head. That I'd escaped was oddly exhilarating.

Next to me, Toni leaned back in her seat, put her hands over her forehead as if trying to keep the thoughts from exploding out of her, and said, "Oh, my God, my God. That jerk nearly blew your brains out. And what was Jenkins doing there? I mean, why'd he show up just then?"

"Good question."

I didn't want to return home. Not yet. When Jenkins found that we hadn't stayed at Liz's but left altogether, he'd probably

212

check my place, either call or stop by. So to avoid Jenkins, we drove to Café Wyrd, a coffeehouse in Uptown, a kind of hip little place with strong coffee, big windows, lots of tables. A perfect place for us to land. As we each ordered a double *au lait,* then sat by one of the windows overlooking Lake Street, I tried to pull back from the edge of danger to a more sane center. Toni looked lost. Her hair was hanging over her face; she kept running her hand through it, shaking her head.

"Never mind about John for right now," I said. "Who knows how he fits into all this, if at all. But if it was Jenkins who killed Chris, you know who he's going to go after next?"

She looked at me as if I were a complete moron. "What do you mean? Us, of course."

"No, I mean if he can't stop us, you know who he's going to try to stop us from talking to?"

She shook her head.

"Tyler. He's the only one from the Dragons that we can positively identify, and he's the only one who can finger Jenkins. I bet he's going to try to kill him, too, to keep him from squealing."

Toni nodded, took a sip of her *au lait.* "You're right."

It seemed logical, all this and what Jenkins would try to do next, and I went on. "Whatever that was all about back there in the basement, Jenkins has got to know we're on the defensive, that we'll be keeping our distance from him. So I wouldn't be surprised at all if he next went after Tyler—you know, just tried to quiet him real quickly."

"I wish to hell we'd found something back at Liz's, something to blackmail Tyler with." Eyes shifting as she schemed, Toni said, "Regardless, we have to talk to Tyler. We have to get him to tell us whatever he knows."

"Yeah, but he's dangerous."

"Of course he is. If we're careful, though, it's worth the risk. The only question is, how are we going to get him to meet with us?"

I took a sip of coffee. Film from Liz's camera. That would have been perfect. Or one of Liz's journals. Then again, did it really matter that we didn't have anything?

I gazed out the window, saw a pack of cars race from the suburbs and down the street into the city, and I said, "What if we just told Tyler we found something? What if we told him we found some film in Liz's camera and had it developed? Or we told him she took some pictures, mailed them out to be developed, and we found them in her mailbox? Pictures of him with the Dragons and some other revealing things? So we need to talk to him because if he tells us what he knows about a cop being one of the Dragons, then we'll be able to help him, steer the cops away."

"How about we just tell him that someone tried to kill us—the same guy who killed Chris and Liz—and now we think he's going after him, Tyler?" She looked anxiously hopeful. "That should do it, wouldn't you think?"

I nodded, took another sip of coffee, then said, "Actually, I do."

We talked about it some more, finished our coffees in plotting silence, and about half an hour later we were back at my place, only this time we were quite careful. We parked down the street, checked for both Jenkins and Tyler, and then hurried in the back entrance.

What could we have done differently? What other choice had we? I kept trying to think of other ways to handle this, but this way just seemed so logical and, in its own crooked method, so simple, the quickest means to an end. If only I'd thought of some other way. Would Toni still be alive? Would that gun never have been fired?

I was silent in thought, in hope, that some great voice would speak to me, call out from another world and another time with wise insights and soothing words. But nothing came. Had I lost that comfort, too? Had I been abandoned?

"No, I'm here," called my guardian, returning to duty. *"Just stay with the story, pull it like a thread and let it unravel. And avoid the rhetorical questions, they'll only confuse you."*

In my mind I closed that black hole of questions, sealed shut that horrible, wormy can. Toni and I were in my living room, we had discussed everything, and she was moving ahead with what we thought was our only choice. I looked up the number again, handed her the phone, and she dialed.

Into the receiver, Toni said, "Hi, is Rob Tyler there?" She glanced at me, smiled. Then: "Hi, Rob, this is Toni Domingo,

Liz's sister. Listen, please don't hang up." Then to make sure he wouldn't, she offered a well-baited hook. "I have to warn you about something—someone tried to kill us this morning and we think he's going to come after you next." Toni paused to listen to him, then tossed in the second hook with the rest of the bait, saying, "Listen, we know you're one of the Dragons. Liz had some pictures . . . she sent them out to be developed and we found them in her mailbox."

We needed to talk, too. That's what she told him. We had proof that he was one of them, that he was in danger, and also that the Dragons had been infiltrated by the police. Did he know that? Apparently not. I stood there, watching Toni nod and concentrate. I stood focused on her, trying to discern what Tyler was saying, if he was agreeing to it at all. Seconds later, she hung up.

"Well?" I asked.

"The good news is that he claims there is some stuff we should know." She tried not to smile. "The bad news is he says you're a pain in the ass. He'll meet me, but only alone."

"What? That's ridiculous. When?"

"Tonight at eight-thirty."

"Here?"

Toni shook her head. "No, at the Thirty-second Street Beach. Where's that?"

"On Lake Calhoun." This wasn't good. Not right. "I don't like this, Toni. You know how dangerous it'd be?"

It would be dark hours earlier, particularly by the lake because all the streetlights were up on the parkway, and the beach was down below. A row of thick trees and bushes was in between. The light would be dim at best. No, this wasn't good. There was lots going on down there, most of it dangerous, all of it murky, because it was difficult to find such a secluded and dark space in a city that was nothing but grid, grid, grid. Why in hell would he want to meet her there? So he could escape easily?

I said, "You have to call him back, pick another place, something public like a mall or a store."

"We don't have a choice, Alex. It's the only place he'll meet me. He said so."

"But—"

"We'll take precautions. I've some ideas, and besides you can wait nearby."

I was searching for a way to talk her out of it, keep her far from that spot. It was hopeless, though. Of course it was. We had to coax some truth, some sort of fact out of Tyler. How else could we do it?

The phone rang its shrill cry and I flinched, stared at the black thing sitting there on the table in the living room. One, two, three, four rings. After the fourth, my attention turned to the grayish box beneath it and on the next shelf down. My answering machine. As it clicked into gear, spit out my message, I glanced at Toni and we mirrored the same question: Jenkins?

The message ended, there was the perfunctory beep, and then a voice said, "Hi, this is Ed Dawson calling. It's about—"

I jumped forward, grabbed the phone. "Hi, this is Alex."

"How's everything?"

"I guess you could say very interesting. What's up?"

"I just wanted to let you know that I'm having a bit of trouble reaching my cousin, the one who's with the FBI. He's up north investigating some trouble at one of the casinos. I've left two messages, so he should be calling back very soon."

"Good."

I guessed that was good, anyway. I'd nearly forgotten all about that. Next to me, Toni was reaching out, wanting the phone.

I said, "Here, Toni wants to talk to you."

I handed her the receiver, she muttered greetings but did not mention—as I hadn't—our encounter that morning with Jenkins.

"Listen," she said, "I just spoke with Rob Tyler, and I'm going to meet him tonight at the thirty-second Street Beach. I think he's got some stuff to tell me, some useful stuff about Jenkins and maybe about Liz." Toni paused, then started shaking her head. "No, I don't want your cousin to come now. No FBI, no police. Not even Alex. He wants to meet me alone, that's the only way—" Toni paused, raised her voice. "Hello? Hello? Are you there?" She hesitated, then said, "Can you hear me now? Good. Well, there's not much else. We'll call you in the morning. Can your cousin meet us tomorrow?" Now she was nodding. "Good, okay. Yes, I'll be careful. Thanks."

She hung up, and looking at me, said, "That was weird. Right in the middle of the conversation the phone started clicking."

Paranoia rushed through me, and I went out on the sunporch and checked the street. Jenkins couldn't be up to anything, could he? My eyes swept the street, saw nothing.

Returning to the living room, I suggested, "Toni, maybe we should have Dawson's cousin come. He could hide in the bushes or . . . or . . ."

"Or bring a whole crew down there? No, we've got to leave him out of it."

"But what if Tyler goes after you?"

"He won't. I'll tell him you're nearby, that you're in some bushes watching."

"So what am I going to do if he does try to pull something, whip out a hankie and wave it?"

"No, I'll get some Mace." She leaned against the couch. "And I'll carry one of the walkie-talkies in my purse. That way you'll be able to hear everything. You'll know if something's wrong."

That wasn't a bad idea; it might work, but again it might not, and I said, "I don't know. This is way too dangerous. Maybe we should get the FBI involved."

"No, Alex, I don't want any FBI types bounding in and screwing this up. If we tell them what's going on, they could decide to play the super jocks and swoop down and arrest Tyler, and then Tyler might just shut up. We might never learn what he knows about Jenkins or Liz or even Chris."

I wanted to say that Toni was just being antimale and superfeminist, that she was just being pigheaded and selfish. But she was probably right. If we brought in Dawson's cousin, then he could decide to do things his way. The FBI could usurp our plan and we could lose control of it all.

"I suppose you're right," I reluctantly said. "Besides, if there was someone else down there, Tyler might catch on beforehand. He might spot an FBI sort and just not show up at all."

"Exactly."

I turned to her, crossed the living room, took her hand, said, "But I still think it sucks. I don't like this, I really don't."

"Oh, Alex." Toni leaned over, kissed me on the cheek. "Tyler could tell me something that might really help."

"Or he might really hurt you. What if it was him that killed Liz?"

"I know, but don't you see I've got to do this?"

Chapter 27

We decided to spend the rest of the day away from my house, away from the phone. The last thing we wanted was to confront Jenkins, or for Jenkins to stop us somehow from meeting with Tyler. So shortly after our conversation with Ed Dawson, Toni and I left for downtown, shopping for the few things we needed, then having a late lunch at the Skyroom at Dayton's. And when I called home well after four and checked the answering machine by remote, there were indeed messages from Jenkins.

"We need to talk."

That's what he said in the messages he left, all three of them. But there was no way we were going to return his call, initiate any kind of dialogue. The soonest I wanted to see him was tomorrow, and then only in the company of Dawson's FBI cousin.

All afternoon I carried a tight sensation in my gut, a feeling of dread; at first I thought I was incredibly hungry, but then I realized I was just incredibly nervous. I wanted to put the brake on all this, and I thought about doing exactly that as we aimlessly strolled Nicollet Mall and waited for the sun to set. I did nothing but stew, however, and by seven forty-five it was dark and we were just about ready to leave, so it was clear I'd missed my chance and there was no turning back. This was really going to happen, this meeting with Tyler, for I knew he was going to show up, just as I knew to expect the worst.

"Don't worry," said Toni, after we'd had yet another cup of coffee and it was finally time to go. "All the stuff we have will help."

Yes, the camera with the infrared film that we'd searched all around for, finally finding it in a camera shop on Hennepin Avenue. The walkie-talkies. We had those, and Toni had a new purse, a big, long one that hung from her shoulder. A bag big enough to conceal a walkie-talkie with a hard rubber antenna, and that was also thin enough so you could hear voices. If it all worked out, I'd be able to hear everything that Toni and Tyler were saying, I'd be able to capture their meeting on film, and if there was a problem I'd be able to come flying out of those bushes at a moment's notice.

"You got the Mace?" I asked as we walked to the car.

"Yep."

"You're going to carry it in your hand?"

"Yes, Dad."

We were going to be early, of course; that's the way we'd planned it, for us to arrive well ahead of time so that I could sink into the bushes, be close by but undetected by Tyler. It wasn't that far from downtown to Lake Calhoun, some fifteen minutes at most. I drove down Hennepin and past my neighbor-hood, skirted Uptown, crossed Lake Street, and then turned right on Thirty-second. It was such a nice neighborhood, the trees and all, the clapboard houses looking so midwestern sturdy, and it was odd to be creeping around like this in a place that looked so damn stable.

"Let me go first," I said, pulling over, shutting off the car. "The beach is right up there. See those steps?"

The street ended in a mass of bushes that were still fighting the spring chill to break into full bloom. Trees, too, a handful of them, that were also struggling to put forth summer leaves. Right in the middle of everything was a wood railing and con-crete steps leading down.

"You just go down the stairs and the beach is right at the

bottom," I continued. "There's a bench off to the left, by some trees—you can wait there. I'll go around to Thirty-first Street and sneak into some bushes on that side."

I glanced over at Toni, saw her nodding, getting it straight. A terrible sensation started clawing at my heart, and I wanted to lean over, hold her, tell her we had to stop, that this was stupid.

"Just keep focused on the details you need to see this time around."

This time around. Oh, Christ. This time around it had been so incredibly wonderful to see Toni. To understand Toni. To put Toni to rest.

"Yes, that's what all this is about—resolution."

I reached out, opened my arms, said, "Be really careful, all right?"

"I will be. Don't worry."

We embraced and kissed, her soft skin brushing my cheeks, and then our lips met, pressed together, and I sensed her warmth and wetness.

As I climbed out of the car, I said, "I'll be watching."

I shut the door of my Honda, started away, my mind loaded with worry, and the nylon gym bag hanging from my shoulder loaded with the camera and the walkie-talkie.

"Can you hear me?" came a muffled voice from the un-zipped gym bag.

I reached into the bag, hit a button on the walkie-talkie, and like a good Minnesotan said, "You betcha."

"Good, then these things work. Stay tuned. I'm putting the tape back on."

After that we said nothing. Which was what we'd agreed to, how we were going to handle it. We didn't want to attract any attention, least of all Tyler's, so we were going to be as cool as possible about the walkie-talkies. I was only to receive from Toni, and to make sure of that, we'd taped down the talk button on Toni's unit. She was going to leave the car, and we didn't want her fiddling with any buttons, for it was possible that Tyler would see her early, and we most certainly didn't want to alert him to my nearby presence. That was our best college thinking, anyway, though it did mean that it would be impossible for me to reach her.

So I headed north on James, walking along through the cool spring night like I was just an ordinary joe out for an evening walk, and then cut over on Thirty-first Street. It was pretty much the same here—the road ended and there were the same bushes and trees, and the same kind of stairs. I descended the concrete steps, and before me the oval Lake Calhoun spread out, bordered on one side by the lights of Lake Street, the rest dotted with lampposts. The waters gently poked at the shores. A calm evening. At the bottom of the stairs I glanced to the right and saw the lights surrounding the stucco boathouse, which would soon be smelling of little but popcorn and engulfed by nothing but sunbathers. I turned a sharp left, continued along the edge of the bike path.

From the gym bag I heard a slamming noise. A car-door–closing noise. At first the bang made my heart jolt, but then I heard footsteps. So Toni was on her way. Here we go, I thought.

Up ahead, near the beach, I thought I saw a figure. Or was it a tree? No, that was a person. Tyler? No. There were two people there, walking along, out for an evening walk, proceeding down the pedestrian path, gabbing about life. Yes, a man and a woman walking briskly, probably doing the whole lake, three-some miles. Real Minneapolitans, out for a spin around the lake, such a tradition here, these two not waiting for brazen summer, just a night when there wasn't snow and ice. And not suspecting a thing. Not realizing that anyone could be in danger down here tonight. As they walked along, their arms flapped, tongues blathered, gabbing while Toni was stepping right into trouble.

I stepped off the path, moved up against the edge of the bushes, blended my shadow into the leaves. Once the people were gone, I moved on toward the stairs from Thirty-second Street, nearing the beach with every step. I paused once, lifted the gym bag to my ear, heard Toni's steps. So far, no problems.

Again up ahead I noticed a shaft of darkness. I slowed, then stopped, pulled over, stepped into the bushes. The stairs were just another thirty feet or so ahead, and that odd figure or shadow lingered maybe a hundred feet away. Then vanished. Nothing. Only darkness. Oh, Christ, had Tyler plotted the way we had, had he salt-and-peppered this dark area with Dragons? I paused in fearful thought. If that wasn't Tyler or any part of his group, then who could have been scoping this murky part of the park?

My heart began to bubble, to roll like I'd had too much coffee. I turned toward the lake, saw nothing but a flat sheet of black, then pressed deeper into the bushes. I put the gym bag down on some leaves, took out the walkie-talkie, lifted it to my ear. Steps. Toni's, of course. I heard them through the little speaker, and then I heard them for real. She was right there now, right at the top of the stairs. I peered through the leaves, caught sight of her, watched as she began her way down, one gritty step at a time. As she descended into the park, I looked around, saw the pale sands of the beach, the water, and the empty guard stand, that tower-monument of the summer months. But no one else.

Wait. I heard pounding steps, heavy breathing. I stood up in the bushes. Jesus, was someone coming after her already? No. A jogger. I saw him, brief nylon shorts, light jacket, breath puffing, steaming slightly into the April air. He pounded by, and disappeared, a misfired threat zinging through the night.

So now again there was just Toni and perhaps that other shadow, the one I'd seen but lost. Toni was at the bottom of the stairs, crossing first the bike path and next the pedestrian path as she headed for the beach. I kept the walkie-talkie pressed to my ear, and reached down, lifted out her camera, looped the strap over my head. Then popped the lens cap, lifted the camera to my eye. Squinted and saw nothing. Total blackness. Toni said it would probably be that way, that I probably wouldn't be able to see a thing through the viewfinder, but that was okay. At such short notice, we couldn't find an infrared lens, only the film, but that would work, she'd assured me. All I had to do was point it in the general direction, set the focus on infinity, and shoot. The film would pick up the images. Well, she'd said, perhaps just the naked skin—the faces, the hands. Perhaps not the clothing, but for our purposes that would be good enough. In case there was trouble, we just wanted to have some pictures. Proof positive. In case Tyler went ballistic, in case there were any other Dragons, in case . . . ?

I lowered the camera, peered out there. Yes. Toni. There she was. I saw her shadow going toward the beach, skirting the sand, and moving nearer to the bench. The one right over by those two trees. She went there, just as we had discussed. I both saw her and heard her via the walkie-talkie. The swish of her. The breathing of her.

Wait. Down there, to the left and behind Toni. Oh, shit. What was that? Who was that? There it was again, that shadow I'd seen and lost. The figure of a woman? Possibly. Or wait, could that be Tyler? It shouldn't be. Not yet. We were early. He wasn't due here for at least another ten minutes. I didn't like this. Toni was sitting on the bench, the figure, the person, behind her and unseen. I wanted to warn Toni, tell her to turn around, someone was back there, but there was no way I could get any kind of warning to her without blowing my presence.

I glanced back. What? My heart seized, then charged. That shadow was gone again. I scanned the park, the short wintry grass, the bushes and trees. No one. Nothing. Not good. Definitely not good. The time dripped by. Minutes later, squinting, tilting it to catch what little light there was, I checked my watch. Anytime now. If Tyler were actually going to show, it could be any moment. I trembled. Any moment, too, I feared the serenity of this park would explode into disaster.

I looked through the park, saw a tall figure coming down the pedestrian path, smoking a cigarette. A lone, thin man. Tyler. He was coming from Thirty-fourth, so he must have parked near there, and now he was walking along quite normally as if he were just a normal guy out for a normal stroll along the lake. I spotted him, recognized him at once, his presence unforgettable after that night he'd jumped me in Liz's apartment.

Over the walkie-talkie I heard rustling, saw Toni now turning, studying, then realizing that, yes, it was Tyler. She stood, moved around to the edge of the bench, stopped there, and I only hoped she had the Mace in hand. As he neared, I rose slowly, tried to get a clearer view. My hand clutched the camera, ready to lift it, shoot picture after picture, and capture him on film.

I heard her voice over the walkie-talkie as Toni said, "Hi, I'm glad you came. I don't want any trouble, I just want to talk about a couple of things."

"Yeah, well . . ."

His voice was faint, barely audible at first, but then he drew closer. At the same time, I could see him slightly better, too. And the orange glow of his cigarette—it was bright and clear as he sucked on it long and slow.

"What the fuck's this all about?" he demanded.

"I need your help."

"What do I look like, the Red Cross?"

"Look it, I know you're a member of the Dragons."

"I don't belong to the Masonic dicks if that's what you're talking about."

"Don't bullshit me, Tyler. I know more than you think, and we're both in trouble."

"So?"

"Listen, you have to help me. I know you broke into Liz's apartment and stole her journal. She wanted to write an article about the Dragons, so you took what she'd written. You searched her entire apartment, checked everything, and you were sure you got it all. Only you forgot to look in one place— her mailbox. She'd taken pictures of the Dragons, yourself included, and she'd sent them away to be processed. That's where we found them, right in there with all her mail."

You're coming on too fast, Toni, I thought. Too hard. Back off. I could hear the anger in her voice. All the frustrations and pain of Liz's death. It was all there in her words. But she was pushing him too hard. Or was she? When she paused, Tyler said nothing and his silence confirmed it all. Yes, it had been him. Yes, he had stolen her journal. He was making that abundantly clear by not refuting anything.

Finally he said, "I didn't have nothing to do with your sister. We had a couple of fights, sure, but it wasn't me who killed her."

"Then who? John, the caretaker?"

"That dork? Fuck if I know."

"Jenkins?"

"Who the fuck's that?"

"A cop—a detective actually. He's the one coming after you."

"What the—"

"Don't bullshit me, Tyler. He's a Dragon, he's one of you guys, you know that."

"What the fuck are you—"

That was the last thing I heard. The last thing Tyler said, because right then an explosion ripped the park. Shit. Was that a car backfiring? Fireworks? Oh, my God, Jesus Lord, no. That was a gunshot. I rushed out of the bushes, dashed out onto the bike path. Was that Tyler, was he firing at Toni? No, God, no. The two of them were bending over, ducking. Someone was firing at them. But who? And from where?

I turned toward Thirty-fourth Street, spotted a figure charging through the dark and toward them. Who was it? I couldn't tell. Couldn't even discern if it was a man or a woman, let alone recognize a face. But I did see an outstretched hand that presumably held a gun.

"Toni!" I screamed. "Toni, look out!"

I shouldn't have shouted because she turned toward me, looked for my help, and didn't see the assailant. Didn't see that shadow charging them, and because of that she didn't bend over, didn't run the right way or duck behind the bench or run behind the tree, and oh, shit. Another shot. The attacker was running at them, the gun aimed right at them both.

"Toni!"

Yet another shot. This time I saw the blast from the gun. The orangeish explosion that burst from the tip of the pistol. And that's when I saw her going down, falling because one of those bullets had struck her and blown her off her feet. I dropped everything—camera, walkie-talkie—and ran, my body pumping, feet tearing into ground, arms pulling at air, at nothing, wanting only to be there now. Toni was down, tumbled on the ground, and I had to reach her, help her, protect her from that dark figure who was charging closer and closer.

"No!" I cried as I tore across the paths, across the beach, feet sinking horribly into thick sand that wanted to grab me, hold me.

Toni was lying motionless, and Tyler was running, streaking toward the bushes, the woods, fleeing like a deer into darkness. And the assassin was shrieking and yelling, racing after Tyler, waving the gun, trying to take aim, wanting to kill Tyler now that Toni was down. Going after him. Chasing him into the bushes.

Toni! I raced across the grass, past the trees, and there she was, my Toni, my college sweetheart, a pile of nothing on the ground, collapsed right there by the bench. I fell to my knees, skidded across the ground, touched her, reached for her.

"Toni, where? Where are you hurt?" I was begging, at first afraid to touch her. "Toni, can you hear me? Toni!"

She didn't respond, didn't move or make any sort of noise. I took her by the shoulder. Oh, God. I touched her, at first didn't see it all. The blood. Black like oil. It curled around from the side of her head, over her ear, down her neck, onto the ground, and into a puddle because she'd been hit, shot, right there in the temple. I clutched her then. Grabbed her and shook her, screamed her name: Toni! But there was nothing. Only emptiness. An empty body. Her eyes were open, unblinking, staring into the night, and I took her into my lap and wrapped my arms around that warm body, spilling blood all over me and the ground. Sobbing. I was sobbing, holding her, wanting to keep her here in this world with me or close by, whatever. But not there, beyond. I couldn't let her go there because she'd never come back.

I heard quick, desperate steps, saw her killer now trotting from the bushes, across the grass, straight toward me. Had there been another shot? Was Tyler dead? I didn't know, hadn't noticed a blast, but I didn't care about Tyler or what was going to happen to me. That was pretty obvious. The gun. That hand. Both pointing toward me. Both indicating it was my turn, I was next chosen, this would be an easy execution.

I saw him, recognized him, shouted, "You fucking bastard, you killed her!"

Before he could kill me, though, I was suddenly silenced and Toni's killer frozen by a bright light. A beam of whiteness burst out of the blackness, aimed at us both, and shot down my words.

"Police!" shouted a voice out there behind the light.

Toni's murderer halted in fear, stopped right then and there, said, "Hey, wait, I'm—"

"No, don't listen to him!" I screamed at the cop behind the flashlight. "He killed her, he shot her!"

"What? No, I—"

The policeman boomed: "Drop your weapon and put your hands on your head!"

He balked, frozen there in the blinding light. "Wait, you don't—"

"Now! Drop your weapon now!"

And the gun tumbled from Lieutenant Jenkins's right hand, hitting the cool April ground with a soft thud.

Chapter 28

Leaning against the balcony door, staring out at the fading sky and Lake Michigan, I took a deep breath, said, "If only it had been that simple."

Behind me on the recliner, I heard Maddy sniffling. I glanced back, saw my sister pushing up her Beverly Hills sunglasses, mopping her eyes with the back of her hand.

"There's more, isn't there?" she asked.

"Of course. That was only the start. Everything got really screwed up after that."

Before me the lake was flat and calm, a throbbing blue, and I looked to the west, saw the last of the brilliant sun slipping away. I'd broken free from my trance, leaped into the present, but it didn't fit, this island, this lake, this sunset. Hard to believe that I was here when everything—Toni's murder, the month of April—wasn't ages but only a few minutes in the past. Perhaps Maddy was right. Perhaps now and then weren't really all that far apart.

I took a deep breath, wished I was a smoker, wished that I could be sucking on a cerebral cigarette, asked, "Shall I go on?"

"Absolutely."

I started pacing, started talking, letting the beginning of

the end come out as quickly and effortlessly as if I were still in hypnosis. I told Maddy about that kid, the child policeman, the young guy who looked like he barely shaved and who was with the park police and who didn't even carry a gun, but who had a booming voice and the balls to carry it off, to get Jenkins to surrender like that. He was the one that shone the light on Jenkins. Next, this child cop radioed for an ambulance, which soon came screaming through the night and into the park. Toni was dead, of course. They checked me, too, because of the blood I had all over me. That was Toni's blood, though. I was okay. Unhit.

Okay except for Jenkins. That pig. That idiot. The cops, a whole bunch of them, were there minutes later, too. And Jenkins kept saying how this was nuts, he hadn't done anything. He'd been called down here, someone had left a message at the office, asked him to meet down here, and that's when he'd heard the shots. He hadn't fired at Toni, he claimed. Someone else had. He'd heard the shots, come running, and had fired his gun at someone else, someone in the bushes.

"That's when I went nuts," I said to my sister. "I started screaming, 'Liar! He's lying! I saw him shoot her!'"

"But Jenkins denied it?"

"Over and over, which only made me shout louder and faster. It worked, I guess, because they arrested him, cuffed him and everything, then stuffed him in a squad car."

"What about Tyler?"

"I was sure they'd find his body over in the bushes, his brains blasted out, but they didn't. He disappeared, not a trace of him." I took a deep breath, pushed on. "Then all the legal stuff started, the depositions and all the cops and detectives and everyone trying to figure out what happened, who and why. It was a mess, really. Jenkins denied it all along. Said I was wrong, wrong, wrong. Nobody believed him, though. Not at first, anyway. Everyone believed me and the child cop who'd seen Jenkins standing there with the gun. So they held Jenkins and posted a high bail. I told them all the stuff about the Dragons. I wanted to get the knife into Jenkins good and deep. So I went into detail about the Dragons and how Toni and I had gone out to the St. Croix and taken the pictures. And I told them about what happened in the basement, you know with John and how Jenkins had been there."

"Go on."

"Well, in the beginning everyone believed me. They brought in John, questioned him, too, but then things started to change. They found the pictures Toni and I had taken out on the St. Croix, and they studied them and it really was Jenkins down there with the Dragons, but he was undercover, it came out. An undercover Dragon, so to speak. He'd been investigating the disappearance of those four women, and so he'd infiltrated the Dragons, tried to learn what they were all about. It was all substantiated, recorded, filed, and approved, too. Okay, so he wasn't a Dragon, not a real one."

Then, I explained to Maddy, Jenkins continued to claim he'd come down to Lake Calhoun because he'd gotten some mysterious message at the office and he was worried about us, Toni and me. It turned out there really was such a message—another officer had taken it—although I was sure it was planted. But the thing that really screwed up everything, that got Jenkins released, was the autopsy. They sliced up Toni, the thought of which made me ill for days, and they carved that bullet out of her head, and it fucking didn't match. It came from a different gun, they said. I can't remember what kind of gun they said it was fired from, but it clearly and definitely was not the gun belonging to Detective Tom Jenkins.

"It was awful, Maddy." I started pacing, passing the window, circling Maddy on the recliner, moving, shaking, trembling. "After that everyone began to question my story. The cops, I mean. It was like they were determined to prove one of their own was innocent, and so they made me go over and over it, wondering if I hadn't gotten something wrong, if I hadn't missed something. They grilled me, interrogated me, you know, like they were the goddamned Gestapo. They started picking apart everything I said, then finding holes, or so they claimed. Something about the sequence of hearing the shots, seeing the shots. And where everyone was, how it all happened, how Toni fell."

"I remember when all that was going on. You called me—you sounded terrible, so depressed."

"I was a wreck."

I was a wreck, I explained, because it was impossible this possibility that they brought up about there being someone else down there. Someone else who in fact killed Toni. That was their theory, and the thing that complicated it further was that Tyler disappeared. Totally, absolutely. He vanished, so there was no one to substantiate or corroborate my story. Tyler was gone; he'd left the city, the state, maybe the country. The last I saw of that guy was him tearing for the bushes. They never found his body over there or even any blood, so he wasn't hit. He ran into those bushes down by the lake, got clean away, and he just didn't stop running. The cops said they checked his house, his friends, the College of Art and Design, but found nothing. Not a trace of Rob Tyler.

It was my word against Jenkins's, and so they kept pushing this investigation and pretty soon, after a month or so, they dropped the charges against Jenkins. Dropped everything, said there was significant lack of proof. The fuckers. The goddamned police watching out for the goddamned police. Something was wrong, I knew it. The main thing that got Jenkins off was the bullet thing, how it didn't match his gun.

"That's when I started thinking, wondering. I mean, that's all I did, just sat around and tried to figure it out."

"And what did you come up with?" asked Maddy, still lying flat on the recliner.

"I think someone in the police force was covering for Tyler."

"Are you serious?"

"Yeah, I think someone switched the bullets. You know, maybe it was bullshit, this thing about Jenkins infiltrating the Dragons. Maybe he was really one of them. And maybe there was someone in the police force who was also a real Dragon. So this other person, well, after the coroner pulled the bullet from Toni, well, maybe this other person took that bullet and left another. You know, switched them so they wouldn't match." I paused, stopped, looked down at Maddy. "It's either that or . . . or . . . Well, what do you think, Maddy? You've got an idea, don't you?"

"Go ahead, finish. Or what?"

"Or Tyler and Jenkins were in it together from the start.

You know, they could have both been Dragons, and they might have tricked us, Toni and me. If it was like that, Tyler could have told Jenkins about the meeting down at the lake, so Jenkins would have been waiting for Toni. And after he shot her, you know when Jenkins ran after Tyler, well, maybe he ran after him and instead of shooting him, he switched guns with Tyler. He could have given the real murder weapon to Tyler, who then disappeared, all according to plan." I caught my breath, returned to the recliner, sat on the edge of it, stared at my sister, said, "It's got to be something like that, don't you think?"

She lay quite still, then started shaking her head. "No, not necessarily. Sure, Jenkins could have killed Toni, but why not you, too? He knew you were both together, so why wouldn't he have gone after you both?"

"Because that kid cop came and stopped him just before he was going to shoot."

"But Jenkins couldn't have been sure you both were there. Toni had promised to come alone, so why would Jenkins have killed her then? That would have possibly meant leaving you alive to talk, to point fingers, which you nobly did." As if this were all a parlor game, Maddy lightly said, "No, if Jenkins intended to kill Toni I'm certain he would have been absolutely sure to kill you, too."

I hung my head, rubbed my forehead with one hand, pulled at my hair, replied, "That's what I keep coming back to. It's the one thing that doesn't make any sense." I burst to my feet again, started pacing. "Well, if Jenkins wasn't involved, then what about John? Maybe he was a Dragon and maybe Tyler planted him in the bushes. It could've been him who fired the other gun. Shit, I don't know. Maybe that's all wrong. It could've been him, though. Maybe John was just a crazy caretaker who was fixated on the women in his building. He had a key to both Liz's and Chris's apartments, he could've gotten in and killed them both."

Pondering a thought out loud, Maddy slowly said, "What about Laura?"

I studied my sister, wondered if there was something more she was trying to get at, said, "Yeah, I've thought about her, too. She'd been in Minneapolis earlier that day, and I suppose she could've followed us to the park. But was Laura that angry

at Toni; I mean, could she have hated her enough to shoot her?
And where the hell is she now? I've written to her, tried to find
her, but no luck."

This was going to make me nuts, push me over the edge.
I had all this information and I kept circling and circling, but
couldn't find the real truth to land on. I eyed my sister lying
there, lounging on that recliner, then gazed out at the blue-
black lake.

"Okay, Maddy, out with it."

"Out with what?"

"Damm it, Maddy, stop playing games with me!" I shouted,
spinning around, staring at her. "You know something."

"Alex, when did you start using such bad language?"

"Maddy, what the hell is it? Did Toni tell you something at
Liz's funeral? Do you know something about Liz that I don't?"
Suspecting something more devious, I asked, "What do you
know about Laura?"

Maddy lay there, put her hands on either side of her
glasses, pushed her glasses up on her nose, then massaged
her temple. Took a deep breath. Then she reached down to
her left wrist and checked her watch.

"Well," she began, "there is something I haven't told you.
But I'm hungry, and—"

"Maddy!"

"Alex, it's going on eight-thirty, and I'm starved. Solange
left some sandwiches in the refrigerator. Let's go downstairs
and get something to eat and I'll tell you everything."

"Jesus Christ!"

"Oh, Alex, stop it. Relax. I'm going to be open with you."

I took a deep breath, looked at my granite-willed sister.
"Promise?"

"Absolutely."

I knew, of course, that I was a fool to believe her, but she'd
always been able to sucker me. Like when we were kids, she
used to pretend she was dying, get all gaspy and roll on the
ground, and she'd beg me to say good-bye to Mom and Dad. I
went for it five or six times, but then I learned. I knew better,
or so I'd thought, because then she'd swear this time it was for
real, that she really was dying. She pulled that another five times
or so, me eventually falling for it each time. It was the meanest

thing she ever did to me, that dying routine, so why did I feel like she was doing that to me now? What was in her voice that reminded me of back then?

"Come on, Alex," she said, pushing herself up. "I'm starved, aren't you?"

I was. Famished. But I wasn't about to admit it.

"All right, but I want to hear it all."

"You will." She reached out baronesslike, hand slightly draped, waiting for me to take it. "Help me, will you?"

I skipped that crap, the hand stuff, went right for her body, asserting my power and strength by wrapping one arm around her waist, the other under her legs and lifting her entirely off the recliner, then settling her into the wheelchair. It startled her, I could see that in her face, could feel it as she wrapped her arms around my neck. Okay, I was trying to say, no more Big Sister, Little Brother shit. Got it? Then without asking, I started to push because I wanted to be in control, wanted to make it clear that she couldn't get away with it now, that she was going to have to tell me whatever it was she knew.

"Oh, Alex, the doors. They're still open. Would you shut them, please?"

I hesitated but didn't let go of the back of the wheelchair. What was she doing, trying to prove that it was she who was really in control? I glanced back at the door, tall and wide. She was right. If it stormed, the rain would come pouring in here, so I went over, closed the doors, locked them tight. Then I returned to the wheelchair, started to push again.

"I can do it," said Maddy.

"I've got you."

I said it flatly, blankly, as if she had no choice, and she was quiet, didn't say a thing as we passed around the Tiffany dome and the skylight above it, as we passed out of this huge room, through the door, and back into the rear wing of the attic. In the smaller room, there was only one light, a dim, naked one in the middle of the ceiling, and dressers and chairs, all draped with dingy, dusty sheets.

"Solange left some cold steak sandwiches and some gazpacho, too, I think," said Maddy. "She makes the best gazpacho—nice and spicy but not too acidy."

It irked the hell out of me the way she was talking and

everything. So lightly. I didn't care if there was caviar waiting
for us. I just wanted to get this over with, so I said nothing
because I knew I couldn't hide my frustration and anger. I just
pushed on and around the abandoned furniture, around the
boxes of junk, and back toward the hall that led to the elevator.
As I pushed Maddy around the last of the stuff and toward that
hall, however, her hands dropped to the wheels of her chair.

"Wait a minute, Alex," she said, braking. "Speaking of windows, there's another one back here that's open. I've been
meaning to get Alfred up here to shut it but I keep forgetting.
Would you?"

I felt all of me tighten with frustration, said, "Maddy, cut
it—"

"Please, Alex. A bunch of pigeons got in last week. I'm sure
they came in through there."

I took a deep breath, forced myself to be patient just a few
more minutes, said, "Where?"

"Over there in that corner bedroom."

She took over, wheeling herself some ten, fifteen feet over
to a back corner bedroom, one of the servants' rooms, long
abandoned. I followed, looked in, saw an old bird's-eye maple
dresser, a sink in one corner, a wicker rocking chair, and pigeon
shit. A whole lot of it on the floor.

She stopped at the doorway, pointed to the back, saying,
"I think it's the rear window. The one way back. There's a
sconce right up on the left, isn't there?"

I stepped into the room, did indeed see a sconce, a tar-
nished brass one with a dangling chain, and said, "What, do
you have this whole house memorized?"

"Just about."

But when I pulled on the chain, nothing happened. I
pulled again. Nothing, burned out.

"Is the bulb no good?" she asked.

"There's enough light."

I moved on, pushing past an old TV stand, two or three
mattresses, some boxes, and back toward the window. When I
reached it, though, I found the window completely shut.

"It's okay, Maddy," I called back. "The thing's all—"

Behind me I heard something creak and slam. I turned
around. The door was shut.

I called, "Maddy? Maddy, what is it?"

I started hurrying, bumping into all that old furniture and all those boxes. Oh, my God. Was it the wind? Or someone else? A stranger? Maddy wouldn't do something like this; so was someone else here as I had once suspected? A rush of panic swept me. Was Maddy in danger?

"Maddy!" I shouted. "Maddy, are you all right?"

I tipped over a lamp, heard something crash beside me, then pawed past the mattresses. Ran to the door. But it was stuck. Or locked? I heard someone fiddling with keys. God, no. It wasn't the wind at all. I tugged on the door. The thing was locked tight.

"Maddy, Maddy! Are you all right? What happened? What's going on? Maddy, speak to me!"

I tugged on the door, then beat on it, my fists slamming against the heavy door. Oh, shit. My sister. She was out there. Alone.

I screamed, "Maddy, are you okay?"

Just on the other side of the door I heard sniffling, then I heard keys jingling, jangling. I froze, was silent, heard nothing except the pounding of my own heart. I was just about to tear into the door again when someone spoke.

"I'm sorry, Alex," said Maddy, her voice low and quiet, just on the other side of the door. "Really, I am."

"Maddy, what the hell's going on?"

"I'm sorry, but I have to do this. I started something and I have to finish it."

"What are you talking about?" I stood there in the dark, shaking my head, clenching my fists. "Maddy, listen to me. Open the door."

"No, I can't."

"Maddy!" I screamed, and kicked the door, its frame, the wall.

But the damn door and everything else were as solid as the rest of the house. I didn't even make a dent in the wood, didn't even cause a crack or a fissure.

"Alex, believe me, I'm sorry. You're just going to have to stay in there for a while. I locked the door itself and then there's a padlock, too. I know how heavy the door is—it's solid oak. You can't get out."

What was this? What was going on? Had my wonderful sister, my filthy rich sister, gone totally nuts? Had her long years of blindness and the recent years of paralysis finally cracked her? Quite possibly. I'd never understood how she could bear it, that darkness and lack of movement. So what was she doing? Why would she need to lock me up?

I caught my breath, forced myself to speak as slowly as possible, my voice nonthreatening, coaxing, saying, "What's the matter, Maddy? What's all this about? Come on, open up the door and let's talk about it." I heard her crying, not a lot, just slightly. "Maddy? Maddy, speak to me!"

"It's all my fault, Alex. All of it—Toni and Liz, I mean."

"What? Come on, don't be silly. That's impossible."

"No, it's not. It's not at all. It's my fault they're dead—Chris, too—so I have to finish it, you see. You'll understand later. Later it'll all make sense."

"Maddy, don't leave me up here! You can't do this!"

"I have to. I don't want you hurt, too. If everything goes all right, I'll be back in an hour or so. Just stay put and stay quiet. This is my business. There's nothing you can do. In any case, Alfred and Solange will be back in the morning."

My God. She had this all planned out. Whatever she was doing, she had plotted and calculated it all. That's why she'd sent them away, Alfred and Solange, so she could lock me up, so she could proceed with . . . with what? I had this horrible notion. Dear God, this couldn't be connected to one of Maddy's former patients from Chicago, could it?

"Maddy?" I called, pounding on the door. "Don't go! Don't leave me! Maddy, what's this all about? What's going on? Maddy!"

"Alex, remember when I asked for your help on something? Remember? Well, you already helped me. I just want you to know that. I wanted your help on something very important, and you did that. You may not know it, but you helped me a lot. Thanks, Little Brother."

"Quit that shit, would you!" I heard the squeak of her chair, the rolling movement, and I pounded and yelled, "Maddy!"

Angrily, she snapped, "Stop it, Alex! There's nothing you can do. I'm not letting you out, so just be quiet and wait there. It's between Toni's killer and me now."

I was still. "What are you talking about?"

"I figured it out yesterday, who killed Toni, I mean. And Liz and Chris, too. You said something in trance, brought a piece of information to the surface, and I knew. So I sent for the killer and that person's on the way here right this minute—should be here in a half hour or so."

"Maddy, what are you talking about?" Could she be serious? "Maddy, listen, if you really did do something like that, that person's dangerous as hell. A lot of people have been killed. Maddy, do you hear me? Maddy? Maddy!"

"Love you."

Then there was nothing, only the gentle rolling of her chair, the sound of her hand touching the wall as she felt her way along it, next, the hum and clanging of the elevator as Maddy boarded it and closed the gates and rode it from the third floor down to some unknown fate below.

"Maddy!" I yelled as I kicked and banged on the door, but she was right. There was no way in hell I was going to bust out of here.

Chapter 29

I stopped kicking and banging against the door about ten minutes later, having had a veritable temper tantrum, the likes of which I hadn't had since I was a kid. It wasn't simply that the truth of Toni's murder seemed to be slipping away. Or that I'd been tricked and locked in here. No. If what Maddy had told me was the truth, then my big sister, the person I was closest to in the world and whom I adored more than anyone, was in a shitload of trouble.

I was sweaty and breathing hard, standing there in the dark until I backed up, dropped into the wicker rocker. What had Maddy done? Had she flipped out, gone totally crazy? How could she possibly be bringing Toni's murderer here? Could she have somehow lured that person to her island? The very thought of it was, pumping me with anxiety. If it was Jenkins, he'd have a gun, and how was a blind, paraplegic woman like Maddy going to defend herself from someone like that? Or what if it was Tyler? What if Maddy had found him—what would a wacko like that do to my sister? What if it were both of them, Jenkins and Tyler? My God. What if they were bringing along a handful of Dragons? Would they mutilate her in some way, make her their sacrifice of the month? And what was I supposed to do up here, just listen to her screams, if indeed I could hear them way up in this hidden chamber? Dragons. I envisioned them overrunning the island, murdering Maddy, later killing me, ruining this house, perhaps torching it, then tomorrow murdering Alfred and Solange. What would the outside world ever know, and why in hell had I asked for the dogs to be penned up?

My head was bursting with worry, the worry sweating out my pores, and I leaped up, charged the door, kicked it, screamed yet again, "Maddy!"

But of course there was no response. Only the doorknob banging as it dropped to the floor because I'd just succeeded in busting it off. Wonderful. Now what?

The room was gray with the last of the day's light, and I turned, saw that back window, the one Maddy had tricked me into checking. Just maybe, I thought as I hurried to the window, beat open the latch with my fist, jerked it up. If you can't get out the usual way, you find another, and so I stood back, gave the screen window a kick. It went flying out, gracefully soaring through the air, into the night, and to the ground some fifty feet below. I leaned out as far as I could. The back of the house was flat, a sheer wall of white clapboard.

I desperately hurried to the other window, pushing past the mattresses, clambering over some boxes. There was a light curtain on it, a tattered old thing, and I ripped it down, hammered my fist against the latch, and lifted up the window. Kicked out this screen window, too. Peering out, I saw about three feet of roof, then a huge old copper gutter.

I hung on to the window frame, leaned around. The elevator tower was there, half of it sticking into the side of the house and the roof, the rest of it protruding. Between that tower and this dormer was a small valley about two feet wide, just wide enough for me to crawl into, yet narrow enough to keep me from slipping right out.

I looked to the ground below, thought, What choice do I have? I clung to the inside of the window frame, lifted my left foot up and out the window, then pushed down on the copper gutter, heard it creak and moan. Still clutching the window, I put more weight on my left foot, found the gutter still true, and so I slowly, carefully swung my right foot out the window and into the air. I glanced over my shoulder, down at the ground. There was no way I'd survive a fall from here.

My hands clinging to the window frame, I inched along. Had to move over about a foot, then pull myself up through that little valley between the elevator tower and the dormer. I couldn't turn back, I knew, and so I let go of the window, threw myself against the elevator tower, and then I was desperately clawing at clapboard and trim. Somehow I was moving up. Not much. I caught my breath, pushed on, and the rest went quickly. Within seconds I was crawling past the green copper dome atop the elevator tower and on up to the next part of the roof, the top section, which flattened into a much gentler slope.

I paused again, pushed myself up slightly. Atop that copper dome was a huge spear of a lightning rod, to my right an enormous vent. One chimney back here. A red brick one in the middle of the house. Yet another chimney, a very big one, up where the roof rose again above the main section of the house. Right, I thought. Up there and underneath that part of the roof was the gymlike attic room, Maddy's trance room, and the Tiffany dome. All under that swell of the roof.

I crawled to the very peak of the roof, then straddled it, sat for a moment, then dared to stand. I was above treetop level, and the wind was fresh, not too strong. The view incredible. The lake seemed to stretch forever into the darkness, a freshwater sea that swelled and rocked, and way out there sailed a tanker or freighter, lights strung along it like a huge party boat. Behind me a long stretch of white light rode the horizon. The Mackinac Bridge? Yes, probably. While in front? The small city of Petoskey. Sure. Something caught my eye and I gazed straight up, saw swirls of yellow and red throb and rush, pulse and fade. The northern lights, dancing away in heaven while we poor slobs struggled down below.

But I couldn't linger, and I caught my breath, tried to think of what next, where next. I was on the roof, but how was I going to get down from here? Were there any ladders, anything perhaps permanently attached? Or a trapdoor, some way for repairmen or chimneysweeps to get up here? I turned, scanned the back part of the house. No, nothing that I could see, not near here, anyway, so I turned, started making my way along the peak of the great house, my arms outstretched as if I were traversing a tightrope.

Off to my left, toward shore, I heard an engine, then saw the lights of a boat. It was a good-sized pleasure boat, actually a speedboat that could easily handle Lake Michigan. Oh, please, I thought, let it be Alfred and Solange. Perhaps they'd changed their minds, decided to return for the night after all. I scurried along, came to the main part of the house, where the roof ran the other way, like the top part of a capital T. The roof was higher there, too, rising perhaps another twenty feet. Undaunted, I bent over, and on my hands and knees scrambled up, hurried past the skylight above the Tiffany dome and all the way to the main chimney, a big red-brick affair that flared out at the top. I took hold of the edge of the chimney, which was easily two feet taller than me, and pulled myself up. My clothes rustled in the wind, and I was momentarily filled with an enormous rush of power, of superiority.

The boat. Solange. Alfred. Where? To the east by the boathouse? Shouldn't they be docking there? No. I heard the engine, followed the roar with my eyes, and saw the boat right in front of the house, pulling up to the small swimming dock. I saw the red and green dots of light on its bow, the white running light at the rear, and I wondered what it was doing there, floating amid the huge rocks in those shallow waters. Alfred would never take a boat there; a single wave would smash a fiberglass hull to pieces on just one of those rocks. I stood next to the chimney, one hand on its bricks, and watched as the mysterious boat slipped up to the dock, hovered next to it for just an instant. A figure jumped out, leaped onto Maddy's swimming dock, and then the boat carefully floated back and back and back, eventually turning, then roaring full engine as it aimed for the mainland.

I stood motionless, my eyes fixed on the stranger, who was carrying a small valise. I edged closer to the chimney, slunk into its shadow so as not to be seen. I had no gun, no weapon. Only surprise, and I had to use that expertly, efficiently against whoever was down there.

I turned, looked behind me. I kept thinking there had to be a trapdoor. My mind scattered, panicked, and ran in ten different directions. I didn't remember seeing any hatch on the inside, and a horrible realization swept over me. I'd crawled out that window, up on this roof, and now I was stuck up here, no way down, more impotent than ever.

I turned from the chimney, started sliding back down, past the large skylight over the dome. As I slid on my butt past the skylight, I looked at the bluish light rising from inside. That's when I saw the ladder I was looking for. I skidded to a halt right next to the skylight. The Tiffany dome lay inside there, some four or five feet beneath these panes of glass, and surrounded by scaffolding. The roofers knew they were going to have to come up here and retar the edges of this skylight every few years, so they'd built a ladder over the dome and right up to the flat skylight. My eyes followed the ladder, and there it was. The one pane that was hinged, that could be pushed open and folded back.

I scurried over, wedged my fingers under its metal frame, pried it open, and was assaulted by a gust of warm air surging from the house. Not wasting a minute, I descended into the house, one foot on the old ladder, another. I sank inside, paused, listened. Then heard the doorbell ring. Shit. How polite a killer.

I scrambled the rest of the way down the ladder, and was soon standing in that big room where I'd lain in trance, where I'd relived Toni's last few days. I dusted my hands, started for the door that led into the main staircase. Stopped. No. I couldn't go that way, couldn't plunge down through the center of the house, the staircase wide open. I'd be spotted in an instant.

Suddenly, oddly, it was horribly black. I looked up at the dome, which was no longer glowing. What had happened? Of course. Welcome to Maddy's house. Welcome to her world. She always had some sort of plan, part of which now obviously meant shutting off the electricity. The dark was her only advantage.

I tore through the door that led into the rear of the attic. Found myself in absolute blackness. Stumbled over chairs. A lamp. Endless crud. I pushed past it all. Lunged on. There was the rear staircase, a steep one that led into the servants' rear hall. I found those steps, skidded, nearly tumbled down and around, and burst through another door at the bottom. I stopped on the second floor, and in the weakest of light, spotted a series of doors, turned and saw another landing. I bolted toward that, hung on to a huge oak railing, came around a corner, and saw a straight expanse of stairs jutting before me.

I started running. Then slowed. Couldn't make any noise. No. Had to be quiet. But still had to be fast. Absolutely. Quickly made my way down, then stopped at the bottom. The elevator was up ahead. Open? Yes, I could tell the gate was pushed up, which meant Maddy was down here, somewhere on the main floor. The kitchen was up and off to the left, the pantry up and to the right.

There was a door to my right. I gently reached for the handle, turned it. Pushed. Towering over me I could make out the huge head of an animal. A moosehead. Then that of an antelope. This was the billiard room, and I stepped into it, one quiet foot, another, dead animals peering down on me with glassy eyes. The entry hall was just ahead, up there on the right, on the other side of the billiard table and through that large opening.

I took a step, froze. Behind me I heard something creak. I turned slightly, heard it again. Was that just the shifting of an old house or could it have been the faint, very slight groan of wood beneath a foot? Was someone back there in the kitchen, perhaps even the rear hall? Could Toni's murderer possibly have made it that quickly to the rear of the house?

From the front hall, a man's deep voice called out, "Maddy? Maddy, are you here? It's me."

My sister replied, "Welcome to the world of the blind. I'm in here, to your right and ahead a few steps."

Shit. Who was it and what was Maddy doing, drawing him, coaxing him toward her?

I heard floorboards creaking, heard him start to move. What could I do? He'd certainly have a gun. And so would Maddy. I knew it just then. She'd have a gun, rely on her hearing, fire at him blindly. Oh, Jesus. Oh, Maddy. To my left I saw a rack of long, tall things. Pool cues. Big, heavy Victorian pool cues. I reached for one, lifted it down.

"Thanks for the invite. It was wonderful to hear from you," he said. "What service, too. Private plane, water taxi. And this place—wow."

I recognized that voice, and froze in shock. But how? How could they know each other, my sister and this man? I cautiously moved around the billiard table, step after step, and saw him standing in the dark, pausing on the edge of the living room.

"Are you on wood or carpet?" called Maddy from somewhere in the living room.

"Ah, wood."

"Then push your toe forward until you feel carpet. Go on. Feel it?"

"Maddy, I—"

"Do you feel the carpet?" she demanded.

"Yes."

"Good, now take four steps forward, two to the left. There's a big chair, a very comfortable one."

"But—"

"No buts. Just do as I say. This is my island, my house, my world. You can be blind just a little bit. It won't hurt. Now go to that chair and sit down."

No, Maddy. No, I thought, begged. She was going to get him in place. Put him in a calculated spot. Then gun him down. I crept into the front hall, the big front door off to my right, the Tiffany dome somewhere high overhead.

I heard some steps, some movement, and in response, Maddy said, "Go on, sit down."

There was rustling, shifting, and the voice said, "Okay, I'm sitting."

"Comfortable?"

"Yes."

"Good. If you lift your right hand you'll feel a table. On that table is a small snifter of cognac. Your favorite kind—Remy Martin. You see, it's been a long time, but I haven't forgotten. When things get a little fuzzy, I do a trance and then I remember it all. It comes back wonderfully clear."

He hesitated, then asked, "How'd you find me?"

"I saw an article on you, and my little brother helped, too."

My heart twisted. I'd thought Maddy had been helping me, but had she merely been using me instead? Had she been conniving, figuring on this right from the start? Was that why she'd invited me here?

"How's that?" he asked.

"Well, you've met him actually."

"Really? Are you serious? What's his name?"

"Alex."

"Alex? No, I—"

"He was a very close friend of someone who was murdered. You knew her, too. Toni Domingo."

A definite pause, then, "What—"

There was nothing but silence floating from the living room, and I halted, didn't take a step, couldn't alert them. I was halfway across the entry hall, nearly at the large arch into the living room.

"Maddy, what are you talking about? What's this all about?"

"I think you know."

"I came here to visit you, not play games."

"Oh, come on now." Maddy's voice was low and slow, and obviously she was having difficulty controlling it. "I loved you so very, very much."

"I loved you, too. You knew that."

"Then why'd you never come visit me in the hospital? Why'd you leave Chicago without even saying good-bye?"

He hesitated, started, stopped, then said, "It's a long story, but I had to. A wonderful job opportunity came up. Please . . . forgive me."

Suddenly my sister burst out shouting, "You can goddam rot in hell, you bastard! I know why you left, I know who you were fucking!"

Rustling, movement, someone getting up, and then Maddy screamed, "Sit down or I'll blow your head off!"

"Maddy—"

A blast. A huge explosion. A pistol that fired a bullet through the living room and into a wall not far in front of me.

"Don't test me!" shouted my determined sister. "I know exactly where you are. If you move again I'll shoot. I might not get you with the first shot, but definitely the next one."

"It's okay, it's okay. I'm here, right in the chair. No need to get excited," coaxed the smooth and professionally soothing voice.

Maddy half-shouted, "You were screwing one of your patients the whole time we were dating, weren't you?"

"Maddy, please."

"This shot's going just over your head, into the ceiling right above you." There was a blast, another huge one, and Maddy quickly demanded, "Well, weren't you?"

By his shaking voice I could tell that the shot had hit the ceiling, probably sprinkled him with plaster, and he said, "All right, yes. That's right. I know I shouldn't have. But it happened. Then I met you and—"

"That was why you left so quickly. I didn't know it then. No one told me. I don't know if that was part of your agreement—that they wouldn't tell anyone—or if the others in our office just didn't have the guts to tell me. But that's why you left so quickly, wasn't it, Ed?"

"Yes. They told me if I left the state, they'd keep it quiet."

I made it to the edge of the living room, stood frozen, billiard cue in hand. It made perfect sense. Maddy and Ed Dawson. Both shrinks. Working in the same office in the Loop. So he was my big sister's one and only love. Mr. Wonderful turned awful.

"That's right," continued Maddy. "I didn't know until last night. I called Bonnie. Do you remember her, she did family therapy? She knew, and I forced her to tell me. Goddam you!"

Another shot, exploding, whistling, shattering into something. Then another. I shrank back. She had no idea I was there and if I moved into the living room at all, one of those bullets would probably hit me instead of him.

"They told me you went to California and took over a clinic."

"I did."

Maddy was crying, her voice unsteady, halting. "But then a couple of years ago I read about your appointment to the executive council of the APO. Congratulations, quite the achievement. I've read your book, too, the one you edited. It was very good, actually. What, did you sell your California clinic for a bundle and decide next you wanted fame?"

"Actually I wanted to do less administration and more therapy."

"Sure, so you moved back to your hometown, Minneapolis, and started a nice little practice." She hesitated, added, "I wanted to come up, I wanted to see you. I didn't, though."

"You were always so proud."

"Yes, and always in love with you. I've thought of you every day. Every goddamned day I've thought of you and your touch on my body. You gave me something extraordinary. You were the only man I ever slept with, did I ever tell you that? But then the accident. I'll never be able to feel anything down there again, so all I have is the memory of you inside me. I didn't understand why you left me back then, why you cut things off so abruptly. I thought it was because I was paralyzed, that the idea of such an awfully handicapped person as me drove you away!"

"Maddy, no. That's not right. I've . . . I've loved you, too. Really, I have."

"Don't say that! Do you hear me?" Another shot. "Don't ever say that again!"

"It's okay," came the trained voice from the darkness. "It's okay."

"I loved you and I thought you were the most wonderful person in the world, even after you left me I thought that. I did. That's why when Toni's baby sister needed a therapist in Minneapolis . . . well, I recommended you. Liz didn't know I knew you. I just gave your name to Toni, and she set it up. But then you started fucking her, too, didn't you? You were Liz's other boyfriend, weren't you?"

"Maddy, you don't understand. Liz was in trouble. She was involved with a terrible guy who was trying to get her into this . . . this cult. I had to get her away from him. It took a lot of coaxing, a lot of nurturing, and then one day she broke down and ended up in my arms. It just happened, I didn't mean for it to, really I didn't."

"But you're a professional, Ed, one of the best! You're supposed to know how to handle countertransference, you're supposed to know the limits! She was at your mercy!" Maddy stopped, fell into several deep sobs. "Do you remember how you used to take me driving on the beach at night, how you'd drive along the edge of the water and make it splash everywhere?"

"Sure."

"It was so wonderful. Such a sense of freedom." She took a deep breath, wiping her eyes perhaps, then caught her breath. "You had a car just like a friend of mine. Hers was a Dodge

Raider. I knew it by touch, which was why yours was so familiar to me. Only a Raider is the American version of a Japanese car, and you had the Japanese one, didn't you? And you still have it, don't you?"

"Yes, a Mitsubishi Montero."

"A black one?"

"Right."

I stood there, knowing, understanding. Of course. In trance, in age regression, Maddy had made me carefully scout the street in front of my apartment building, and I'd seen a vehicle of some sort. I'd thought it might be black, couldn't tell much more except I'd seen MITSUBISHI emblazoned across the grille. That was what had tipped Maddy off. That was why she broke off the trance last night. She thought it might be Ed's car, so she ended the trance, returned to her room as quickly as possible, called that other therapist from work, and learned that Ed Dawson had been thrown out of their practice for sleeping with a client. I'd known it was something like that. Maddy wouldn't cry over lost money. Right, she'd figured it out, had stayed up late, plotted how to get Dawson here, probably had him flown on a private jet.

"I know it all, Ed. I do," continued my sister. "That note of Liz's, the one she wrote about not being able to go on—she was talking about you two. She wanted to end it, your affair, not her life. She was stronger than you thought, healthier than you believed. And I wonder if Liz wasn't planning to write an article, not about that cult, but about patients who fall victims to their therapists! In any case, I'm sure she wouldn't have kept quiet. That wasn't like Liz."

"Maddy, no, you've—"

"You've always been ambitious, Ed, and you killed her to keep her from ruining your career, and then Chris, too, you killed her because she'd seen you two together! And Toni—she told you she was meeting with Tyler, so you called and left that message for Jenkins and—"

"Stop it!"

I heard him jump to his feet, heard heavy steps.

"Ed, no! Sit down!"

"Go ahead, fire."

"I will!"

Then came a blast, a shot. It reverberated through the room, the house. I edged around the corner. Dawson was standing there. I saw his dark shape trembling, shaking.

"You missed." He forced a laugh. "And I do believe that was six shots."

From across the room I heard a gun click. Then another click of an empty gun. And now Dawson was charging across the room. I jumped forward.

Shouted: "Don't you dare touch her, Dawson!"

In the shadows of the room I saw him stop, saw him turn around. For a terrible instant all of us were frozen, Maddy, him, and me.

"Alex, no!" shouted my sister. "Get out of here!"

Dawson reached into his coat, pulled out something, hit a button. A glinting switchblade popped into the night.

"Maddy, he's got a knife!"

I charged into the room, ran around that chair, right toward him, and swung the pool cue back, whipped it around, smashed him and cracked it right in half. I'd never known myself to be so strong. He stumbled slightly, then held out the knife, lunged at me, but missed. Pulling back, he raised his arm, readied himself to attack again.

Suddenly a strange voice called out, "I wouldn't move if I were you, asshole!"

Dawson and I stood rigid. I looked toward my sister, who sat several yards away in her wheelchair. Clearly, it hadn't been her, and my eyes raced past her, scoured the room, then saw a dark, vaguely familiar shape emerging from the dining room, gun in hand. So I'd been correct. There had been someone else in the house.

A woman demanded, "End of game. Put down the knife, Dawson!"

He moved slightly, studied her, said, "Who the hell are—"

"A lady with a bad attitude. I'd advise you to do as I say."

I knew immediately who it was. Same long hair, same tall figure. I was about to say something, to call out to her, but then things started happening much too quickly. Dawson would never have given himself up. Maddy obviously knew that, for as soon as he began lunging toward her, knife poised to stab her, my sister shouted to me.

"Get out of the way, Alex! Drop!"

My instinct was to go to her side, to try to protect her, but I knew that warning tone and I knew, too, that Maddy would never let herself get caught. She wasn't the sort. So I heeded her, dove forward, landed on the floor.

And then, when Dawson was only feet from her, Maddy screamed, "Laura!"

Toni's widowed partner hesitated not an instant. I saw a blast. Orange and red. A brilliant, violent snap. Then another. That was all it took. It was over that quickly. Quite dead, Toni's killer toppled and hit the living room floor.

Epilogue

Afterward—after we'd called the mainland, after the police had come and taken statements from us all, after the body had been removed and the house cleaned—I spent another week on my sister's island. So did Laura.

I walked the paths of Madeline's island, strolled the beaches. I found two Petoskey stones, some green sand-worn glass, and a small piece of driftwood that at the time seemed utterly remarkable. A month or so later when I picked up the newspaper and read that they'd finally pinned the murder of those four Minneapolis women on two alleged Dragon members, I pulled out the piece of wood. Staring at it, I couldn't recall why I'd picked it up at all. I still have it, though. Probably always will.

We talked a lot, the three of us. I was still a bit angry at Maddy for her secrecy. To borrow her shrink terms, she acknowledged that, accepted that. And then we had a few good laughs. I made her promise never to address me as Little Brother again.

Laura, I learned, had arrived on the island the day before I did, brought there by Maddy in case my trance had failed to reveal Toni's killer. A sort of backup subject who might be mined for information. Maddy had purposely kept Laura and me separated so as not to influence my trance—Laura had spent those days hidden in the servants' quarters—but after all the commotion was over, Laura and I spoke freely and at great length about Toni. Maddy chimed in, too. We spoke of Toni's struggle to be honest with herself and the world, her beauty, and what a good doctor she'd been.

I think it was hardest for Laura. She cried a lot and made us laugh a lot, too, even in her pain. It was hard for her because Laura had been in the midst of her struggle with chemical dependency when Toni had died. As she put it, at the bottom of the barrel, and she'd thrown all of her self-hatred, all of her anger at Toni. That's what she regretted the most. She just wished that instead of shouting at Toni that morning in front of my apartment, she'd told her how much she cared. Unspoken love. That was, I knew, the hardest of all wounds to heal.

But of course Maddy, the great seer and healer, tried to do exactly that. She hypnotized Laura a handful of times and finally got her to the point where she could regress. I never learned the exact scene, but I knew that Maddy led Laura back through her unconscious, and in trance created some fictional meeting where Laura made amends to Toni.

As for myself, I shied away from hypnotism, at least for that week, content that I would never again return to Toni in trance. I'd found her once, discovered new dimensions in her as well as myself, resolved a great deal, and now it was time to release the past and move again back into the present.

The present? I wasn't quite sure what that meant. Maddy offered me a job, wanted me to come to her island and work for her. I spent a lot of time pondering that. Leaving my work as a technical writer and going into the field of forensic hypnosis, being my sister's eyes and legs. It was tempting, to say the least, particularly if I never had to talk about garage door openers again.